MW00817978

SEA STORMS

NELLIE KRAUSS

Jessica,

love comes on the tides

Nellie Krauss

ACKNOWLEDGMENTS

I wish to acknowledge the people who have supported and encourage me to write the story of Banji and Santiago. My thanks to the San Antonio Romance Writers critique group for their patience and positive feedback. Special thanks to my editor, Ms. Patty who patiently corrected my grammar while encouraging me to write the best story possible.

To my readers, I thank you for your positive comments and hope you enjoy reading this book and much as I enjoyed writing it.

ALL RIGHTS RESERVED

No part of this book may be reproduced, scanned, or distributed in any printed or electronic form without prior written permission from the author, except for the use of brief quotations in a book review.

This book is not intended for anyone under the age of eighteen(18) due to sexual content and language.

This is a work of fiction. Names, characters, places, brands, media, and incidents are the product of the author's imagination or are used fictitiously. Any resemblance to actual persons living or dead, business establishments, events, or locales, is entirely coincidental. As a work of fiction, this book should not be used in any way as a guide.

ALSO BY NELLIE KRAUSS

NEWSLETTER SIGNUP

If you would like to stay up to date on news and releases, please sign up for my email newsletter at NellieKrauss.com

If you liked this book, please leave a review and check out these others:

Galveston Island Series

#1 The Moon Over Sea Wolf Bay

#2 Desperado Lucky

#3 Valentino's Fire (forthcoming in Winter 2021)

Other full-length titles

East of Baghdad

Crossing Love Lines

Sea Storms

Short Stories

Queen of the Black Roses Ball (Short Story)

Keep reading for a look at:

Amazon Link: https://www.amazon.com/Nellie-Krauss/e/B08LF2K8K6?ref=
sr_ntt_srch_lnk_1&qid=1611815262&sr=8-1

CHAPTER ONE

BANJI AMBLED ALONG THE TIDELINE, looking for something that might have washed up on California's beaches during the storm, like the ruins of her career, or a clue to her future. Anything was better than another fruitless day of searching for a way to fix her professional reputation and coming up empty.

She glanced up and spotted the notably large man from up the coast. He liked to walk at sunset. For days she'd watched him and wondered who he was. A middle-aged, well-proportioned handsome man like him walking alone day after day was unusual. Well, in California anyway. If he'd been jogging alone, that would put him in a different category. Lots of married people jogged alone.

Curiosity was her downfall. It killed the cat, and her job. If she hadn't been so damn curious she wouldn't be an outcast living like a hermit in her Gram's oceanside summer cottage with freaking winter closing in.

Usually, they passed with only a quiet, "Hello." But today she was going to say something. He drew closer and she inhaled a steadying breath. She plastered a friendly smile on her face and said, "Hi! The storm was sure a wild one last night."

"Yes." A slight nod while he kept walking.

Great. The strong, silent type. The width of his shoulders and the denim hugging his muscular thighs hinted at his conspicuous strength. The worn-thin flannel shirt told her the cold didn't worry him. He was definitely very attractive for a middle-aged man. His shoulder length, coal-black hair matched his neatly trimmed moustache. And there was something about his dark brown eyes that conveyed he had seen more of the world than she wanted to know about. There was nothing innocent or naïve about him.

She glanced at the churning grey waves and shoved her hands deeper into the pockets of her burgundy parka. Even though it was fraying at the cuffs, it was still comforting on a chilly evening.

She looked down the beach at his receding figure. Ah-ha. She caught him. He glanced back over his shoulder at her. Yes! She stifled a giggle. She would work on him a little at a time until she got a complete sentence out of him. She'd found her new purpose in life. Well, at least until she found a job.

She continued her walk a little longer and then turned around. The deserted beach and a few seagulls made for peaceful company and a routine ending to a quiet day.

Santiago glanced over his shoulder at the interesting woman who had spoken to him. She was pretty but the dark circles under her weary eyes told him she had history. Her speaking to him also told him she wasn't afraid of him. That was unusual. He was large and not particularly friendly looking. His appearance was intimidating, always had been and nothing he did seemed to change it.

He knew this stretch of beach between Kington House and the Betmunn estate by heart. He lived and worked on the Betmunn estate. Twenty-six years of building race cars and restoring antique vehicles made him a good living. Walking the isolated tract of sand seemed to help keep the loneliness away.

He could say something to her next time they crossed paths. His English was near perfect when he chose to speak. Today, she'd taken him by surprise. He'd do better. He stopped beside the dunes and watched her climb the hill to the widow's little house. For years,

Missus Lori made the best apricot pies and shared them with the neighbors. Then one day she didn't wake up. After that, the property manager rented out the house every summer. A tenant in the winter was something new.

He could ask his daughter, Alena, if she'd heard anything about the new tenant, but that might bring up questions he didn't want to answer. Alena Betmunn had adopted him to be her *Papi* when she was a child. She'd made it legal when she turned twenty-one and started racing stockcars with her own team.

As his daughter she had also adopted all the accompanying rights to snoop in his life. He chuckled softly. Without Alena, he'd have no one. And she could snoop all she wanted. There was nothing happening in his world outside of work. But that might be about to change. The woman had spoken to him first. It wouldn't hurt to talk to her. Maybe she was lonely too.

Banji locked the kitchen door and shucked out of her coat. A cup of hot chocolate sounded good. She'd have to settle for the store-bought, instant version but it would be fine. She was not known for any cooking ability. More like inability. Odds favored her burning whatever it was to tiny meteorites regardless of how many cookbooks her friends gave her for Christmas.

While the water heated, she looked through Gram's vinyl albums. Another antique feature she enjoyed. Watching the turntable spin always fascinated her. The old songs resonated with her current life, a little raw and scratchy but still good.

She placed a black vinyl album on the spindle and pressed start. The walk to the kitchen accompanied by the pulsing drumbeat lifted her flagging spirit. She was still standing, barely, and she could get past the wreckage. It would take time but she'd figure it out.

Her phone signaled an incoming call from her least favorite person in the world. She could answer it now or later but eventually she would have to talk to her father. Lloyd Preston could be extremely and annoyingly persistent when he wanted to be. Since he held her responsible for dragging the Preston family name into the gutter, he'd been determined to make her life a misery.

She answered, "Hello."

"Finally. I've been trying to get ahold of you all day."

"I've been busy sending out resumés." Auction houses were few and far between thanks to the internet, and the few remaining weren't looking for disgraced appraisers. Art, and estate and antique jewelry were her specialties. At least they had been.

"What's that god-awful racket?" Lloyd's tone did nothing to hide his annoyance.

"Gram's stereo."

He grumbled, "More worthless junk."

Banji sighed loudly. "What do you want?"

"I'm losing business. People don't want anything to do with Preston Auction House in case you're working for us. You have no idea the influence the Floods have."

"I can't do anything about that. You can make a public service announcement and tell the world I've never worked for Preston Auction. That insurance appraisal has nothing to do with you."

"The Floods are threatening to file a law suit for the damages you've caused them."

"They won't. The test results back up my reports and they wouldn't want to have that confirmed in open court. The tests don't lie. It's more country club gossip." She leaned against the tile counter.

"And where are those documents?"

Ah, now the real reason for the call. "In my safe deposit box."

"Which bank?"

"None of your business. I don't work for you."

"You don't work for anyone, and you're not going to at this rate."

"If there's nothing else, I need to go." She didn't bother masking the heavy exhaled breath. She'd had enough of this useless conversation.

"There is one more thing. We'd appreciate it if you didn't come to Madison's wedding. We'd like it to be a pleasant occasion."

"No problem. Give my half-sister my regrets, or not. I really don't care."

"That's the problem with you. You don't care about your family."

Banji rested her fist on the tile countertop. "You're right. I don't care about the man and his affairs that drove my mother to suicide."

"She was depressed. It wasn't my fault."

"It's never your fault. Don't call me again. Do the world a favor and crawl in a hole and pull the dirt in on top of yourself." She disconnected the call.

Well, that had gone better than expected. At least he hadn't yelled obscenities at her. That was a nice change. She walked back to the living room, turned up the volume on the stereo, and gazed out the window toward the open sea.

Freedom was out there. Better days and blue skies were waiting for her on the horizon; she'd get there. It was only a matter of time.

The tall, dark, and handsome man standing in the dunes glanced up and caught her gazing out the window. Okay, now that could make any girl smile. He was a fine-looking devil. Well, for a man his age. Lucky for him she liked antiques.

CHAPTER TWO

Banji stood at the edge of the porch staring at the faded, peeling paint. Sand Dollar Cottage needed a make-over. Not a lot, but enough to put the past behind and make it her home.

The salt spray tended to weather even the hardiest outdoor paint. And it was depressing. Winter was only a few weeks away. The days were still warm and a fresh coat of something bright and cheerful wouldn't hurt. If she hurried, she could get the outside done and move on to the inside before winter's dreary cold and rain set in.

She spent the morning looking at paint samples and finally settled on pale cream with bright Caribbean sky-blue trim. Okay, so it wasn't original but it was definitely in keeping with being oceanside. A few groceries, some staples from the in-store deli and she was headed home.

After lunch she tied up her hair and went to work cleaning off the outside walls. Painting over a salt film was a waste of time and energy. And she had to scrape the loose paint off. Her project kept growing and the afternoon light kept fading. Afternoon became evening. It was either set up work lights that she didn't have or quit for the night. She put her supplies away and strolled down the trail and through the dunes.

Too tired to walk on the beach, she found a dry spot and plopped down on the sand. With her arms wrapped around her bent knees, she leaned forward watching the sun sink slowly on the horizon. She jumped when a deep voice rumbled behind her.

"The weather will be calm tonight."

She looked over her shoulder at the man who had been tickling her imagination. Up close, she could easily discern his ruggedly handsome features. His thick chevron style moustache added to his confident, distinguished appearance. It was too soon to judge, but something about him encouraged her self-confidence. She lowered her built-in defensive system replies and said, "I hope so. I just spent hours washing walls so I can paint tomorrow."

"May I?" He dipped his head toward the space next to her.

"Oh, sure. Have a seat." She watched him fold himself down beside her. Sitting next to her, his physique became more impressive. The ragged sleeveless chambray work shirt revealed his well-defined biceps, triceps and deltoid muscles on the arm nearest to her. His physical strength was real. The unusual ink tattooed into his skin would require careful study. It wasn't anything local. And the dark stains on his fingers confirmed he worked with his hands. "What kind of work do you do?"

His gaze met hers. "I am a mechanic. I fix old cars."

"My Gram had a Firebird Trans Am back in the day when muscle cars were hot. She might have been old but she wasn't slow." Banji giggled. "Those were some good days."

"What color?"

"Oh, ah, white with a red firebird on the hood. The red upholstery was the finishing touch. I loved that car."

His gaze met hers. "What happened to it?"

"I don't know." She blinked and her brow wrinkled as she did her best to remember. "I never thought to ask. I always assumed she sold it or traded it in for something newer." Banji focused on his bottomless brown eyes and he didn't look away. His inner strength stared straight back at her. There was nothing wishy-washy about him. She liked that.

"Too bad. That was a good engine."

She didn't know anything about engines other than they got her car from one place to the next, usually. Lately, it was touch and go. Maybe the darn thing would start and maybe not. Moving on.

"I'm Banji." She stuck her hand out.

He looked at it and slowly met her handshake. "Santiago."

His warm, rough skinned and callused hand totally engulfed hers. She inhaled and noticed a distinctly male scent on the evening breeze. A faint wisp of aftershave mixed with a touch of sweat and musk teased her senses.

"I'm staying at Sand Dollar Cottage." Duh. That was stating the obvious since he'd seen her standing in the window. "I'm going to fix it up a little."

"It is a good sturdy house."

"It was my grandmother's." She looked at him. "Have you lived here long?"

"Yes, a long time. I knew Missus Lori."

Sitting quietly had its merits. From the corner of her eye she glanced at him. He didn't seem to be in any hurry to jump up and go home.

She said, "I would visit her in the summers. She would sit in her beach chair while I played in the water. Those were the best days."

"You were happy here." His voice carried softly on the evening breeze.

"Very happy. I never wanted to leave." Banji rested her chin on her knees and looked out to sea.

They sat in companionable silence for several minutes. The sun turned into a ball of fire sinking below the horizon taking the temperature down with it. She shivered.

"You are cold. You should go in." He stood up and reached out to her.

"Right." She put her hand in his and let him pull her to her feet. "I enjoyed the visit. Thanks for sitting with me."

"It was my pleasure." He turned toward the dunes. "I will walk you back to the house."

"You don't have to. It's not far."

He gave her a curt nod. "Okay. I will watch until I see you turn on the lights. I want to be sure you are home safe."

8

He didn't argue or try to pressure her. That was a relief. Having a man she didn't really know on her doorstep was not a smart move. Self-preservation 101. She was pretty sure she didn't need to worry about Santiago. A man that strong could take what he wanted.

She took several steps, turned and waved. "Good night."

Santiago stood with his back to the sea watching her walk away. He whispered into the fading light, "Good night, *Carida,* sweetheart." Hers was a face he'd be happy to wake up to in the morning. Up close, she was younger and prettier than he'd first thought. And she had an easy way about her. She'd been content to sit quietly next to him.

He slowly moved up the beach but stopped and waited until he saw her lights come on. Satisfied she was safely inside, he continued on to his house not seeing the dunes or rocks leading up to the cliffs. His mind was on something else. Something with long wavy hair the color of fine scotch whiskey and golden sun-kissed streaks. Unruly waves that reached past her shoulders and blew wildly in the wind finished off her untamed appearance. He imagined looking into her summer-sky blue eyes and kissing her sinfully rosy lips.

Miss Banji was very pretty. This stretch of the coastline didn't attract uninvited visitors, but that didn't guarantee someone wouldn't wander this far. She shouldn't be alone on a deserted beach. He would keep an eye out for her, do his best to ensure her safety.

And he shouldn't be thinking the thoughts that were stealthily creeping into his mind. He walked into his kitchen and turned on the lights. Dead silence. That was his life now and had been for the past two years. It was time to admit he was lonelier than he'd ever imagined possible.

His phone beeped breaking his train of thought. Alena was his life-line. His finger pressed to answer the call. "Yes."

"Hey, *Papi,* Gabriel's in the city. Come on up to the main house for dinner and keep me company. I hate eating alone."

A slow smile crept across his lips. "Okay."

He walked back out into the night, hiked up the hill, past the garages, swimming pool, gazebo, and across the wide expanse of lawn. Alena wasn't good at taking no for an answer. He could go to her or she'd bring their dinner to him. It was nobody's fault but his own since he was the one who had taught her stubborn determination determined one's future.

He took a seat at the kitchen table. When it was the two of them, they didn't need to sit in the formal dining room and shout at each other from opposite ends of a table for eight.

She slid his plate of pot roast in front of him. "Gabriel is held up in the city. I'll make him a plate. He can eat when he gets home." She waved her fork in his direction. "Dig in, before it gets cold." She sat across from him. "Have the parts for the new car come in?"

"They will be here next week." He sliced off a chunk of beef. "We will be ready." He chewed and swallowed.

"Great." She sipped her wine.

"Someone is staying at the old Sand Dollar Cottage." He prodded his baked potato with a fork and smeared butter and sour cream over it.

"That's good. It's been empty about a year. I asked the property management company if it might be coming for sale."

"Is it?" He mashed the melting butter mixture into the potato.

"No, but they said they'd call me if it did. It's a nice piece of property. It would be a great addition."

He picked up his water glass and took a drink to clear his throat. "Yes." He put his glass down. No. If it sold, Banji would move away, maybe before he got to know her. Or, if it wasn't too expensive, he could buy it. He'd always liked that place. The wide porch facing the ocean was perfect for watching the sunset. It was his favorite time of day. He would put up a swing and hold Banji in his arms under a warm blanket. Yes, he liked that idea.

"*Papi*, are you listening to me?"

"Hmm, what? Sorry I was thinking about that cottage."

"I've been thinking that since Carmen has been gone for two years, you might be ready for a change."

Damn, he had to force his throat to work. There were things he'd never told Alena. Even when Carmen was alive, he'd been lonely. "We never know how much time we have." He hated coming home to an empty house. At least when she was alive, the lights had been on and the aroma of dinner cooking had been comforting.

"You did everything you could. We got the best doctors." She put her fork down. "I worry about you." She leaned forward. "Miss Mari, at the bakery, asks about you every time I go in. You could ask her out."

"No. I do not want to marry again." He stared at Alena.

"Being alone is not healthy." She tapped her index finger on the table. "A man needs company. You don't have to get married to have company these days."

"No."

"Fine. How about Miss Sara at the fish market? You like fish."

"Alena, I do not want to go out."

"I could invite her over for lunch." Her lips flattened to a thin line.

"No."

She raised her voice at him which was unusual and asked, "Why not?"

"Because." He stared at her unflinchingly.

"Because why?" Her fist with the knife pointing straight up rested next to the left side of her plate.

If he ground his back teeth together any harder he was going to break them. He forced his jaw to relax so he could answer. "Because I have met someone."

"When, where? Was it that lady with the old Barracuda? That thing was a rusted wreck. It should have been rebuilt years ago." Alena snickered. "She was nice but not really what I'd picture for you."

"No, not her." He winced.

"Well, who?"

His hand gripped his fork with excessive strength. "The woman staying in the cottage."

"What's she like?"

"I do not know what you mean."

"Is she young or old, fat or skinny? Is she pretty?" Alena grinned from ear to ear.

"Maybe she is close to your age. Not fat or skinny." His lips turned up at the corners. "She is the right size for me."

"Really? Now, that's interesting. Is she as tall as you?"

"No."

Alena's eyes narrowed to slits. "What aren't you telling me?"

"We only met a couple days ago. There is nothing to tell. Leave it alone."

"Fine. For now." She picked up her fork. "Eat your dinner. You don't want to get skinny and have your pants falling off your butt. It's not a good look. Especially on a man your age."

His jaws clamped down tight and he ground out, "My pants will not fall off."

"They might. Everyone knows that men lose their butts when they get old. That's why they invented suspenders."

"I am not old."

"Not yet. But why take chances."

His pants were in no danger of falling off, but he might take them off if Miss Banji asked him to.

CHAPTER THREE

BANJI FINISHED APPLYING the blue painter's tape around the windows and doors. The porch ceiling was next. If she didn't want wet paint dripping on the floor she'd have to put down tarps. Damn, she should have thought of that while she was in town. She looked around contemplating if there was anything she could use for a drop cloth. An old sheet would work.

Gram used to keep stuff like that in the shed to cover the delicate plants in winter. The plants were long dead, but there might still be some rags in there, if they hadn't been eaten or carried off by rats and mice. Sheds and rodents went together like peanut butter and jelly. Rats didn't bother her but she hated spiders and their sticky webs. Well, standing there staring at the floor wasn't going to fix her problem. She'd have to find the key to the shed and take a look.

She went into the kitchen and grabbed the key ring off the holder by the door. Gram kept every key to the place on that ring so she'd be able to find them without a lot of fuss. That was Gram, no fuss, no muss. Boy, after all she'd paid for Banji's education, she'd be in a tizzy over the spectacular depths to which Banji's career had plummeted. Talk about fuss. *Sorry Gram.*

Prepared to do battle, she tucked a can of insecticide in her back pocket and firmly gripped the key ring in her right hand.

The short walk to the shed did nothing to lessen her arachnophobia. With the lock in her left hand she tried each key in turn. Nothing worked.

She shook the lock. "Damn it!"

"What is wrong?"

Squealing, "Ah! Shit!" She let go of the lock and flung the keys. She spun around and glared wide-eyed at Santiago. "You scared the crap out of me." He moved quietly for a man his size.

"I am sorry." He looked from her to the lock.

If the smirk partially hidden under his moustache was a clue, he wasn't all that sorry. She picked up the keys. "Do you have a bolt cutter I can borrow?"

He bent down and moved the clay pot at the corner of the shed. His fingers plucked up a key and he handed it to her. "This is what you need."

She took it and shoved it in the lock. It worked. "How did you know?"

He shrugged. "Missus Lori kept it there. I did not have to disturb her when she wanted me to work on her car." He reached past her and pulled on the door handle. It needed a good strong tug to get it moving. The sunlight hit the interior and illuminated the cloud of particles floating in the air like fairy dust.

Banji waved her hand in front of her face and coughed. "Oh, my god. This is awful. Nobody's been in here for years."

Santiago ducked his head, walked inside and stopped next to a large mound in the middle of the floor. He lifted the edge of a dust encrusted car cover. "Hold your breath and close your eyes."

Banji did better than that. She put her hands over her closed eyes and muttered, "Ready."

He pulled the cover off sending dust and grime flying. "It is her Trans Am."

"What?" she dropped her hands and peered into the gloom. "It's Gram's. I'd know it anywhere."

"The tires have dry rotted." He squatted down by the front fender and dug at the black mess with his fingers. "But the rims are still good.

I can put tires on it and tow it to my garage." He stood up. "I can rebuild it for you." He smiled.

"I need a drop cloth, not a Trans Am." Banji ran her fingers along the rear spoiler.

Her eyes met his. He asked, "Do you have the title to it?"

She cleared her throat. "I have her will. It's all mine. Everything she had came to me when she passed. I can get the title put in my name. Why?"

"You can sell me the car, if you do not want it."

"It's Gram's. She'd have a stroke if I sold it." Her eyes widened and she burst out laughing. "I can't believe I said that."

Santiago stepped toward her. "Are you okay? I could get you some water. Do you want to sit down?"

"I'm not going to faint or fall apart. Sometimes I forget she's gone." She wiped at the gritty film on the passenger window and peered inside. "I don't have the keys to it."

Santiago opened the driver's door. "They are here." Missus Lori always put them over the sun visor." He reached in, pulled out the keys and held them out to her.

"I don't need them. It's not like it's going to start." She patted the roof. "You keep them."

She stepped back. "I need to paint the house. The car can wait. It's been sitting here for the last four years. A few more days won't hurt anything."

Santiago shook his head. "Let me take it to my garage. I can fix it."

There was an almost desperate quality to the request. She took a few seconds to really look at him. "You really want to do this, don't you?"

"Yes. I am a very good mechanic. It will run like new."

She waved her hand over the car. "Fine, take it. It's not like I can fix it." She laughed. "This just keeps getting better and better. I need a drink. Something with rum in it."

He turned and rummaged on the shelves behind him. "Here are some old rags you can spread on the floor." He pulled a sagging cardboard box out. "I will take this to the porch for you."

"Thanks." She followed him, getting a great view of his backside.

He filled out his work pants nicely. Oh, my god, she was reduced to ogling a man's ass. How long had it been since she'd been on a date? She needed to check her calendar. Her social life had dried up, right along with everything else. She could count the friends who were still speaking to her on one hand and nobody dared to be seen with her.

Santiago carried the box to the porch and disappeared as silently as he'd come.

Banji sprayed the open box to be on the safe side, then proceeded to pick through the rags watching for the dreaded spiders. While she did that, her mind wandered to images of Santiago.

She didn't know much about him, but it was obvious he liked fixing things. He wasn't shy or retiring and that was good. She'd been known to run over timid men like a locomotive. She gave up and dumped the box out on the floor and muttered, "There, problem solved." Now she could see all the rags without sticking her fingers into the unknown.

Her ears registered the sound of a diesel engine and tires crunching up her driveway. She looked up and sure as Christmas there was a tow truck backing up to the shed. He had to be kidding.

The car was sitting on flats. It wasn't going to roll out of the shed on rims. Even she knew that much. She walked over and met Santiago at the back of the truck. "What's all this?"

"I am picking up the Trans Am." He pulled a mounted spare tire to the edge of the flatbed.

"I see that, but it's not moveable the way it is. It needs tires."

"I brought some temporary wheels. It will be fine."

"Okay. Do your thing." She backed away. Talk about a man on a mission. This guy didn't waste time.

"I will take it to the garage and I will come back and help you."

"All right. I'm not going to turn down help." She sauntered back to the porch. Somewhere along the way she'd lost half a day already.

Santiago had a treasure. The Trans Am was salvageable. He could fix it. It would take time to find and replace all the dry, rotted, and cracked

16

rubber and plastic parts. Then all the fluids would have to be drained and the tanks and pans cleaned. He would replace the wiring and fuses. All that would take time and it guaranteed that Banji would be within reach. It would give him enough time to get to know her.

He slid the jack under the frame and sprayed the lug nuts with lubricant. He let that sink in before loosening them and lifting the rims out of the dirt. With the old rims off and the temporary wheels on, the car was good to roll. He crawled inside, put the transmission in neutral, and released the park break. He glanced at the sky. The day was slipping away. One look at the porch told him he would be working late making up for the time Banji had lost fooling with the car. That was okay. It would be time spent with her.

He towed the Trans Am to the garage and left it. He would unhook it later. Getting back to the cottage and to Banji was his priority. There were spontaneous signs of life twitching below his belt. Those had been infrequent to say the least since Carmen had discovered she couldn't have children. She didn't believe in sex unless it was to conceive.

Banji was to blame for reminding him that he was still a virile man with wants and needs. He wanted to hold somebody warm and willing, he ached to be touched, caressed, loved. He needed company and he wanted Banji's. In the bright sunlight, with her hair piled on top of her head she appeared much younger than he'd originally thought. She might prefer a younger man.

In case he was wrong, he jogged back to her cottage and almost had a heart attack when he saw her standing on the top step of a ladder swiping paint on the porch ceiling. His first instinct was to yell, but if he startled her, she would be in more danger of falling. He picked up his pace and didn't slow down until he stood firmly below her. "Be careful. You could fall."

"Nope, I'm good." She lowered her arm and looked him in the eyes. "I think I need a bigger brush."

"I think I should paint the ceiling, while you work on the walls." Not that he didn't like looking up at her backside from where he stood. It was a very enticing round, firm backside. He had no trouble at all imagining it minus the jeans.

She climbed down the ladder and bumped into him along the way. He hid the grin, and hoped that she'd bump into him again soon. From the front would be nice. He couldn't remember the last time he'd been touched by a pretty woman, on purpose or by accident. But if she told him to step back, he would and he would know she wasn't interested in him. At least not in that way.

She turned, he didn't back up and got his wish. Banji's breasts brushed against him when she moved away from the ladder. Holding the paint brush out to her side, he hoped she wouldn't slap him with it. Not that he didn't deserve it, but he was not ashamed of being a man who could appreciate a beautiful woman.

She looked up. "If you help me finish this porch, I'll fix us some dinner." She bit her bottom lip. "If you want to stay and eat?"

"Yes."

"Great. Here." She waved the brush at him. "I'll get another one for the walls."

She slipped away leaving him holding her dripping paint brush.

Once he started, it didn't take long to finish the ceiling and move on to help her with the walls. By the time the sun was sinking low, they had put the lids on the paint cans and washed the brushes. There was more to do but they'd gotten a good start.

He followed her into the kitchen. Missus Lori's place hadn't changed. Cheerful seaside ambiance, comfortable but not fancy. Banji glanced over her shoulder at him. "You can wash up. The bathroom's that way." She pointed to the hall.

He gave her a nod. He wanted to be reasonably clean and comfortable for their meal. He'd like to stay and visit a while afterward. In no hurry to go back to his solitary existence, he sauntered down the hall to the bathroom while glancing through the open doors at the bedrooms. Like taking a step back in time, hardwood floors and oceanside complementary pastel-colored throw rugs in turquoise and soft coral, nothing had changed.

On his way back to the kitchen he stopped in the living room. The old albums lined up along the dark-walnut stained shelf by the stereo caught his eye. He called out, "Do you play these records?"

"Every chance I get." Some noises indicative of cooking emanated from the kitchen and she added, "You can pick something and we can listen to it after dinner."

His prayer was answered. "I would like that."

Dinner was a quick and easy menu, green beans from a can, instant mashed potatoes from a pouch, grocery store premade hamburger patties that she hovered over to make sure they didn't burn. Santiago stepped up to the stove and turned down the flame.

She glanced at him. "So, you don't have to turn the knob all the way?"

"No. Low is good most of the time." He grinned.

Or was it a smirk? She couldn't tell for sure. Either way, he'd saved the burgers from becoming her usual scorched-to-black chunks, resembling charcoal briquettes. The smoke alarm hadn't even gone off once.

It didn't take long to eat the simple but edible dinner she'd put on the table. Peering over at his empty plate, she made a mental note to make bigger portions when he came to dinner. There was nothing petite or even average about him. And he didn't need to watch his weight. What would it be like to have him around all the time?

"I've never had to cook for myself. I've lived on deli food and take-out for years." She frowned. "I worked so much I didn't have time to cook."

"I know the basics." His lips curved up on one side. "We can help each other learn."

"That would be great." She breathed a sigh of relief and carried their dishes to the sink. "Go put on whatever album you want to listen to. Sit down and get comfortable while I fix us a couple glasses of wine."

He got up and sauntered to the living room. She poured two glasses of sweet red wine and followed him. So far, he'd been good company. Getting to know someone took time, but she wasn't known for being patient. She took a sip from her glass and handed him his.

Banji settled next to Santiago on the forest-green chenille uphol-stered couch. Looking out the picture window, the silver moonlight

19

shimmering on the water added its own magical spell to the evening. He'd chosen an album of mellow, soulful love songs. Who knew the man was a romantic? She put down her glass and lit several candles in a colorful array on a glass stand. The flames flickered and danced on the mirrored coffee table.

She gazed unashamedly into his sinfully dark eyes. Something in them beckoned her. Exploring their depths could take a lifetime. Santiago was not a simple man. She blinked breaking their connection. "I think I understand why Gram moved here permanently. It's very peaceful."

"Yes, peaceful."

"She told me she was fond of a merchant seaman who was lost during a storm on a voyage to Australia. She felt closer to him with the ocean right outside her door." Banji sighed. "I think she never stopped loving him."

"He was a lucky man. Missus Lori was a caring woman."

"Did you know her very well? Gram was kind of quiet after she lost him. His name was Ritter. She hardly ever talked about him. I think it made her sad."

"I fixed her cars. She would bring us apricot pies when she baked. Those were my favorite."

"She did like to bake." A short snicker escaped. "I was a plump kid back in those days. Gram's kitchen was my favorite place in the world." She shifted around to study Santiago without having to turn her head. "Did you get to try her cookies with apricot centers? They were delicious."

Banji made another mental note. He liked apricots. He couldn't be too dangerous. What ax-murderer likes apricot pie? On her next visit to the bakery, she'd ask if they could make her one.

And why would she do that? Well, because she was starting to really like Santiago. He was quiet and polite. And every once in a while, he smiled.

"I did. My wife liked strawberry, so I got them all."

Wife? What wife? "I didn't know you were married." Keep it casual. This was the first mention of a wife.

"She died two years ago." He turned his attention toward the window. "Before she got sick, she would take Missus Lori good Argentinian empanadas, and bring home pies and cookies."

"I'm so sorry. I had no idea."

He shrugged and turned toward her. "You would have no way of knowing." He took a sip from his glass. "You are painting the house. Are you going to sell it?"

Banji's hand flew to her chest. "Lord, no. I have to live here." Well, that wasn't supposed to have come flying out of her mouth. He'd dodged talking about himself and turned the conversation to her. Might as well put it out there and get it over with. The cat was definitely out of the bag and running around the room. No way Banji could stuff it back in the sack. She lowered her hand from her chest and inhaled. "I'm not working and I need a roof over my head. Gram's cottage is mine and it's paid for."

"I understand." He nodded once.

She was pretty sure he didn't have a clue. Nobody got it. And she was tired of defending herself when she hadn't done anything wrong.

"Um, no, you probably don't understand, but it's okay." She leaned away, putting more space between them. The old, high-backed couch came with three square cushions. There was only so much room she could put between them.

He shifted his weight, turning in her direction he bent his knee and pulled his leg up to partially rest on the worn middle cushion.

"If I do not understand then you should explain it so I can."

Wow, what was the deal with that? Talk about being direct. She wasn't used to it. For years she'd had to read between the lines at home and at work.

She'd suck it up and tell him the truth. "I'm the estate appraiser that discovered the Flood's ruby wasn't from the Mogok Stone Tract mine, and the Borger's sapphire was actually from Montana and not Burma. I did my job and I got fired."

"For telling the truth?"

"That's the way it goes. You don't cross people with old family names and fat bank accounts. I have the original test reports in my safe deposit box so I can prove my appraisals are correct."

"I believe you."

"Well, that's nice, but it doesn't fix my reputation or career. I'm pretty much finished. The word going around the trade grapevine insinuates I was likely mistaken and didn't have enough experience to be reliable." She finished the wine in her glass and stared at the last drop in the bottom.

"What will you do?"

"Well, that is the million-dollar question." She laughed. "I think I'll sit here by the sea for now." She glanced at his wine glass. "Can I get you more wine?" She could open another bottle. She could use another glass of sweet red wine or maybe two.

"It is late. I must go. I have to work in the morning but I will come help you later in the afternoon." He stood up. "Good night. Thank you for dinner."

"Sure." She got up and led the way to the door. "I'll see you tomorrow."

"I will give you my phone number. You can call if you need help."

A couple of minutes later, she pocketed her phone, leaned against the edge of the door, and watched Santiago walk down the path to the beach trail. He was a gentleman. Most guys would have been trying to weasel their way into her queen size bed. Yeah, he was one of the last few who didn't presume because he'd done some work on her house and she'd fed him, that he got rewarded with a roll in the sheets. She'd need a much bigger bed to roll around in with him.

Santiago ambled along the beach trail leading to the Betmunn Estate. He'd had an interesting day with Missus Lori's granddaughter. His lips turned up at the corners. It would take some time to get to know her, but he suspected it would be time well spent.

He would help her tomorrow and every day for as long as she needed him. They could go walking together on the beach in the evenings. He imagined how warm her hand would be and how it would fit perfectly in his. And when the time was right he would lean down and kiss her.

The zipper of his jeans cut into his erection. He adjusted his anatomy trying to get comfortable. Eventually, she might give him a sign she wanted to get more involved. He'd like that.

Missus Lori had loved a seafaring man. He'd always wondered why a pretty lady like her didn't have a man in her life. Now, he knew. She also had the stereo on all the time. She said it kept the loneliness away. In the summer she'd have her windows open and he'd hear the songs playing late at night while walking in the dunes below her house. He liked the idea of slow dancing in the dark with Banji. That thought made his erection press harder against the damn zipper.

All in all, he'd had a very good day. Smiling, he opened the back door and walked into his kitchen. He spied a note on the kitchen table.

I saw the Trans Am in your driveway. Whose is it? Any chance they want to sell it? Let me know. Alena

CHAPTER FOUR

THE NEXT AFTERNOON, Santiago closed up the garage and walked along the beach trail to Banji's. He would help her paint until dark. They should be able to finish the outside. She might fix them dinner again. He'd do his best to keep her from burning it. He smiled to himself. She meant well but she definitely needed more practice. Alena might be willing to help her learn someday in the future, if things worked out the way he hoped they would.

Tonight, he'd ask to play another record and he'd pick something good for slow dancing. A glass of wine and soft music would be perfect for asking her to dance. He'd get to hold her in his arms for a few minutes. They would sway to the music and he'd be able to pretend he was a younger man and she was his sweetheart.

He might be fooling himself for the few minutes the song played but it would be worth it. He'd tamped down his feelings for so long, he wasn't sure they still existed or that he could find them. What he did know was that his manly parts were definitely awake and ready to get acquainted with Banji. She had that effect on him without even trying.

He topped the hill and her cottage came into view. A few more hours and he would hold his *Carida* in his arms for the first time.

Banji glanced over the dunes at the setting sun. It had been a long day but her house was looking good. The fresh paint made a huge difference. It went from sad and lonely to bright and cheerful. She was home at last. There was no mistaking the warm feeling wrapping itself around her heart and soul. This was where she belonged.

As soon as Santiago got the brushes cleaned and put away it would be time for dinner.

The cooked rotisserie chicken from the store was warming in the microwave. It would be fine with the potato salad she'd gotten from the in-store deli and the pre-cut tossed green salad she'd flung in a bowl with some cherry tomatoes on top. She'd gotten three kinds of salad dressing. He was bound to like one of them. Okay, so she was not domestically inclined. It was only food.

The best part was, she'd gotten apricot cookies at the bakery for dessert. The Napa Valley bottle of sweet white wine she'd taken half-an-hour to pick out would be delicious. He would be delicious with the taste of apricots and Moscato on his lips. Okay, so she had ulterior motives.

The night before she'd gone to sleep thinking about the possibilities. She could live in Sand Dollar Cottage and make a new life for herself. She could do something fun and different with her education. Being an appraiser had made her a decent living but it had never been her passion. Antique jewelry was her thing. There were stories behind the pieces. They had history. She loved digging in the archives and finding out their significance. It was doubtful she could make a living doing only that, but she'd figure it out as she went along. She had to start somewhere.

There were treasures out there waiting to be discovered and have their stories told. And then there was Santiago. She needed the story to go with the man.

She called out, "Dinner's ready."

"*Sí, Carida.* I am here." He walked up and stood beside her.

The microwave binged. "Grab the wine and we'll eat." She carried the chicken to the table and set the plate down near him. "I hope I got it hot enough."

"It will be fine." He opened the wine and filled their glasses.

25

"Tomorrow is Saturday. I was thinking if you didn't have to get up early we could listen to some music after dinner."

"I would like to listen to more of your records." He cut up the chicken. "Which piece would you like?"

Banji held out her plate. "The thigh and leg. I like dark meat." She needed to rein it in before her mouth got her in trouble and that was so not her style. Any wild thought skittering across her brain was likely to come babbling out of her mouth. She glanced over at Santiago. Was he smirking at her, again?

They continued loading their plates. So far, so good. At least he hadn't gotten up and walked out. Banji did her best not to fidget. She twisted the cap off the balsamic vinaigrette and poured it over her salad. She glanced at Santiago as she placed the bottle back on the table. "I got us apricot cookies from the bakery for dessert."

She was rewarded with a smile and a quick look of surprise in his eyes. If she wasn't mistaken, her not so subtle attempt to please him was well received. She would ply him with wine and cookies, then maybe get a hug and a kiss for her efforts. She'd be good with that. At least it would be a start.

After working on the house, they were both hungry and their food disappeared quickly and quietly.

She stacked the dishes in the sink, looked over her shoulder and said, "Go pick out some albums and I'll bring the dessert."

"Would you like me to light the candles like last time?"

Smiling, she reached for the bakery box. "That would be perfect."

She carried their glasses to the coffee table, put them down, and went back to for the dessert plates and napkins. The perfect romantic evening. Soft candlelight, music, wine, sweet confections all fell into the romance category.

It didn't take long to arrange the plates and napkins neatly on the coffee table. The first strains of music drifted out of the speakers. He'd chosen something soft and dreamy. An old movie soundtrack. Her gaze met his.

She whispered, "I love the soundtrack from this movie. It has a happy ending."

He turned and held out his arms to her. "Would you like to dance?"

"Yes, I'd love to." She glided into his arms. Her left hand rested on his shoulder and her right hand lightly held his large, warm hand. She leaned in and looked up into his eyes. "This is nice. Do you like to dance?"

"Yes, with you." He pulled her close.

She glimpsed a shimmer in his eyes and rested her head against his chest. It was so easy to let herself float on the soft notes, slow rhythm and the masculine scent of Santiago.

He pressed his lips to the top of her head and she melted against him.

Santiago swayed gently to the slow-moving song with Banji in his arms. Soft and warm pressed up against him, she fit comfortably against his chest. His heart beat increased, his blood flowed to his penis and he couldn't stop the hunger building deep inside. He'd been starving for so long. This was not the time to lose control.

It was no secret he was getting older, but that was no excuse to mislead Banji. She deserved to know what she was getting.

The song ended and he led her to the couch. His heart was available if she truly wanted it. Would falling in love with him make things harder for her? There was only one way to find out.

They sat close together. She reached for her glass. "That's going to be my favorite song for the rest of my life." She gazed into his eyes and took a sip of wine.

One thing was for certain. She came right out and said what was on her mind. He didn't have to guess what she was thinking.

He sat back and straightened his shoulders. "I never had a favorite song to dance to before." He trained his eyes on her watching for a reaction. "My wife, Carmen, did not care to dance."

"I'm sorry." She put her glass down. "If I'm doing something that makes you uncomfortable, you need to tell me."

"I must tell you things from my past before we get closer."

Banji glanced at the apricot cookies. "All right."

"We were young when we married. When we realized we had made a mistake we had to live with the vows we made."

"I see." She turned toward him.

"Tonight, I found something that has been missing from my life for a long time."

She scooted closer. "I think you should kiss me now, real slow. Take your time, there's no rush."

He wrapped her in his arms and glimpsed the promise in her eyes when he pressed his hungry lips to hers.

She kissed him back, slowly ran her tongue along the seam of his lips encouraging him to open for her. Her hands cupped his cheeks. It must have taken him too long to comply because the next thing he knew, she caught his lower lip with her teeth and tugged. His mouth opened and she swooped in. Lord have mercy, he was being French kissed for the first time in his life. Her fingers threaded through his hair and held his head firmly in place.

She'd taken him by surprise and his body was begging him to move. To run his hands over her hips, cup her butt, pull her close and press his erection against her. He leaned into her, pushed her back against the cushions and broke their kiss. "*Carida*, you tempt me beyond reason."

Banji caught her breath and mumbled, "I could say the same about you." She grasped his upper arms.

"I must go before we do something we might regret." He pulled away breaking her hold on him.

"You must be talking about yourself, because I don't regret kissing you one damn bit." Her lips turned downward in a frown. "Unless you didn't like it."

He took her hand and pressed it over the bulge in his pants. "I liked it." He rubbed her hand down his length. "It is too soon." He released her hand and moved away. "I will see you tomorrow." He was up and gone before she could scramble off the couch and follow him to the door.

Banji muttered, "What in the hell? Men are so weird."

CHAPTER FIVE

SATURDAY AFTERNOON, Banji pointed at the master bedroom suite. "We need to take this apart and move it to the guest room. I want to paint this room next so the new furniture can be delivered."

Santiago asked, "What is wrong with this furniture?"

"Nothing. But I want a king size bed." So far, they'd avoided talking about the previous night. "The old guest room furniture can be donated. Gram got it for me back when I was a kid visiting in the summers." Her voice softened. "That was before she sent me to see all the art museums in Paris and Rome to round out my education."

"And what about the back room?"

"That's mostly boxes and storage. I'll have to go through it and clean it out. That's a rainy-day project."

"I will get my tools." He headed out the back door.

"I'll fix some sandwiches for lunch."

Sandwiches were easy and she couldn't burn them as long as she didn't do anything fancy that required grilling. She was the queen of burnt grilled cheese sandwiches.

While she retrieved the sandwich ingredients, she heard Santiago down the hall taking apart and moving the bedroom set in the guest room. She'd spent her grade school and high school summers and holidays in that room when she wasn't out roaming the beach with the girl next door.

Alena Betmunn had gone off to college in Houston, Texas and eventually married a Marine. Banji had read her tarot cards and the Wheel of Fortune had been in Alena's favor. It had been a close call but Alena had made it happen. She'd also followed her instincts and done what she loved most. It had been a rough road but the hard-earned comeback on the stock car circuit had been worth it, and she was taking Betmunn Racing to new heights of success.

Banji should call her, but she really didn't want to cry on Alena's shoulder. She'd do that if and when she got desperate. Today she was on cruise control. Santiago was in the other room and they were having lunch together. There was something about that man that lifted her spirits. Nothing could be wrong when he was close by.

She smeared mayonnaise on the hoagie buns, stopped and looked out the window. *That's it! I'm going to do what I love most. If it worked for Alena, it can work for me.* She'd get out her cards and see what they had to say. A quick glance at the sandwiches brought her another thought. Santiago had better be in the cards for her or she'd get a new deck. She was not giving up, she was starting over.

Santiago walked up behind her. "I will take the furniture to town for you Monday."

"Great. It can sit out on the porch till then."

"There is a storm coming. It will get wet."

"Oh, I guess with the bed frame taken apart we can lean the mattresses up against the wall good enough to fit Gram's dresser and night stands in the guest room for now."

"Yes, but your bed will not fit."

"Uh, well, we can push it into the center of the room. I can work around it. If we put stuff in the shed, the mice will gnaw on it."

"They have chewed the wiring and hoses in the Trans Am. It will all have to be replaced."

"I figured it was going to be a mess under the hood." She piled lettuce and tomato slices onto the buns. "If you don't want to bother with it, we can haul it to the junk yard." Banji cringed at the thought of Gram turning in her grave. "Or we can put it back in the shed."

Uh-oh. The indrawn breath behind her let her know she'd said the wrong thing.

"I said I would buy it, if you do not want it."

She turned and her chest mashed into his. Wow. She put her hands on his shoulders. "It's a lot of work. I don't want to keep you from doing more important things."

His hands gripped her gently at the waist putting space between her and the growing bulge pressing against her abdomen. Oh, my, god, and damn good thing she'd gotten large condoms on her recent trip to the store. It hadn't seemed quite so big or so hard last night.

"There is nothing more important." Santiago gazed into her eyes.

All she had to do was slip her arms a little higher and hug him. And it would change the whole dynamic of their relationship. She patted his chest. "All right. It's up to you." Doing her best to execute a nonchalant turn back to the counter should ensure everything would return to normal, for now.

He stepped back. "I will start on your room. Call me when lunch is ready."

She listened to his retreating footsteps fade down the hall. She was glad to know he was definitely still interested in her, unless taking apart furniture gave him a hard-on.

Santiago went to the master bedroom, pulled the drawers out of the dresser and carried them to the guest room followed by the night stands. After that he'd have an easy afternoon of it. His dick needed to back off. He didn't do casual, and had no intention of rushing her. There were still many things about him she needed to know before they got naked. Well, before he got naked.

He didn't see the scars and ink anymore when he looked in the mirror but she would. Before he had time to dwell on those thoughts she called him to lunch.

Sitting at the table, he noticed she was quieter than usual. But he caught her glancing at him when she may have assumed he wasn't looking. He was always looking. It was hard to keep his eyes off of her.

If he was a younger man, he'd say he was infatuated. But at his age, infatuation was a thing of the past. He knew better now.

She said, "I'll clean up the dishes while you finish moving the furniture." Her eyes stared at her plate. "It'll take me the rest of the afternoon to clean the room and tape the windows." She looked at him. "You don't have to stay for that. I can do it."

He'd made her uncomfortable and she wanted him gone. He couldn't argue with her. It was her house. "Okay. I will help you paint tomorrow."

"Great. That works." She got up and carried her plate to the sink.

He put his plate on the counter and went back to her bedroom. Right room, wrong time. He'd have to figure out what he'd done wrong and fix it tomorrow. He put the sliders under the dresser and moved it to the guest room. Five of the six drawers slipped back into place perfectly but the sixth one wasn't cooperating. He pulled it out and felt around to the back of the dresser. Nothing. Then he ran his fingers back along the bottom. Nothing. He examined the drawer. Looking closely, he discovered a latch.

He carried the drawer to the living room and called out, "Banji, come look at this."

"What?" Her head poked around the corner from the kitchen.

He nodded toward the couch. "Your grandmother's dresser has a hidden compartment. This drawer has a false bottom."

Banji hustled to the couch and plopped down next to the drawer. Her fingers gripped the front edge. "I don't see anything. Do you know how to open it?"

His fingers brushed over the inside hardware behind the decorative lock, a slight push and the catch released. He pulled at the frayed ribbon in the corner and the bottom lifted. From her indrawn breath and wide-eyed stare, he was almost afraid to look closer but curiosity got the better of him.

"Those are very old letters." He bent closer. "They were mailed from foreign countries. Some are from South America. I recognize the stamps."

Banji picked up the one nearest to her on the top of the pile and turned it over. "Oh, my god! It's from her sweetheart. Look, the return address is only his name, Third Mate, Ritter Davis."

Banji put the letter back on top of the others, scooped them all together and lifted them out in a messy stack. A solitary key fell out and bounced on the table. She looked at Santiago. "What do you suppose that goes to?"

"I do not know, but you should keep it with the letters. The answer could be in one of them."

"I'm going to read these one at a time once I put them in order. I'm going to find out what happened. She took the key from his fingers."

"Missus Lori must have hidden them for a reason."

"There's got to be more to the story. She wouldn't have spent years living here alone if he wasn't somebody very special." Banji's forehead wrinkled. "Gram was still married to Grandpa Bancroft when he died. I'm not sure how Ritter fit into her life but I'm going to find out."

He picked up the drawer. "I will put this back in the dresser."

"Thanks. I've got to empty out a couple shoe boxes so I can put these in order." She gazed at Santiago. "This is so amazing. I can't believe you found them. It's like a message from the fates telling me not to give up."

"I do not understand. Give up on what?"

"Give up on finding things, on living my dreams." She hugged the letters to her chest. "This is it. I can feel it. There are answers in these papers. I only have to find them."

He nodded and carried the drawer to the guest room. He'd never expected to find old love letters. Hidden compartments were usually used for important documents like deeds and wills, or maybe jewelry, things of value. He scratched his head. Missus Lori must have thought those letters were valuable. If Banji thought they held answers, they must be important.

He would have to ask her if she found what she was looking for when she was through reading them. They were private and he had no business prying into things that were not meant for him.

By the time he'd finished moving the furniture and walked out to the living room, the afternoon sun had slipped behind a bank of angry storm clouds looming on the horizon.

He looked over his shoulder and called out, "The storm is almost here."

"I saw it. I'm closing the windows. I'll fasten the shutters next."

"I will get them." He didn't want her to struggle with the heavy shutters. The storm might be minor but judging by the dark clouds closing in, he didn't think so. "Get your candles ready."

"Got it. No problem."

The back door slammed. Where was she going? He went out on the porch and caught sight of her disappearing around the corner of the shed. Following her, he learned two things. The wind was picking up and it was cold. He pulled up short when she pushed open the door and held out two storm lanterns toward him.

She said, "Put those in the house and I'll get the oil."

He left the lanterns on the kitchen table and finished closing and securing the storm shutters. From the corner of his eye he kept track of her whereabouts. They were on a mission to get the house prepared to ride out a Pacific storm.

She twisted the oil container cap closed and met his gaze. "I've got this. I'll go with you and help you get your place ready."

"No." His heart skipped several beats and he stopped breathing for a second. "I can do it."

"Oh. Well, okay. If you're sure." She looked away.

He didn't miss the hurt in her eyes and disappointed tone of her voice. He'd been gruffer than necessary but she'd caught him off guard. He didn't have time to explain it. He wasn't ready for her to step into his world, to see the way he'd lived.

When Carmen died, he took the sheets off the bed and closed the door to her room. The only time he'd gone back in there was to get her favorite dress and take it to the funeral home.

"I should go." He stepped back.

"Right. Stay safe. I'll see you when it's over." Her half-hearted smiled faded and she added, "Thanks for all the help."

"You might want to fill a few pots with water in case things get really bad." He opened the back door. "Call if you need me."

"Will do." She raised her hand and waved.

34

He didn't like leaving her there alone but the storm was only minutes away. He had to hurry.

~

He jogged to his house and got things secured in record time. It was small and didn't take much to keep the wind and rain out. He pulled candles out of the drawer and set the matches next to them. He was ready.

Santiago sank onto an old chromed-tubular framed chair at the worn kitchen table and listened to the wind whistle under the eaves. It was going to be a wild night once the rain started. He turned on the radio and heated a can of soup for dinner. The music helped fill the void in his life and kept his mind off Banji for a few minutes, but his eyes kept straying to the door.

He didn't have to live alone for the rest of his life. He only had to take a chance and give Banji the opportunity to wound him. No, not doing it. Back and forth he went. One minute he desperately wanted to be in love and the next he wanted to lock out the world and avoid the inevitable pain falling in love would bring.

Lightening lit up the gloom. Shit! He hated lightening. Then the thunder rumbled in the distance sounding like a war drum calling him to battle. Something stirred deep in his heart. Something that hadn't surfaced in many, many years.

He grabbed his raincoat off the hook and stepped out into the storm.

CHAPTER SIX

A STORMY NIGHT was a good time to walk on the beach and rage at the world. Santiago's anger and frustration matched the howling wind and pounding rain. He fought the urge to open his mouth and scream into the darkness. The evil genie of hope refused to be stuffed back into the bottle from which it had surreptitiously escaped. An hour later and chilled to the bone, he glanced across the dunes. He picked out the faint outline of Sand Dollar Cottage and turned back to face the crashing waves.

The salt spray burned his eyes. He couldn't stand there all night. He could go home and no one would ever know he'd finally given up, or he could go to Banji. He could try one more time to find the love and acceptance he craved so desperately.

With her he was allowed to be the man he truly was. She let him express his masculinity without shame. He didn't have to hide that side of himself.

One kiss, one slow dance was all it took for his *Carida* to bring him back to the land of the living. He would be a fool not to accept what had appeared on his shore.

Every hour he spent with her reminded him of what he'd once believed love would feel like. She filled the empty spaces in his heart and he kept her from burning down the house. He chuckled to himself. He didn't mind cooking. It was a small price to pay for her affection.

He wanted to make love to her. Yes, he could wait. No, he didn't want to. It had been so long and he'd learned the hard way that every day was precious. Every day he hoped to see her face each time he looked up. Every night his arms ached to hold her. He was worse than infatuated. He was in danger of falling in love.

She was all alone and the storm was getting worse. He should go to her, wrap a blanket around her and hold her safely in his arms while the storm raged around them.

As long as the power stayed on, the stereo would keep playing. She'd picked an album of broken-hearted sad songs. For some crazy reason they seemed to match her mood. She shuffled through the album jackets in hopes of finding something more cheerful. It wasn't over. *It,* being her love affair with Santiago. He was a fire she was not willing to put out. Hell, she was just getting started.

She pulled a likely nineteen-eighties candidate from the shelf. One kiss and she'd known he was the one. Last night he'd gone home like a perfect gentleman. A perfectly panicked gentleman. And today he'd been polite and kept a respectable distance. He had only invaded her personal space and bumped into her once. And she'd messed it up somehow. She mulled it over carefully and couldn't figure out what she'd done wrong. She liked him being near, close, bumping up against her.

What was that awful thumping? Had one of the shutters come loose? Now was not the time for that. She hated getting rained on. Frigid water running down her arms and legs was one of her least favorite things. Thinking about it made her shiver. Nope, she did not want to go out in the rain.

The back door opened with a swoosh. There, dripping water on the kitchen's faded linoleum floor stood a soaking wet Santiago. Mystery solved. From the looks of him, the storm was the least of her problems.

She scrambled to the kitchen leaving the album forgotten next to the stereo.

"What happened? Are you all right?"

"*Sí, Carida.* Now that I am here." He threw off his raincoat and wrapped his arms around her.

Her arms hugged him of their own accord. That was a telling sign if there ever was one. Her arms welcomed him even soaking wet and shivering. She gasped, "You're freezing." She inhaled while a tremor ran through her. "And you're all wet."

"It is raining outside." His hand cradled the back of her head. "I thought you might be scared being here alone, so I came back."

She was definitely not scared of the storm, but if that's what he needed to tell himself who was she to argue? It was as good a reason as any. Once she got him out of those wet clothes and into something warm, it would be a wonderful night. Mother Nature absolutely knew how to liven up the dark.

"Get out of those clothes and I'll throw them in the dryer before the power goes out."

"I must get your generator out of the shed and hook it up first."

"That thing is ancient. I'm not sure it even works."

"I brought some gasoline for it. You can help me get it from the shed."

"Fine. Let me get Gram's old rain slicker." She dug through the old jackets and ponchos on the hooks lined up in the utility room. She pulled the stiff yellow rain slicker out of the jumble and dropped it over her head.

The shed was not that far away on a normal day, but in the gale-force wind and rain it was too far. She followed him into the darkness with only their flashlights to illuminate the ground. Opening the shed door was not the best idea they'd ever had. The wind threatened to tear it off the hinges and Banji hoped her weight leaning into it would be enough to keep it from being ripped out of her hands.

If she ever got back to the safety of her living room, he was going to get a lesson in just how much she hated being cold and wet.

He rolled the generator out of the shed and helped her secure the door before proceeding to pull the red box on wobbly wheels to the front porch. The outdoor outlet that would connect the generator to the house was located there. Gram had believed in being ready for every possible disaster. Banji, not so much.

Santiago poured gasoline into the tank and gave the starter cord a yank. The handle came off in his hands with the frayed fragments of the cord poking out.

Banji's snicker morphed into a chuckled before becoming a full-throated laugh. "Come on, let's go inside, get out of these wet clothes and get warm."

"I should go home." Hc looked toward the dunes.

"No. The storm has gotten worse and it's not safe to be walking around outside." She grinned. "Guess you'll have to stay with me tonight."

"I have nothing dry to wear."

Was he smirking at her? No, he wouldn't do that. She peered closer at the edges of his moustache. Hmm, he might. And the twinkle in his eyes was a definite improvement over the dull sadness that clouded them earlier.

"You can change in the bathroom and dry off while I get you a blanket."

Santiago followed her down the hall, veered off into the bathroom and closed the door. He peeled off his soggy clothes and dropped them outside the door. The fluffy pink towel he used to dry off smelled like tropical flowers. She was such a girl. He buried his face in the towel, inhaled the scent and grinned. His towels were black and smelled of laundry detergent.

The knock on the door signaled his blanket had arrived. He stood behind the door with her pink towel wrapped around his middle and opened it a crack allowing her hand to pass him the sunny-yellow blanket. He dropped the towel on the counter and wrapped the blanket over his shoulders and snuggly around himself. He looked in the mirror. How pathetic. He looked like a giant cartoon bird.

Her voice came through the door. "I've made us some hot chocolate with a touch of Irish Whiskey. It'll take the chill off. There are still a few apricot cookies left. I didn't eat all of them last night after you left."

"I will wait for my clothes."

"It'll get cold by then." Silence. "What's wrong?"

"I am wearing your yellow blanket. I look ridiculous."

The lights flickered and blinked out.

She chuckled. "The bright yellow will help me find you in the dark. You won't be able to hide in the shadows. I'll go light the lamps."

One click and darkness had descended but he wouldn't be alone this time. He rubbed his chest to ease the discomfort in the vicinity of his pounding heart. He rested his forehead against the door. Was he making a terrible mistake?

He heard her call out, "Okay, it's safe to come out." Was she laughing at him? His lips curled into a full-fledged grin and he snorted softly.

He stepped out of the bathroom and padded barefoot to the living room. The soft light from the hurricane lamp held back the darkness and gave the room a sentimental glow. He folded himself onto the couch close to the coffee table. A quick arrangement of the blanket insured that only his head, forearms and hands were visible.

Banji brought two steaming mugs and put them safely within reach before making herself comfortable. She lifted her purple hibiscus-print robe out of the way and tucked her feet off to the side. Her gardenia scented perfume mingled with the smell of their hot chocolate.

She asked, "Are you warm enough?"

"Yes." He reached for his mug. His temperature was rising and it had nothing to do with the yellow blanket.

"I checked your clothes. Your t-shirt and briefs are still damp and the rest is very cold and wet. I'm afraid you're stuck with wearing that blanket toga for a while."

"I could wear my briefs, they can dry on me." His penis would shrink and his balls would shrivel from the wet chill but it was better than being naked under the hideous yellow blanket.

"Not happening. You'll be cold and miserable. I'll finish drying them when the power comes back on."

"We should have looked at the generator sooner. I will fix it so it is ready for the next storm." He picked up a cookie and bit into it.

"I was fine. My clothes weren't wet." She poked his upper arm through the blanket, laughed and reached for her mug.

His first instinct was to reach for her. The blanket would fall open and she'd see the monster underneath. He clutched the covering tighter.

She looked at the illuminated dial on her watch. "It's closing in on midnight. We should probably try to get some sleep." She sipped her drink and put the mug down on the table.

"I will sleep here." He patted the couch.

"I don't think so. This thing is ancient. It's barely fit to sit on. You're sleeping with me."

"It is not right."

"It's right enough under the circumstances."

She glared at him, at least it looked like she did. It was hard to tell in the flickering light. "I cannot."

"Yes, you can. The power is out. It's going to get cold. I'm going to get cold. If you don't want me sleeping on top of you on this lumpy couch, you will get in bed with me."

This was not how he envisioned their evening going. He was supposed to wrap them in a blanket, stretch out on the couch and keep her warm. He grumbled, "Go get ready for bed. I will be there soon."

"If you're not, I'll come looking for you." She pointed her index finger at him. "Don't make me come looking for you."

He caught her satisfied smile as she walked away. She picked up a flashlight from the kitchen counter as she passed. Miss Banji had a touch of her grandmother in her when it came to saying what was on her mind. Every day he learned more about her and every day his attraction to her grew. She was strong under the pretty.

He heard her shout. "Okay, bathroom's all yours. Time to blow out the lanterns and come to bed."

Gulping down the last of his chocolate and whiskey concoction he contemplated his options. He could put on his freezing wet clothes and go home. Or he could get in bed with Banji and keep his hands to himself. If he went home he'd be cold and alone. Mind made up, he carried the lantern down the hall to the room they would share. He preferred to be warm.

It was time to lie down next to his *Carida,* and pray. Pray for forgiveness, pray for strength, and pray she didn't run screaming from the sight of him. He blew out the flame and slipped under the covers.

~

Somewhere in the hours before dawn, Banji had nestled herself up against Santiago's back. His body heat had drawn her close and his skin, smooth as velvet in the night, had beguiled her subconscious into making her stay.

The first foggy-grey light of day peeked around the edges of the shutters. She inhaled deeply and exhaled slowly. He smelled delicious, clean and male, yummy. Rainy days were for lying in bed skin to skin under her Gram's cozy comforter.

Santiago still slept soundly next to her. She snuggled into his warmth.

She rubbed the sleep from her eyes and did her best to focus in the dim light. She stifled a gasp. Who had done this to him? Puckered crisscrossing scars covered his back. And the raised marks of brands burned into his skin suggested hours of torture. Her fingers followed the marks while her mind tried to make sense of them.

Her arm snaked over his ribs, her hand rested against his chest and she pressed her forehead to his back.

His voice rumbled deep in his chest. "Good morning, *Carida.* "

"I'm sorry. I didn't mean to wake you." She pressed closer. "You're so warm. It feels good."

"Do not let those old scars frighten you. It was a long time ago. We were very bad men doing terrible things. It is in the past." His hand rested over hers.

"I'm not scared." And that was the unvarnished truth. She was not afraid of Santiago or where he'd been, and being with him did feel good. It might not make sense to the rest of the world but she didn't give a damn about that. For the first time in a long time, she was content with where she was and who she was with. She wasn't doing the walk of shame this morning. "I'm so sorry this happened to you. I wish I could make it all disappear."

"I would not be the man I am."

Such softly spoken words she was barely able to hear them.

"All right then. I like you the way you are." She rubbed her foot up along his calf. She liked touching him, the feel of him. He was quickly becoming her obsession.

"You must tell me your age, *Carida*." He tightened his hold on her hand.

"*Carida* is nice. I like that." She flexed her knee and brushed it over his thigh. "I love rainy days lounging in bed." She didn't want to talk about her age. Or his for that matter. "A couple of stupid numbers do not dictate happiness." Well, at least not to her they didn't. She was all done being dictated to. "It's too early to get up."

He released his grip and patted her hand. "Sleep, *Carida*. I will make breakfast for us in a little while."

"No rush. The sound of the rain on the roof is perfect for dreaming."

Heaven help him. The rain and lazy morning were perfect for other things as well. Things like rolling around in the blankets with a soft and sexy woman. His *Carida* was made for what he had in mind. At forty-two he was still strong and hard bodied. The arduous nature of his work kept him in shape. Everything was in working order and he liked the idea of being able to please his woman.

There was only one small problem. He needed her age before things went any further. No honorable man would take advantage of a young woman half his age. What kind of future could they have? She'd have to take care of him in his old age while her best years slipped away. It wouldn't be fair. And considering his past, he didn't deserve her.

"I cannot make love to you until you tell me the truth." He held his breath and waited.

"Later. I'll tell you later. Right now, we're good like this." She draped her leg over his thigh, and exhaled slowly.

Santiago listened to her even breaths. She'd dozed off to sleep so easily. She truly wasn't afraid of him. There was a chance she would come to accept him, all of him. It would take time. He would wait.

He rolled to his back and snaked his arm under her shoulders, pulling her against the side of his chest. "Come *Carida*, let me hold you." He closed his eyes. "You are safe with me."

The next time her conscious mind surfaced, she kept her eyes closed and savored the feel of the man pressed against her. Oh, yeah. If she wasn't mistaken that was one big, hard cock pressing against her abdomen. She snuggled a little closer and hugged him a little tighter, her hand resting on his chest.

Santiago's voice rumbled. "*Carida,* you are making it very hard for me to be an honorable man."

"You worry too much." Her fingers brushed over his nipple. "Um. So nice."

His hand grasped hers. "You must learn to trust me. I cannot make love to a stranger."

She peeked at him through her sleepy eyes. One look at his face made it clear he was not in the habit of having meaningless sex. He wanted her but only on his terms. Santiago was not only old, but old-fashioned. More and more it was looking like he could really be her one-and-only. What had she gotten herself into? Well, that was a stupid question. She wouldn't be in bed with him if he wasn't definitely a real possibility. That realization had hit her days ago when she was picking out condoms. Large, ribbed, colors, warming, so many decisions. She'd settled for the variety pack. Now, she wondered what it would be like to ride him bareback. That was definitely a sign she was thinking about making him more than an affair. In the meantime, they could try them all and figure out which ones worked best.

Nervous or not, she really needed her cards. She wanted to know what they held, and at the same time she didn't just in case it was bad news. They were in one of the boxes she hadn't unpacked yet and she had no clue which one. She'd been in a hurry when she'd unceremoniously thrown her life in the cardboard containers and left town.

Once she found them, she'd shuffle the deck and pray they'd reveal her future with Santiago. Maybe then she'd be able to breathe easy. In the meantime, she'd hold him and pretend he was hers. Heaven knew she was good at pretending. She inhaled the masculine scent that was uniquely his and closed her eyes, content to be held in his familiar arms. This was much better than dancing.

She had no idea how long she'd slept but her ears were responsible for forcing her out of her warm, comfortable dream and back into reality. Rain pounded on the roof loud enough to wake the dead. The storm wasn't letting up. The mattress jiggled and she cracked open one eye. Santiago moved slowly getting out of bed. She watched until he walked out and disappeared down the hall. Okay, she had to slow her rapid pulse. Slow, deep breaths didn't help. The broad shoulders, sturdy hips, toned thighs, and taught butt cheeks had her attention. She pushed the blanket away in hopes of cooling the sudden rush of warmth that flooded her body. If she could block out the sight of him standing naked at the bedside, she'd get back to normal. Yeah, that was a nice thought that went absolutely nowhere. She pulled the covers up to her chin to ward off the chill. One look at him had her temperature rising and the cottage was chilly. No man alive had ever had that effect on her. Not until Santiago.

She rested her forearm across her eyes. Just breathe. She could do that.

Banji reached out and ran her hand over the warm sheet where Santiago had been moments before. She missed him, the soft sound of his breathing, the warmth of his skin on hers.

The morning brought with it a secluded, secret rendezvous vibe. There was nowhere to go in the storm. They could cuddle on the couch or lounge in bed. She rolled over, buried her face in his pillow and inhaled. He smelled right, felt right, sounded right, looked wonderful. The only thing left was to get a taste of him. The five senses were never wrong. She couldn't exactly walk up and bite the man, but she could get a little lick, if she snuck up on him from behind. She kicked off the covers and grabbed her robe to guard against the chill. Her hot-pink chemise was cute but not made for warmth.

CHAPTER SEVEN

BANJI TRUNDLED her way to the kitchen. The smell of food was tantalizing but the sight of Santiago standing over the stove was the clincher. She walked up behind him, wrapped her arms around his waist and laid the side of her head against his back.

With her hands under his t-shirt and openly pressed against his abs, she held him in place. "Thank you for everything."

"It is my pleasure, *Carida.*" He tipped his head to the side toward the coffee maker. "The power is back on. There is coffee ready if you want it."

"In a minute. Right now, I want more of this." She closed her eyes and inhaled slowly. Letting go could wait. It would have been nicer if the power had stayed off longer. But no such luck. And he knew how to operate a dryer. Now, he was safely tucked back into his clothes. Damn the bad luck.

He said, "Breakfast is ready. You should sit down. I will bring your plate."

She let go, strolled the few steps it took to reach the table and took a seat. He'd heated Gram's old stoneware plates and loaded them with bacon, scrambled eggs and toast. Simple but it worked and it wasn't burnt beyond recognition.

47

For the next few minutes they ate in companionable silence. She picked up her last slice of bacon.

"*Carida.*" The warning tone only deepened his already deep voice.

"What?" She bit into the bacon and chewed.

"How old are you?"

"Old enough that it doesn't matter." Her face crinkled with a frown. "Why?"

"It matters to me." He sat back, crossed his arms over his chest and held her gaze. "Are you half my age? Will you be satisfied with an old man in your bed?" He raised an eyebrow. "Tell me."

"You're not old." She sniffed.

"I am forty-two."

She grinned, "That's perfect." Mr. Inscrutable didn't budge, didn't smile. "Uh! Fine, I'm going to be thirty next August. Like over-the-hill, spinster-on-a-shelf thirty. Have to turn in my jeans and wear stretch pants, thirty." She winced.

He pushed back from the table and held out his hand.

She glanced at his working-man's hand and calloused fingers, then at the unreadable expression she found so-him, and muttered, "What?"

He curled his fingers. "Come, *Carida.*"

Was it a trick? "Why?" She threaded her fingers through his.

He huffed out a breath. "Because I want to hold you."

Uh-oh. She was about to get what she'd been after since she'd woken up comfortably warm with him in bed this morning. Suddenly, and a little too late, her self-confidence deserted her. Santiago was no ordinary man. Did she really want to go there? "Are you sure I'm not too old for you?" Her bottom lip curled out in a challenging pout.

"I am an honest man and I say what I mean." His fingers remained intertwined with hers. "There are some things you should know about me before I make love to you."

"Okay, fine." She got up and moved around the table.

He pulled her onto his lap and wrapped his arms around her. "Ah, this is much better."

She ran her index finger over the edge of his moustache. "This is nice. And it's softer than it looks."

His lips turned up at the corners. "What would you like to do now?"

"I think I'd like a nap." She glanced at the shuttered window over the sink. "It's still raining."

He stood up with her in his arms. "I will help you relax so you can rest."

"Okay, but you have to stay with me. No getting up and sneaking away."

For a brief moment she caught a twinkle in his eyes while he said, "I will not leave you." His steps quickened and she landed in the blankets and pillows before she had time to come up with an answer. The line of his jaw and the dark stubble along his chin had distracted her. She liked everything about him.

He laid down next to her and pulled the covers over them. "I do not want you to get cold."

She rolled to her side facing him. "I won't. I have you to keep me warm." Her fingers found the hem of his t-shirt and she slipped her hands underneath. Her leg slid over the top of his. "These pants gotta go."

"If you are sure that is what you want."

"I can close my eyes, if it'll make you more comfortable. But I already saw your back. I'm okay with it."

"Perhaps the front is worse."

"If you're trying to scare me, it's not working." She snickered and slid her leg up a little higher on his thigh. "Maybe we should take a bath together and you can hide under the bubbles."

"Later." He disentangled himself from her, rolled away and stripped off his clothes.

While he stepped out of his pants, Banji pulled off her chemise and flung it past him. He wouldn't have to guess what state of undress she was in. Bring it. She didn't want anything getting in the way.

Santiago turned around giving her the full view. And it was impressive. Nicely defined pecs and abs. A small, neat patch of black hair perfectly framed the root of the generous length of his cock. He was a living dream. She held out both arms to him. "Come keep me warm."

The ink and scars covering his chest weren't any worse than the ones

49

on his back. Whatever hell he'd escaped from hadn't broken him. He'd survived and made his way to this secluded stretch of beach. Her beach.

"With pleasure, *Carida*." He slipped into bed beside her.

She wrapped her arms around his shoulders as he wrapped his around her waist and pulled her to him. Her skin pressed tightly to his was the best feeling in the world. And it was only the beginning. Had she ever wanted anything as badly as she wanted Santiago? That was a clear, no. Somehow over the past couple of weeks he'd slipped quietly inside of her outer defenses. Now she was wrapped in his solid arms. Her leg between his thighs. A little higher and she'd nudge his already erect cock. "I got large, ribbed, lubricated condoms."

His hand slipped between her legs and his fingers deftly worked their way to her center.

"I have not used them. I have only been with my wife." His gazed held hers.

"That's okay. I can show you, and it's easy." She brushed a hand down his arm. "I'll make it good for you."

His smile caught her attention, but his words let her know she was right about him. He was ready to please. She could feel his breath on her lips when he whispered, "I think you should kiss me first." He slipped a finger inside her warm, wet entrance.

"I'm going to kiss you all over." She pressed her lips to his. His lips were soft and warm. His arms strong and secure. His skin velvety smooth against hers. If there was a perfect man for her, Santiago was it. Her inner walls hugged his exploring finger. The invasion of the second digit made her whimper, "That's so good."

She teased his lips open and delved deep with her tongue. He tasted like breakfast. She could spend the morning kissing and tasting, but another fire was already burning out of control. Moving slowly, she gently urged him onto his back. His fingers slipped out as she glided over him. His hands strayed to her hips and held her snuggly in place. His rigid length tucked between her slick folds. This alone was perfection, but the promise of what was to come hinted of ecstasy. And that couldn't be rushed. He deserved to be loved.

She broke their kiss. "Let me love you."

"*Si, Carida.*" His fingers pressed into her flesh and deliberately positioned her clit over the broad head of his cock. With a slight rocking of his hips he rubbed her sensitive nub.

Banji whimpered in the back of her throat and murmured, "You have to stop or I'm going to come. Please, baby, I need to feel you inside me."

"Later."

She groaned. "Later will be too late." He thrust his slick member back and forth over her clit in short strokes while holding her hips firmly in place creating an unbearable friction. "That's so good." Beyond aroused and ready to tip over the edge into oblivion any second.

Her inner walls clenched, her thigh muscles bunched as the building tension of her impending orgasm took over.

"Come for me, *Carida.*"

Her fingers curled into his pecs and she wailed, "Yes, oh yes!" She pressed down on his hard length eliciting the final burst of pleasure as her orgasm rippled through her body.

His hands slid up along her sides and pulled her to his chest. A smooth roll and she was under him. "Now, *Carida*, which condom do you want me to use?"

Her breaths came in short gulps of air and her body thrummed with pleasure including the tingling in her toes. "It doesn't matter. They're all good."

Santiago picked up the first packet his fingers landed on. Ribbed, lubricated and warming sensation. Great. He could do this. He'd used condoms twenty-two years ago before he got married, not much had changed. At least he hoped not. Damn, being with a younger woman was already a challenge and now this.

The mattress moved under him and her hands slid across his shoulders and down his arms. "Let me do that." She kissed the side of his neck. "There's something I'd like to do first." She took the packet from his grip. "It's our first time together and I want to make it special for you."

She scooted back and brushed her fingers along the comforter. "Lay down here and let me take care of you."

Truth and vulnerability collided deep inside, crawled up his throat and made it hard to breathe. No one had ever offered to take care of him in that way.

"*Carida*, you do not need to do this." The pounding in his chest increased, his ability to think faltered.

How many times had Carmen told him that his desire for physical pleasure was wrong? A man couldn't do the things he'd done and expect to be rewarded. Banji's touch brought him back to the present, to the ecstasy and the hunger thrumming through his veins.

"I know, but I want to." She slipped her fingers through his hair starting at his brow, gently moving past his ears and around to the back of his neck. "If there's anything you don't like, tell me and I'll stop."

Her caresses reached into his heart, easing the uncertainty that had tortured him since their first meeting. Some self-destructive inner demon compelled him to tell her, "I have not done this. You must tell me what to do."

"Relax, lay back, close your eyes. I'll take care of everything." She pressed a soft kiss to his inner thigh. "It all starts with a kiss." Her lips brushed against his sensitive skin. "Just one kiss can start a fire."

Santiago's eyes closed and his body pulsed uncontrollably to the beat of an old song. He had known heartache and pain. Banji was warm and offering him a chance to change his solitary life. He would let her show him love. She owned him, everything he ever was and ever would be as he stifled the pitiful whimpers threatening to escape from his throat. Her soft kisses pressing up and down his inner thighs quickly brought him to a state of heightened arousal the likes of which he had never experienced before.

When he thought he couldn't stand anymore she wrapped her fingers around his aching cock, her thumb playing with the underside, rubbing just below the head. A new and desperate craving ignited deep inside. He wanted to feel her affection. His knees bent and his heels dug into the mattress raising his cock in an offering to her warm breath caressing the crown.

His hunger for her to take him, consume him, became almost unbearable. His body ached for release. He would give her all of himself.

The soft press of her lips to his crown and the slow skim of her tongue over the center drew a strangled moan from him. "*Carida.*" He drew in a ragged breath. "Please, I need you."

The loss of warmth over the crown of his penis was the signal that she'd heard his plea. The sound of the condom wrapper tearing gave him ease and allowed him to breathe easily as she slid it over his engorged length.

He had never been so helpless, so desperately craving a woman's touch.

Banji straddled his abdomen and slid lower. Her hands pressed into his pecs. Her words flowed over him. "You're perfect the way you are." She positioned his cock at her entrance and slowly sank down. He was hard, aching, and needed to move to increase the friction that would bring him release.

He was big and she was tight. The slow descent stretching her, turning her into a snug glove around his pulsing erection. It was the most exquisite torture, one he'd only been able to dream about. His hands found her hips. "Please *Carida*, take what you want."

Banji slid all the way down and stopped when he was fully seated deep inside of her. She rubbed her clit over his pubic hair and hissed, "Yes, that's so good. You fill me up just right." She glided back and forth, short strokes, slowly at first. As the tension increased so did the length and speed. Her pussy pulsed around his dick, but when she ground down on him and her inner muscles clenched around his length, a groan tore from his throat as he came hard, pumping semen into the condom glove buried deep inside her core.

Moans mingling together, his deep, hers a high wail, he held her hips firmly in place while her orgasm rippled through her. Her cries filled the space around them. Nothing had ever sounded sweeter to his ears. He had brought his woman to euphoric completion. She crumpled onto his chest, her skin damp, her body sated.

Small spasms racking both their bodies, she lay sprawled on top of him. His legs tingled and his testicles slowly relaxed. Soon his erection would recede. He shifted his weight rolling them to the side. "*Carida*, I must remove this covering."

Her hand stroked the skin over his ribs, her fingers digging into his flesh. "Stay where you are a little longer. It feels like heaven."

Their mouths tangled together as her hand moved to his cheek. He leaned into the gentle caress. Never had he been treated with such love and tenderness. He would remember and treasure this day for the rest of his life.

She nibbled on her bottom lip, a smile creeping across her face she said, "The first time is always the most uncomfortable. It'll get better, I promise."

Had she read his mind? If it got any better, it might kill him. It would not be a bad way to die.

CHAPTER EIGHT

BANJI HEARD the chime and glanced at her phone. Alena? Wow, could the timing be any worse? Santiago was barely out of sight headed to his house and she was still in her robe enjoying the afterglow. The man was amazing.

She inhaled and answered the call. "Hi! What's the scoop?"

"Where are you?"

That was Alena, direct and to the point.

Banji grimaced. "Home, why?" It wasn't exactly a lie. The cottage was her home. Her San Francisco apartment was long gone.

"Just wondering what you're doing for the holidays. The racing season is wrapping up and I'm home working on next year's car. I thought you could come visit me."

"Let me check my schedule. I'm pretty sure it'll work."

"Banji, your sister called." That warning tone was a dead giveaway that Alena knew all about the disaster zone otherwise referred to as her life. "I know you're persona non-grata in the city these days and you were let go from Nerbert's Auction.

"It's no big deal. I'm an independent appraiser at the moment. And I don't have a sister. There's only Madison, the spoiled-rotten half-sister."

"So, you're unemployed with zero prospects and zero social life. It's the perfect time to visit me."

"Wow, who peed on your breakfast this morning?"

"Nobody. I woke up this way. I couldn't sleep with all the noise from the storm last night."

"Well, grab Gabriel and go back to bed. You'll feel better in no time."

"You're the Queen of Wands, not me."

"What's that supposed to mean?"

"You're the one who likes things wild and spicy." She snickered. "I'm more the reserved and quiet type."

"Liar!" A full-throated laugh escaped. "You're lots of things, but none of them fall under quiet or reserved."

Alena wheedled, "I miss you and you're not busy. Come see me."

"Maybe. I have to work some things out."

"Okay. Well, let me know." She hummed and added, "I know you're at your Gram's cottage. So, work them out quick and get over here before I come looking for you."

No point in lying. "Yeah, I need a roof over my head and this one is paid for. I'm fixing it up."

"Do you want me to come help you?"

Oh, shit, no! That wouldn't be a good idea. Calm, she needed to sound calm. "Um, no, I've got it under control. I'm almost done."

"Well, okay if you're sure?"

"I'm sure." Banji giggled. "But I do have more boxes to unpack." Alena hated packing and unpacking. Like she'd rather eat lint than pack a box. Ask anyone who went to college with her.

"Yeah, no. I'm not good with boxes. Hmm, I was wondering whatever happened to your Gram's Trans Am? That was a great car. I'd love to put it in a show."

Deflect and avoid. Brain not working. No reasonable excuse popped into her head. "Uh, I had it towed. It's been collecting dust in the shed and it's in real bad shape." There, that was kind of true, more or less.

"Well, let me know when it's fixed. We can work something out. It's a classic."

56

"Right. Classic." Kind of like the man fixing it, but Alena didn't need to know that particular detail. What would she say when she found out Banji was sleeping with an older man? The older man who would be back any minute. "I have to get dressed. I've got someone coming by to pick up my old bedroom furniture."

"Are you really going to be staying at the cottage permanently?"

"Yeah. I like it here." She walked down the hall toward her bedroom. Her world wouldn't fall apart if she fell in love with Santiago. "It's got some things I can't get anywhere else."

Things like a man that could make her come undone with a touch of his hand and a whisper in her ear. No man had ever made her come twice so quickly. Amazing.

CHAPTER NINE

THAT AFTERNOON BANJI sat at the kitchen table, sipping on a wine cooler and sorting Ritter's love letters by date. She was immensely grateful for the lack of wi-fi back in those days. These letters wouldn't exist and she'd have no idea how to find out what had really happened to make Gram move to the edge of the world. Without Gram there would be no Santiago.

Her musings were interrupted by loud knocking on her front door. She wasn't expecting any deliveries. She pushed back from the kitchen table and muttered, "Really? Now that I have something to do, people come knocking. This better be good."

One twist of the knob was all it took to reveal her third least favorite relative. "Madison, what are you doing here?" Banji didn't hate her, that would take too much effort, but she didn't like her either.

"Hi! Banji. I'm sorry to arrive unannounced but it's important."

"You have my number. You could have called." She stayed firmly planted in the doorway and took in her half-sister's appearance. Nothing had changed. Madison still wore a white blouse with a non-descript grey skirt and matching sensible shoes. Boring.

"I was afraid you'd hang up on me. Can I come in?" Madison's eyes darted past Banji to the interior of the cottage.

"Why?"

"I need to show you something."

"Like what? The new car Dad bought you? I can see it fine from here."

"That's like three years ago."

"Really? Feels like yesterday when I became a certified gemologist and earned my appraisal certification. You got the summer in Europe and the brand-new Mustang Dad promised me." She pointed at the driveway. "And I got that. The cheapest third-hand, bargain-of-the-day car he could find."

"That's not my fault."

"Right. Not your fault." She tightened her grip on the door.

"You could have traded it in. You had a good job."

Banji stared at the offending vehicle. "I keep it to remind me of how much Dad loves me."

Madison held out her left hand. "I think I have a problem with this." She twitched her left ring finger. "I don't think it's real and I don't know who else to ask."

Banji glanced at the sparkling engagement ring and back at her half-sister's pinched up face. "I've never seen it before." She exhaled loudly. "I wasn't invited to your engagement party or your bridal shower. And I've been disinvited to your wedding. Whatever is wrong with it isn't my fault."

"I need you to look at it and tell me the truth. Is it real?"

"Are you kidding?"

"No. I'm not kidding." Madison winced and pulled her hand back.

Banji inhaled and exhaled slowly. "Well, all right. Come in and sit down at that table right there." She pointed at the kitchen table. "You don't get to go wandering around in here plotting what you can borrow and forget to return. Those days are over."

"I didn't know it was really your stuff. Mom told me those things were supposed to be ours and you didn't want to share." Madison slid onto the chair Banji pointed at.

"That makes zero sense but you've always been a little on the gullible side."

"I tried to get your Mom's earrings back but they're locked up in

59

the safe." She twisted the engagement ring around her finger. "Why are you still so mad?"

"Ah, because you got everything and I got kicked out of the house." She fished in a kitchen drawer and pulled out her magnifying jeweler's loop. "Gram took me in and paid my tuition or god only knows what I'd be doing for a living at this point."

Madison's gaze followed Banji's every move. "What was I supposed to do?"

"Same as always. Keep quiet, take the education, the car, the clothes, the vacations and smile." She plopped onto the chair opposite Madison. "Give me the ring. Let's see what you've got." She held out her hand. "I'm going to do this one last thing for you and then you are leaving and never coming back. Do you understand?"

"Sure, Banji." She twisted the ostentatious ring off her left ring finger. "I've never been as brave as you. It terrified me when Mom would lock me in my room. There was no way out. I've never been able to stand up to them the way you do."

"One of these days you'll figure it out." Banji held the ring up to her eyepiece. "This is a very good imitation. The split shank is a lovely style. The brilliant cut, round side stones in the crown are real but the center stone isn't." She handed it back to Madison.

"It was when I picked it out."

"And then what happened?" Banji raised an eyebrow.

Madison sniffled. "Bennett took it to be cleaned."

"Crying won't fix it. Tell me what happened next?"

"I was out shopping before my bridal shower and I wanted it to be really sparkly for everyone to see and I stopped at the jeweler in the mall. The clerk cleaned it and said it looked as good as the real thing."

"Sounds about right. A real center diamond this size is extremely expensive. Cut, clarity, color, and carat all go into the value. If it was D, it was colorless and very expensive, H-J is near colorless and still good. You'll have to look at the certificate to know what you had. Bennett had it taken out and replaced with this. The real one is probably in his safe. You'll never see it again."

"But it's mine. It's my ring." Madison's eyes teared up. "I picked it out."

60

"Sorry. You can ask Bennett to give it to you or have it reset, but he won't. He paid for it. It's an investment as far as he's concerned. It'll never be yours."

"I won't wear this. It's not real." Madison dropped the ring into her purse.

"Ah, yeah, that's great today but what are you going to do on your wedding day? People are going to expect to see it." Banji rested her hands on the table. "You'll need a good excuse."

Madison's lips pinched tightly together and she stuck out her chin. "I'm not getting married. Any man who would give his fiancée a fake ring doesn't love her. And I'm not marrying a man who doesn't love me." She pushed back from the table. "I'll have to send out notices to my guests."

"But you love Bennett."

"Not anymore." Madison stood up and put her purse strap over her shoulder. "Not in a long while actually."

Banji shrugged. "So, when did you fall out of love with the most wonderful man in the world?"

"After I accepted his proposal, he started changing. He hasn't been wonderful for a while. He says it's all the stress from his work and the upcoming wedding but I don't think so."

Banji made a circle on the table top with her finger and looked over at Madison. "I'm sorry things aren't working out the way you wanted. Do me a favor and leave my name out of all this. I've got nothing to do with it and I don't need any more trouble. If you want a second opinion, there are some very good jewelers in Carmel. You can ask one of them to take a look at it."

"That's okay. I believe you. You've never lied to me." Madison let herself out, turned and said, "I'm sorry for all the things the folks did to you."

"Fine, and for the record, I tried to be your big sister when you were little, but you were too caught up in being their favorite to notice."

Madison winced. "Mom wanted to be sure I didn't disappoint Dad like you did." She bit her bottom lip. "By the time I figured out what was really going on, it was too late and you had gone off to

Europe. There were times I was so scared and wished you'd come home."

"Well, we can't fix any of that. Even if I wanted to, there's nothing I can do now. I've lost my job, my apartment, and my reputation. I've got nothing to work with. This is what you can expect when Dad turns against you. He wants this marriage and he's going to be royally pissed if you call it off."

"But I don't want to marry someone I don't love and who obviously doesn't love me." She rubbed the empty space where her engagement ring used to be.

"All I can say is, good luck, you're going to need it."

Banji watched the disillusioned bride shuffle to her car. At least she had a decent car to drive away. That was more than Banji had. She ran her fingers through her hair. Wow, what a mess. Madison had no idea the shit-storm she was going to set off when she got home and canceled her wedding. She'd better be prepared to pack her bags and get out of Dad's house fast. He'd been counting down the hours to the day Madison would marry into Bennett's family.

Banji watched Madison pull out of the driveway. She jumped and spun around when Santiago asked, "Who was that?"

"Where did you come from? And stop sneaking up on me." She closed the front door.

"I did not sneak up on you. I used the beach door like always." He chuckled, "You were not listening."

She walked back over to the table and plopped down. The old love letters were right where she'd left them. Waiting for her to return. "I was working on these letters when my half-sister showed up. There's a problem with her engagement ring."

"Did you fix it?"

"Yes and no. Yes, I answered her question and no, her problems are just starting." She sat back and looked directly at Santiago. "We've never been close. Our father sent me here to spend summers with Gram while they went to Orlando's amusement parks. I was here for most Thanksgivings and every Christmas while they went skiing in Colorado, Vermont or New Mexico."

He sat down across from her. "I am sorry but if you went with them, you wouldn't have had the time with Missus Lori."

She frowned. "If he hadn't cheated on my Mom with Madison's mother, maybe mine wouldn't be dead and I could have had more time with her."

"*Carida*, you would not be the woman you are today."

Her chin trembled and she inhaled a deep breath. "Maybe I'd be somebody better and smarter with lots of friends. Maybe I'd have a wonderful future and I wouldn't be sitting here all alone reading someone else's old love letters." She reached out and poked the box holding Ritter's letters.

Santiago's eyelids partially closed and his head tipped down. "I am sorry." He got up and walked out the way he'd come.

The door latch ticked shut and it hit her. What had she done?

"Wait." She swiveled around and jumped out of her chair but it was too late. His long strides had made short work of the distance. He was already descending the trail to the beach. She ran after him and stopped at the edge of the dunes. Barefooted she couldn't go any further. She yelled, "Come back!"

He didn't turn or look in her direction. Maybe he couldn't hear her. "Damn it. I wasn't talking about you."

She trudged back to her kitchen and flopped down at the table staring at the pile of old love letters. If she didn't rein in her careless mouth, she'd be alone forever. She'd stabbed Santiago in the heart judging by the pained looked on his face right before he walked out on her. The drooping shoulders were another clue. If she wanted to know what pain looked like, she only had to memorize the disappearing figure of the man tramping away from her.

There had to be a way to fix it.

Santiago's march to the beach was sightless and soundless. His only goal was to get far away from the pain in his chest. He didn't count, he was nobody to her. He could fix cars and do all the odd jobs around the house, like paint, close the shutters and move furniture. He could sleep next to Banji and have sex with her but he meant nothing to her.

He did his best to walk off the dreary thoughts swirling around in his head. The sun sinking low on the horizon cast shadows along the path. Shadows dark enough that he didn't see the dip in the sand. His next step faltered and he went down cursing. The pain shooting up his leg from his ankle told him he'd done more than simply twist it.

He struggled to his feet and limped slowly home. The ankle was throbbing hellishly when he reached his door. By the time he flopped down on the kitchen chair, propped his foot up on the opposite one and peeled his sock down the purple bruise covering his ankle had migrated half way down his foot.

He knew enough to know it wasn't broken but it wasn't going to disappear overnight. He called Alena. "I have sprained my ankle, can you come help me take care of it?"

Asking for help wasn't something he liked doing. He preferred to be independent and self-sufficient. Letting people get too close got his hopes up only to have them crushed. He'd been overjoyed to find Carmen. Too late he realized she cared for him as a friend but she wasn't in love with him and never would be.

With that sorrowful thought rolling around in his head, he leaned back and inhaled deeply. He thought being with Banji would be different. His scars and ink didn't bother her.

Alena's feet landed on his porch and a second later his door opened. She was on him in a flash. "What happened?" She stood over his extended leg and pulled off his sock. "This is awful." Her cold fingers gently pushed at his swollen flesh.

He winced and hissed out a breath through his clenched teeth. "I was not watching where I was going. I tripped." He sucked in a breath. When he couldn't stand it anymore he groaned. "Enough. Can you wrap it up for me? There are bandages in the bathroom drawer under the counter."

"You need an ice bag. This is going to hurt for days. No working. No standing on it for hours. You'll be staying off of it."

His grin was interrupted by a shooting pain from her next stab at his ankle. He growled, "Stop. I will not walk on it."

"Good." She let go of him and went down the hall toward the bathroom.

He had taught her too well. She could make him do damn near anything when she set her mind to it. She was the daughter he'd raised even if she wasn't his biologically. That was a small technicality. She'd legally changed her name to his and taken him to be her *Papi*.

She had him and her father. Montgomery Betmunn was in England visiting his family. Alena had taken over running Betmunn Racing and taken her place on the Board of Directors. He was very proud of her, even if she was a bit bossy. She got the *bossy* from her grandfather.

Before he had time to delve too far into the past, she was back and muttering about men being high-maintenance. She went about the chore of wrapping his foot like the expert she was. When she finished, she gently pressed her hands against his ankle and looked up at him. "There, all better. You are so lucky I became a registered nurse when I was living in Texas, otherwise you'd be waiting in some clinic for hours."

"Yes, you are right. I am a very lucky man." He tried to smile but couldn't quite make it happen.

"Okay, what's wrong? This isn't like you. You don't just trip. And you always watch where you're going. You taught me a long time ago to always check the ground for snakes."

"There are no snakes here." He stared at his bandaged ankle.

"There used to be. Who knows, maybe one got homesick and came back. Or maybe someone let one of their pet snakes loose when they got tired of taking care of it." She stared at him.

What could he say? Nothing new was wrong. It was the same as it had always been. He wasn't good enough. "It was the shadows. It is getting dark earlier these days."

"Right." She looked around the kitchen. "I'll fix you some dinner and I'll come back and check on you in the morning." She moved across the room to the cupboards. "Be sure to elevate that foot on two pillows overnight." She glanced at him over her shoulder. "I'll be back, so don't think you can fool me."

CHAPTER TEN

BANJI READ the same love letter for the third time and still didn't know what it said after, *My Dearest*. Her mind was not on the page. It kept wandering to the man who had walked out of her house and probably out of her life. She might be able to salvage their relationship if she did something fast to stop the hurt she'd caused from settling in.

But what could she do? She didn't know exactly where he lived. It was somewhere between her cottage and the Betmunn estate. But there were several vacation homes along the road in between. She couldn't go walking in the dark looking for a blinking arrow pointing to his house. She could call him and see if he'd answer the phone. That was a long shot.

She put the brittle paper down before she wrinkled it beyond recognition. She stared at the yellowed page. She could write him an apology, a love letter. And just exactly how would she deliver it? Damn, back to the drawing board.

He had towed Gram's Trans Am to his garage. Find the car and find the man. That had possibilities. She patted the love letter. "Thanks Gram. You're the best. Love the car."

All she needed was writing paper and a pen. And she didn't have any stationary so the pen was useless. Last resort, she picked up her phone and pressed his contact.

"Hello." He sounded gruffer than usual. Not surprising but still not a good sign.

"Hey, I want to say I'm sorry. You left before I could explain."

"You do not owe me any explanations. Do not worry."

"You don't understand." She inhaled deeply and let her breath out slowly. Crap! She sounded like a whining teenager. "Um, I've never told anyone this before. I guess because there really wasn't anyone to tell. I've been alone since Gram died. With her gone, there's nobody left to care what happens to me. If something goes wrong, I'm on my own. It's nothing to do with you."

"We have been together for weeks. We share your bed. You are not alone anymore. Why would you say it has nothing to do with me?"

The muffled grunt at his end of the connection caught her attention. She asked, "Are you all right?"

"I am okay."

"Then why don't you sound okay? Did something happen on the way to your house?"

"I twisted my ankle. I will be fine in the morning."

"I can come take care of you. You shouldn't be alone."

"No. I will call you tomorrow. Goodnight, *Carida*."

The call disconnected. Banji stared at the screen and her finger hovered over his contact. He'd hung up on her. Damn. She didn't want to push her luck by calling him back. This was not the time to argue.

Tomorrow couldn't come soon enough. She picked up a few of Ritter's letters and carried them to the couch. She could see the moon-light playing on the waves. There was something comforting about reading his letters with the ocean a stone's-throw away. She could swear he was out there on the water waiting for her to discover his secrets.

She picked up the page she'd put down earlier and got comfortable. *We will start a new life together. I have found a good place for the three of us.*

Three of them? What three? Who was he referring to? Banji had a new mystery to solve.

~

67

Santiago put the phone down on the nightstand next to his bed. His cold empty bed was no comfort to him and his throbbing ankle only made everything worse. The ice bag would help eventually along with the three anti-inflammatory pain pills he'd swallowed.

The ache in his heart was a little better since Banji had called. When he was able to walk in the morning, he'd go see her. There were things he needed to clarify. He huffed out a breath. If he'd asked her what was going on and not walked out assuming the worst, he might not be lying there like a beached whale.

He'd gone over to her house hoping to spend the night. Instead, her words brought up sad memories from a past not forgotten. He could ignore them when he worked or walked on the beach. But in the stillness of his empty house Carmen's words came back to haunt him. He would never be good enough. Men like him didn't deserve to be loved.

Banji had inadvertently ripped the scab off his deep festering wound. It was time to drain the poison and heal his heart while there was enough of it left to give to his *Carida*. He sighed heavily. It would be painful but it had to be done or he might as well resign himself to being alone for the rest of his life.

He wasn't used to explaining himself to anyone but if he wanted his relationship with Banji to move ahead, to turn into something long-lasting, he'd have to do better starting first thing in the morning. He glanced at his swollen ankle. It would have to stand the strain come daylight. He needed to see her face to face. He'd crawl to her house if he had to.

CHAPTER ELEVEN

BANJI SNIFFED, opened her eyes and sniffed again. Bacon, she smelled bacon and coffee. Santiago was back. She kicked off the covers and breathed in the aroma wafting around her head. Thank god and all her guardian angels for bringing him back to her. She would beg for forgiveness and promise to never, ever hurt him again.

She wrapped her robe around herself, scampered down the hall and skidded to a stop in the kitchen doorway. She hadn't fully appreciated him until that very moment. He wasn't a passing fancy. Santiago was the real deal.

"Come, the coffee is ready, *Carida*." He didn't look up from the stove. "Can you get the plates?"

She didn't have the words she needed to tell him all the thoughts whirling through her mind. She walked over and slipped her arms around his waist hugging him tightly. She sniffled, inhaled and sighed. With her eyes closed, she pressed her open hands against the soft cotton of his t-shirt, into the firm muscles beneath and murmured, "I missed you last night."

His arm moved as he turned the bacon in the pan. "I did not like sleeping without you next to me."

"It's different having someone in my life. I'm not used to it, yet. Please forgive me. I didn't mean to hurt you."

He turned off the stove. "It is my fault. I did not give you time to explain." He exhaled. "After breakfast we will talk so we do not have this misunderstanding between us."

"Promise?"

"Yes." He looked over his shoulder at her. "I promise."

"Okay, I'll get the plates." She squeezed him and let go.

He wanted them to stay together or he wouldn't be standing in her kitchen, head hung down and looking like he'd lost his last friend.

She watched him limp to the table and sit. The grimace bracketing the edge of his mouth was an indication he was in more pain than he wanted to admit. She shoveled her breakfast into her mouth and chewed. It was all her fault. If he hadn't gone home, he wouldn't have sprained his ankle.

She picked up her dishes and carried them to the sink. "I'll do these dishes later after I get you comfortable." She looked at him. "I'll go get the extra pillows to prop up your ankle while you finish eating."

"You do not need to do that. It will be fine." He took a sip from his coffee cup.

"You should elevate that ankle." She walked over and gently touched his hand. "Why don't you come lie down? Let me make you feel better."

"*Carida*, we need to talk."

"I know. We can talk in bed. You can stretch out and get comfortable."

"If that is what you want." A slight nod of his head and a soft-spoken reply let her exhale the breath she'd been holding.

"I'll go fix up your side of the bed."

A few minutes later, she helped him lose his clothes right down to his boxer briefs. Her fingers slipped behind the elastic band. "And these are way too tight. A man needs freedom to rest well." A slow descent and carefully sliding them past his swollen ankle only took her a few seconds. She stood up and surveyed her patient. Au natural was the best view. When had she become so obsessed with him? "Okay, lie back and I'll put a couple pillows under your leg."

By the time she was through, he looked like a very pampered man. Fluffy pillows under his head and shoulders, soft snuggly blanket in royal-blue tucked around him with his dreadfully swollen ankle propped up on two pillows.

She stepped back and examined her work. "There, that looks good. How do you feel?"

"Cold." He turned his soulful eyes on her. "You must come lie down next to me and keep me warm."

"That's the plan." She walked around to her side of the king-size bed and slipped off her robe. The snort behind her made her turn and stare. "What?"

"Is that my t-shirt?"

Was that a smirk under his moustache? The twitching at the corners of his mouth was a dead giveaway that he was failing to control the laughter behind the smile spreading across his face.

"I told you, I missed you." She plucked at the soft cotton material. "You left it here a couple days ago. It smells like you. It was the only way I could get any sleep."

He held out his hand to her. "Come, we will talk and then we will sleep."

Banji slid into bed, pulled the covers over herself and snuggled close to Santiago. When he put his arm around her shoulders and pulled her tightly to his warm body, she sighed and draped her arm across his midriff. "This is much better."

"Yes."

"What did you want to talk about?" Her fingers moved in lazy circles over his skin.

"I was married for twenty years. I do not know how to build this new relationship."

"Well, we're in uncharted territory. I've never had a real relationship." She tilted her head up and looked him in the eyes. "I know I want one with you. For the first time, this thing with us feels right."

He rested his hand over her fingers on his chest. "Those brands are from my days in Argentina working with some very dangerous men."

"That's over twenty years ago." She rested her head on his shoulder. "You're here with me now and that's the only part I care about."

"You might not say this if you knew the things we did."

And you might not want me, if you knew about the things I did in my younger days. I was a bit of a wild child. And it only got worse when I got to Rome."

"Tell me."

"Really? I guess you have a right to know before we get in any deeper." She inhaled deeply and exhaled. Any courage she might have had deserted her. It was time to suck it up and spit it out. "I drank too much and stayed out too late. Had more than my share of boyfriends I'd like to forget."

"After the terrible things I have done, that does not seem so bad."

"Maybe not to you, but it's embarrassing to me." She somehow managed to slip lower. It wasn't like she could hide from him.

"I am ashamed of the things I did." His head turned away from her. "I did not want to do them but it was the only way to survive. If I did not do what they wanted, they would kill my family."

"But you left."

"My brother made a mistake. He took what he should not have. It cost my sister, my father and mother their lives." He inhaled deeply and exhaled. "After that I had no reason to stay."

Banji's hand slipped out from under his and drifted slowly across his chest taking in the sensation of his warmth and strength. "You must have been terrified."

"I did not want to become an animal like the men who killed my family."

"How old were you?" Her fingers drifted back and forth over his skin.

"Seventeen. I ran and kept running. I met Carmen along the way. I did my best to protect us." His hand settled over hers and pressed it against his chest. "Sometimes, I think she married me so she wouldn't be alone here."

"I'm so sorry you had to go through all that."

"I am here now and that is what is important." He turned toward her."

72

"My mother walked into the ocean and drowned herself. My father threw me out of the house the day after I graduated from high-school. Gram was all I had and she was getting so old and tired by the time I finished college. I knew one day I'd wake up and she'd be gone." She sniffled. "I always end up alone."

"Ah, now I understand better." His hold on her tightened. "*Carida*, I will not leave you, but I will not try to make you stay, if you choose to go."

Her fingers circled his firm nipple. "I'm not going anywhere. I like it here just fine."

Her warm hand glided up and down his stirring length. Teasing fingers gently massaged the root of his cock and pleasure flooded his body. Her personal touch meant more to him than all the words in the world.

"*Carida*, we will not get any rest if you continue to torment me." His hand closed over hers cupping his length against his abdomen. "We will continue this later. For now, I am content for you to hold me."

CHAPTER TWELVE

SANTIAGO DIDN'T KNOW how long he'd slept but his eyes popped open when he heard Alena shouting, "Banji, where are you? Why is *Papi*'s truck in your driveway?"

He snatched the blankets up over his chest just in time for Alena to poke her head in the open doorway of the master bedroom.

He blinked. "What time is it?" He glanced at the empty space next to him. Where was Banji?

The sound of the shower running answered that question.

Alena peered over her shoulder at the bathroom's closed door and focused back on him. "It's almost eleven o'clock." Her eyes narrowed. "What's going on? Why are you in Banji's bed?"

He wasn't prepared for this. "Go wait in the kitchen. Let me get dressed."

"Get dressed? Oh, good gracious, are you naked under there?" She slapped her hand over her mouth. "Don't answer that." Alena backed out into the hall unable to stifle a giggle. "I'll just go wait in the kitchen."

How was he going to explain it? He threw back the covers and reached for his pants. He pulled on his wrinkled white t-shirt and hobbled out to the kitchen. He'd no sooner arrived than Banji called out, "Santiago, why don't you put on some music? Prop your ankle up on the couch. I'll fix an ice bag for you and we can watch a movie."

Alena turned toward him and crossed her arms over her chest. "Really? You and Banji laying on the couch watching movies. You never hold still that long." She chuckled. "I can't wait to hear this story."

"My ankle hurts too much to stand on it very long." He momentarily glanced at the floor. "I will let her tell you." He rubbed his hand across his mouth and smoothed down his moustache.

Alena dropped her arms and broke out laughing. "Are you kidding me? Amazing. And at your age. I can't believe it. You're having sex with Banji."

His *Carida* chose that moment to walk up behind him, slip her arm around his waist and say, "Well, believe it. Best sex ever."

He looked up at the ceiling and silently prayed for deliverance.

Alena stopped laughing and stared. "Banji Aloysius Preston, what is my *Papi* doing in your bedroom?"

"He fixed breakfast and needed to rest." She shrugged and tilted her head to the side. "What are you doing in my kitchen this early? Do you need your cards read?"

"No, I do not need my cards read." An amused huffing sound escaped as she gently shook her head. "I went to *Papi's* to fix him something to eat and check his ankle but he wasn't home." She shot a glance at Santiago then turned her attention on Banji. "His truck wasn't home and he didn't answer his phone. I was afraid his ankle had gotten worse overnight and he'd gone to the clinic in town." She backed up till her butt pressed against the cabinets. She reached back and rested the heels of her hands on the counter. "On my way to check the clinic I see his truck in your driveway and find him tucked up all comfy cozy in your bed."

"After we had breakfast he needed to elevate his ankle. Bed seemed like the best place to do that."

"Yeah, right. Like you're going to get me to buy that. How long has this been going on?" She pointed back and forth between Santiago and Banji.

Banji looked around the room and cocked her head to the side, put her finger to her lips and said, "I think I've heard those words in a song." She grinned. "Actually, I'm sure of it."

"Alena, I am a grown man. You wanted me to find a woman and I have." He pulled Banji closer against his side. "This one."

"Don't try changing the subject. I know you've been over here. That Trans Am gave it away weeks ago, but sleeping together, really, I'm not sure which one of you two surprises me the most."

"He's been spending the night since the big storm." Banji leaned her head against Santiago's chest. "It was a very cold night and he's nice and warm."

"Is he? I guess that's good to know." She looked back and forth between them. "Um, guess there's nothing to do but roll with it." She smiled broadly. "Gabriel's gone to the office and won't be back till late tonight. I thought I'd come see if you were hungry. And since *Papi* is here, we can all eat together. What do you say?"

Banji frowned. "Is that a trick question, because you know I don't cook?"

"No, it's not a trick. I have a nice pot of beef stew simmering on the stove and a homemade loaf of bread I just took out of the oven."

"It's okay with me." She looked up catching Santiago's eyes.

He nodded. "I will drive the truck home and meet you at the main house at lunchtime."

Alena tipped her head in his direction. "You could have told me this is who you're seeing."

His eyebrows furrowed and released. "Why?"

"Because Banji and I have been friends since grade school."

"I did not know Banji was your friend. You always told us you were going to play with the girl next door."

"Well, we're next door." She looked at Banji. "Are you sure about this?"

"I'm good." She tightened her hold on Santiago. "Better than good."

Alena grinned. "Great. I'll go set the table for three." She headed for the back door. "I can't wait to hear how you two met."

Banji waited until Alena was out the door and off the porch. "Wow, that went well."

"I did not know you were friends with Alena."

"We've known each other a long time. Whole years have gone by with only phone calls. We've been all over the world but not together and not at the same time."

"But you did not come to her wedding. I would have seen you."

"I got held up finalizing an appraisal at the Maritime Museum and then the next flight out of London was delayed." She turned and wrapped both arms around his middle. "Something tells me it all happened for a reason."

Banji stood in front of Alena's kitchen sink looking out the window. "Santiago should be along any minute." She bit her bottom lip. "He acts like he doesn't want me to see his house." She glanced over her shoulder at Alena. "Is there something wrong with it?"

"Not that I know of. He and Carmen lived in it since they got here." Alena put the bread basket on the table. "Would you mind getting the butter out of the refrigerator?"

"Can do."

"I'm glad he's found you. I've been worrying about him being alone. Carmen passed away two years ago." Alena opened the cupboard and reached for the bread plate. "I totally get wanting to be alone for a while after losing someone." She put the plates on the table. "But *Papi* is still a relatively young man and lately he's been too quiet. I was getting worried." She went back to the cupboard, took down two bowls and handed them to Banji. She reached up and grasped a third bowl. "He's been there for me through the good and the bad. All I want is for him to be happy."

Banji put the bowls on the counter next to the stove. "There's something about him that really works for me."

"Are you sure about that?"

"Absolutely."

The back door opened and Santiago stepped in. He shucked out of his coat and hung it on the back of his chair. "It is very cold today." He

77

smiled at Alena. "Thank you for making lunch." He put his hand on the small of Banji's back. "Come, sit, *Carida*."

He held the chair for Banji and she slid onto it. She stared across the room at Alena. "So, Santiago is your *Papi*? You never told me his name. I always pictured some really old guy, all wrinkly with grey hair."

"I never said anything of the sort." Alena giggled. "Where do you get these crazy ideas?"

"I don't know. Where do you get your crazy ideas?" She closed one eye, scrunched her face, relaxed it and sniffed. "Lunch smells delicious."

Banji glanced at Santiago. Something was wrong. He had that stunned into silence look that never bodes well. His butt landed in the chair to her left with his eyes focused on the table in front of him.

Alena slid onto the chair directly across from Banji. "How much remodeling are you planning on doing?"

Scrunching her lips together, Banji hummed and cleared her throat. "Gram's cottage is my home now. I don't have any plans to make big changes." She took a bite of stew. "Some fresh paint and new bedroom curtains. Maybe fix up the back room for an office." She glanced at Santiago. "Whatever Santiago thinks will work."

They both looked at Santiago who was staring silently at his untouched bowl.

Alena glance at Banji before turning her attention to Santiago. "What's wrong?"

"I should not have a relationship with my daughter's friend." Head down, he gazed at his bowl. "People will say it is wrong."

"Oh, hell no." Talk about being blindsided. Banji glanced at Alena and her forehead wrinkled. "There's nothing wrong about us. We're both consenting adults."

Alena nodded. "That's right. Banji being my friend doesn't put her off limits. We're not little kids. She's old enough to know what she's doing."

Banji's upper lip twitched and she shot a look at Alena before focusing on Santiago. "There, we're old enough to know what we want." She put her hand over his. "It's okay. Alena's not upset. Right?" She speared Alena with a quick glance.

"I'm totally fine with the two of you getting together." Alena leaned back in her chair. "Actually, I thought about it on the way home and I think it's perfect." She grinned. "I can't wait to tell Gabriel."

Banji nodded. "Exactly. I knew it. I read it in the cards. The Four of Cups reversed, came up for me. This new relationship is one of the positive changes in my life."

"If you are sure, *Carida*." He turned his head to meet her gaze.

She moved her hand up his arm and pulled him close. "I'm more than sure." She kissed his cheek.

Alena picked her spoon up. "Wonderful. Now that we have that settled, tell me what's up with you." She pointed at Banji.

"Not much. I let the apartment go and sold the furniture. No point in hauling the past around with me. I'm making a new life for myself." She stirred the stew in her bowl. "My degree from the Art Institute along with the gemologist certifications will get me a job. Something will turn up."

"Your furniture was all antiques. Those pieces can't be replaced. They were worth a small fortune." Alena's forehead wrinkled and her mouth turned down.

"They wouldn't fit in Gram's."

"Have you applied to the museums and auction houses in Los Angeles?"

"Yeah, like the day after I got here. I've looked through the ads and sent out inquiries, but no takers. No surprise there. I'm stepping back and rethinking things for now."

"Been there. It took me a long time to get back to doing what I love." Alena looked at *Papi* and then at Banji. "When was the last time you really put everything aside and asked yourself what you'd do if you could do anything you wanted?"

"That's easy. I'd stay here. I always hated it when summer would end and I'd have to go back to the city."

"Well, see, that's a start. You used to paint the prettiest watercolors. Have you thought about painting?"

"I haven't picked up a brush in years. No time. No inspiration.

Who has time to sit on the beach and paint?"

"Um, it was just a thought."

Alena got that thoughtful look that Banji knew only too well. Something had gotten the wheels turning. Whatever it was, she could forget about Banji painting seascapes.

Changing the subject, she said, "Santiago found Gram's old love letters from Ritter. I've been reading them when I'm not painting the walls." She glanced at Santiago and grinned. "I'm glad she saved them. He was so in love with her. I can see why she waited for him."

Alena took a sip of her tea. "But he never came back. Right?"

"He was lost at sea during a storm. She told me living here, close to the ocean, made her feel nearer to him. I never really understood that until now."

"Okay, that has to be some kind of a good sign." Alena raised another spoonful and blew on it. "Check the cards. Maybe there's a clue in there somewhere."

"I don't need the cards to tell me how lucky I am to be home. It's the wreckage all around me that's the problem. It's what comes next that's the mystery."

Alena chewed on her top lip. "I'm real familiar with that. You can do it. You're here for a reason." She looked pointedly at *Papi*. "I think you've come home to a good place and family."

Santiago met Alena's gaze. "Banji belongs with us."

"There you have it. It's official." Alena looked at Banji. "You're one of us. You're not an orphan. Get used to it."

Banji put her hand on his thigh. "We're together now." She glanced towards Alena. "And you've always been there for me. The past is just that, the past. No looking back. Today is what counts."

Alena exhaled audibly. "Wow, when did you get so smart?"

"I think it started in Verona. I went to Juliet's house and I didn't have a note to put in the wall. No letter asking for her advice on how to mend a broken heart or find a true love. I had nobody." She looked at the man sitting next to her. "I hadn't met Santiago yet."

"Okay, so no advice for the lovelorn. Not exactly deep philosophy there." Alena brushed her hair back from her face.

"Right, but after that I went to England and did an appraisal for the

Maritime Museum. It was a once-in-a-lifetime opportunity and it changed everything."

"I remember that. You missed my wedding because of some long-lost pirate treasure." Alena put her spoon down and leaned forward in her chair.

Banji took a drink of her iced tea and set the glass down within easy reach. "The runaway princess of Genoa and her pirate lover's treasure." She looked at Santiago and squeezed his thigh. "Princess Alessia loved the corsair Salvatore so much, she ran away with him. Her enraged betrothed followed them to the Bahamas and killed them in a battle at sea. Salvatore's ship, *El Anochecer* sank with the treasure onboard."

Santiago grumbled, "A corsair was a very bad thing to be. Only the worst of all pirates could be such a devil."

Banji let go of his thigh and intertwined her fingers with his. "Apparently, Alessia didn't care about his past. They stole away in the dead of night and married. They sailed to the Bahamas hoping to make a new life for themselves."

His eyes met hers. "*Ay, Carida*, he should not have taken her if he could not protect her."

"The point is, Alessia loved Salvatore for the good still in him. They wanted to start over and spend the rest of their lives together. After hearing that story, I had to seriously rethink a lot of things."

Alena's phone chimed. She glanced at it and said, "It's Gabriel. I'll be back and I want to hear the rest of this." She got up and left the room.

"*Carida*, do you really believe a man can change that much?"

"I saw the locket Salvatore gave Alessia as a symbol of his undying love. When I held it in my hands, I knew everything was going to be okay. Their love was real. And yes, I believe love can change a person."

Alena hurried across the room and plopped back onto her chair. "Okay, so what happened?"

"What? Oh, Salvatore was wounded and they died together on his sinking ship."

"You missed my wedding for that?"

CHAPTER THIRTEEN

BANJI SAT in the front seat next to Alena while Santiago stretched his legs in the back. She ran her hands over the Tundra's soft leather seats. "This is really nice."

"It's Gabriel's. He took my Mustang today. Some excuse about it being easier to maneuver in town. Like I'd believe that." She grinned. "He likes to drive fast when I'm not looking."

"Santiago is fixing Gram's Trans Am." Banji smirked. "Girls like to drive fast, too."

"Hell, yeah." Alena glanced up at her rearview mirror. "*Papi*, do you want me to drop you at your house?"

"No."

Banji and Alena's gazes met briefly.

"So, take you back to Banji's?"

"Yes. I want to lie down. My ankle hurts."

"Got it. And that king size bed isn't bad either. Let's you spread out and relax."

"It is very nice."

"I'll call and check on you tomorrow. If that ankle isn't better, I'm taking you to the clinic."

Banji looked over her shoulder catching Santiago's attention and smiled. "I'll keep him off his feet. Promise."

~

Banji handed Santiago three anti-inflammatory tablets and a glass of water. "Do you want to lie on the couch or get back in bed?"

A lock of his untamed hair covered his brow and he brushed it out of his eyes. "My ankle is throbbing. I need to lie down."

"Let's stretch out in bed. I could use a nap." She ambled down the hall with her hand in his. "I'll help you get comfortable."

"I would like that." Lately, he lived for it. The gentle touch of her hands roaming over his body, the soft sound of her breaths in the night while she slept next to him soothed his soul.

He stood beside the bed and pulled off his shirt while Banji's nimble fingers divested him of his pants and briefs. As soon as he sat down, she slipped them over his feet and placed them on the bedside chair.

With his clothes jettisoned, he settled back against the pillows and raised his leg for Banji to adjust the support for his swollen ankle.

It wasn't the only part of him that was swollen. He pulled the covers across his midsection to hide the unruly part of his anatomy that he feared would appall her. They had already spent the morning satisfying their desires for each other. Would this display be too much?

She dropped her robe at the foot of the bed and slipped under the covers next to him.

"You don't have to hide this from me." Her hand slipped over his blatant arousal.

"It is too soon to ask this from you." He inhaled sharply as her hand tightened judiciously around his erection.

"Don't say that to me ever again. You don't hide your needs from me and I don't hide mine from you. That's the deal. Take it or leave it."

Her hand slid slowly up to the crown and down to the base. His legs tensed and willingly separated. "I will take it."

She pushed the covers down past his knees. "Good because I have this urgent need to taste you." "A little something for dessert." She slipped into the space between his thighs.

"*Carida,* you must not say such things."

"Why not?" She licked him from root to tip.

"I will not be able to control myself."

Her lips closed over the crown and she swirled her tongue around the ridge. "So, don't. I want the real you." She took him deep into her mouth and sucked as she pulled back. Her fingers teased and tickled his testicles as she repeated the stroking and flicks of her tongue on the tip of the crown.

His head thrown back and his neck exposed, he let a tortured moan escaped him when she took his penis deep in the back of her throat and hummed. Sparks of desire shot through his body as excitement built at the base of his spine. One heel dug into the mattress and his legs strained pushing his cock deeper into the wet heat. His heart pounded harder than ever before and he feared it would burst with her next squeeze of his engorged member.

Labored breaths and strangled gasps that he couldn't control were the only sound in the room. His hands fastened on the sides of her head and his fingers threaded through her hair. "You must stop."

Her hands slid along the inside of his thighs. "Tell me what you need."

The urge to roll toward her and pin her under his large frame was overwhelming, and it took all of his self-control to quell the insistence of his desperate need to connect to Banji on his most primal level. Was this the animal deep inside that Carmen had accused him of being? A monster with lustful and indecent desires?

His balls pulsed, his swollen cock throbbed with every beat of his heart, and his legs tingled letting him know his orgasm was right there when he was ready to let go.

His hands gripped her under the arms and lifted her to his side, pillows fell off the bed, covers twisted, and he gave in to his basest instincts. Burning in hell would be a small price to pay to be deeply connected to his *Carida*.

He insinuated himself in the cradle of her legs and his cock nudged at her entrance.

She murmured, "It's not nice to keep a lady waiting."

Santiago sank deep into her welcoming heat, withdrew and sank in deeper, rooting himself in the enveloping wetness. Banji's legs wrapped over his hips allowing him to seat his full length snuggly inside her tight depths.

"Yes, that's it. So, good." Her fingers dug into his shoulders.

His knees took the majority of his weight, but the occasional twinge in his injured ankle made him grit his teeth. He would not let pain stop him from this chance at unbridled completion.

Her raw edgy cries resonated in the air around them. His *Carida* shuddered under him. Her inner walls clutched hungrily at his sensitive shaft stealing his last shred of resolve. Hot semen rushed through him, pouring his physical and passionate release into the accepting woman wrapped around him.

Her quiet, shuddering gasp turned into a low moan. "This is heaven."

His head hung as wave after wave of long-denied ecstasy rolled through him. The afterglow of euphoria began to slowly wear off and was replaced by trepidation. "*Carida*, I beg you to forgive me."

"For what?" She stroked her hands down and up his sides, caressing his damp skin. "You're perfect."

He moved to her side. Looking into her eyes, his fingers glided over her soft skin. "I did not protect you."

"From what? We're fine, better than fine."

He touched his forehead to hers. "From me."

Those words had the same effect of throwing a bucket of ice water on her. Her moment of comfort and belonging was shattered. "But you told me you haven't been with anyone except your wife."

"And I have not. But you are still a young woman."

"I got checked before I moved here. I'm starting my life over and I wanted to be sure I was healthy."

"I am sure you are."

Silence hung in the air between them.

He hugged her close. "Whatever happens I will take care of you."

"Oh, oh, you mean if I get pregnant." Banji closed her eyes and inhaled. "Wow, that is a whole new subject. I'll have to think about it."

The cool air on her still damp skin caused her to shiver. She nestled down into the pillows and wiggled closer to Santiago. "You're nice and warm."

"*Carida*, you must tell me. Are you angry with me? Am I forgiven?" He let go of her long enough to grab the edge of the blanket and pull it over them.

Her hands drifted to his hips and tugged him in her direction. She draped a leg over his and ran her foot along his calf. "I'll think about it. Maybe you should kiss me to make up for scaring me. I thought you'd gone and done something really bad."

She could breathe easy. A little Santiago running around the house hadn't been on her list of things to do, but it wasn't a bad idea. She hummed contentedly, "Hmm, you need to rest."

She had tested his sensitivity and found out how good it felt to be nestled between his massive thighs when she blew him. Getting him to stay on his back was the challenge. She'd work on that later.

"I want to kiss you." His finger pressed under her chin encouraging her to tilt her head back.

She murmured softly, "Yes, anything you want is fine with me."

Their eyes met. His irresistibly devastating grin caused a quiver in her heart and between her legs. It promised a future of pleasurable indulgences.

CHAPTER FOURTEEN

Banji walked along the beach trail to Alena's. The day was a little on the cold side but her parka was warm and her thoughts were warmer. She was falling deeper in love with Santiago one day at a time. No rush, slowly learning to appreciate all the little things he did for her. She took her time climbing the hill.

The garages were on the way. She stepped inside and looked around. It wasn't hard to spot him leaning over an open engine compartment. She waved when he straightened up and looked her way. She wanted to tell him the good news. She'd gotten a call for an interview and scheduled it for the next day. A few strides and he was standing in front of her.

"*Carida*, is everything okay?" He wiped his greasy hands on a shop towel.

She rested her hand over his heart. "Yeah, I'm going up to the house to have lunch with Alena. I had to walk right by here. I wanted to see you for a minute is all."

"I am working." He carefully brushed her hair back from her face with his fingers. "I will see you tonight."

She kept smiling. "Right. See you later." She patted his chest and dropped her hand to her side.

This might not be the time to talk about her job interview. He had real work to do and she didn't, not yet anyway. "I'll be at Alena's for a while." She left the shop. Note to self—do not disturbed Santiago at work.

Santiago had been polite. He hadn't said anything wrong. But he hadn't seemed thrilled to see her. Her world might light up when he came into view, but it didn't mean she brightened his. She was so not into going down a one-way road. That never ended well.

She reminded herself to smile as she went through the back door to the kitchen. "Hey, Alena, I'm here." She chanted, "Come out, come out, wherever you are."

"Sit down. I'll be there in a minute." Alena's voice floated from some far corner of the rambling house.

True to form, Alena walked into the kitchen a minute later holding her phone and scowling. "What a mess. I've got parts scattered from one end of the Detroit terminal to the next. The Kington driver is not happy. He's having to help find the boxes and load them."

Banji ran her hand along the counter top. "Will that make his delivery late?"

"No. And we're not under a tight deadline but Tate's been on the road for days and he wants to get home."

"I get it." Banji watched Alena move around the kitchen pulling out their lunch plates from the warmer. "I stopped at the garage to see Santiago."

Alena put the plates on the table and went to the refrigerator. She came back with two tumblers of water. "I have hot tea or hot chocolate. Which do you want?"

"Tea, the chocolate will put me to sleep." Banji settled in to her seat at the table.

Alena placed the thermal carafe of tea in the middle of the table and took the seat across from Banji. "How did it go when you stopped to see *Papi*? He doesn't like to be interrupted at work. If he makes a mistake, the engine could fail during a race and our driver could be injured."

"He didn't say anything much." Banji shrugged and took a bite of her chicken pesto panini. "It seemed like he was pretty busy. I was going to tell him about my job interview tomorrow but it really wasn't a good time. I'll tell him later."

"Who's it with? Is it an auction house?" Alena smiled over the top of her sandwich and bit into it.

"It's a small company in Los Angeles that buys and sells estate jewelry. I applied back when I decided to move here. I'd forgotten all about them. I was surprised when the secretary called this morning." She chewed and swallowed. "They need someone to look up the history of the pieces and make sure there's nothing unpleasant attached. Not too many people want to wear something that was involved in a murder or a family feud."

She sipped her tea and put the glass down. "It's exactly the kind of thing I'm good at. I really love antique pieces. They're so unique and the workmanship is beautiful." She sat back and played with her napkin. "That old locket at the Maritime Museum was rumored to have a curse on it."

Alena stopped chewing and swallowed. "Did it?"

"Absolutely. A really old one." Banji dabbed at the corners of her mouth. "But I couldn't find many details. The woman who brought it in didn't know much about it." She poured some tea into her glass and took a taste. "I wanted to catch the plane home so I didn't waste time worrying about a curse."

"So, what happened to it?"

"I gave her a realistic estimate of the current value for each piece." Banji bit into her sandwich and talked around the food as she chewed. "I looked it over carefully. There's something inside of it. I could hear it rattling when I turned it. It was beautiful but it wouldn't open. There's a secret to the clasp. It'll take a really good jeweler that specializes in antiques to work with it."

Alena dipped her head, shivered and stared at her plate. "That's creepy." She inhaled and looked at Banji. "You could ask Cami. Her grandfather was a jeweler. She worked with him a lot before he died."

"I'd forgotten about that. But it's too late now."

"Will this new place let you work from home?" Alena picked up her tea and sipped it slowly.

Nodding, Banji answered, "I'll go in, take pictures and do the rest from the comfort of my kitchen until I turn the back room into an office." She put her sandwich down. "I'll keep track of the hours and turn in a time sheet with the report." She looked from her sandwich to Alena. "I've got better things to do than waste time commuting."

Alena pushed her empty plate away from the edge of the table and pulled her tea glass closer. "You're the best. They'd be fools not to hire you. We'll celebrate when you get home."

Banji winced. "Being the best isn't always a good thing. I'll call and let you know what happens."

~

Deep in thought, Banji hurried home and glanced at the garage as she passed. Santiago would see her tonight. Those words had a familiar ring to them. They were code for later, after the important stuff was done. She shrugged and inched the parka zipper higher to ward off the chill. She'd never been important to anyone but Gram. Nothing new there.

Banji traipsed up the stairs and went inside. The sunny yellow paint she'd applied to the cabinet doors relieved the previously stark white with a cheerful glow. A hot cup of tea should lift her spirits. The citrus aroma of Gram's favorite blend always made a foggy day better.

A few minutes later, she wrapped her fingers around the warm stoneware cup while she stood staring out at the grey swells in the distance. Winter's icy cold fingers gripped the coast but that did not account for the cold trickle in her stomach. That first thread of doubt needed to get the hell out of her life.

She flipped through Gram's records looking for something reminiscent of happier days. But every album she picked had a slow, sad song on side two. Not a good sign. She didn't want to be an afterthought to a man who had better things to do than be in love with her. Her mother had been trapped in that kind of relationship and all it had gotten her was depressed and dead.

There was some comfort in knowing she wasn't the only person who'd ever been in danger of having her heart broken. Dwelling on those sad thoughts were not going to help her get ready for her one and only job interview in six months. Next time she went to Verona, she might very well have a letter to leave for Juliet but not today.

Some people, herself included, had the misfortune of being the something that got in the way of other people's aspirations. She looked around the living room. Gram understood. That was one of the reasons she'd built her seaside hideaway with its weathered wood paneling and seaside decor. It was out of the way. Nobody went there, ever. Nobody except Banji. Sand Dollar Cottage wasn't on anyone's map. Here, she wasn't supposed to be in anyone's way.

Banji finished her tea. If she'd left well enough alone, kept her mouth shut, she wouldn't be in this mess. But no, something about Santiago had called to her and she'd gone and spoken to him. She'd disturbed his peaceful life. Staring out the window wasn't helping. Running away to sea wasn't an option.

She needed to get her interview presentation ready. This evening would not be a good time for him to come over. She'd see him when she got back. She put her empty cup in the sink, picked up her phone and left him a voice message, *"I have a job interview in the morning. I'm kind of tired and not in the mood for company tonight. I'll talk to you tomorrow."*

She spent the rest of the afternoon putting together a few appraisals she'd done with the detailed descriptions and history of the pieces. Her fingers brushed over the glossy photos of the pirate treasure she'd examined for the Maritime Museum. The golden heart-shaped locket caught her eye. She ran a finger around the image. It was a symbol of undying love and it was cursed. There had to be more to the story. What would it take to uncover the truth, the whole truth of a devil falling in love with a princess? Why would a princess sacrifice her life for a pirate?

Banji had the name and contact information for the young lady for whom she'd done the appraisal. It would be easy enough to contact her once she figured out which box the work order copies were in. She'd start looking for it when she got home from her interview. First things first, she needed a job, something to keep her busy.

The folders containing examples of her work and reports went together easily and were ready to show to her prospective employers. She loaded them in her briefcase, ready to go.

After picking at a microwaveable dinner and she was all set for the night. She sat on the couch with a glass of red wine and mellow music flowed from the stereo while she read Gram's old love letters. Ritter wrote tonight's missive from Santos, Brazil. He was lonely, he missed their walks on the beach and the sound of the fog horns at night. He would be coming home soon.

CHAPTER FIFTEEN

SHE TOSSED and turned all night and looked suitably haggard by morning. One cup of coffee later she was out the door leaving her bed unmade. It could wait. She added getting a set of softer sheets to her shopping list.

The long drive to Los Angeles didn't do anything for her mood but it did give her time to organize her thoughts for the presentation. The Spanish colonial style office complex on the outskirts of the northern end of the city was easy to find. She checked her makeup in the rearview mirror, got out and brushed her suit into place before she went inside the brightly lit office.

"Good morning. I'm Banji Preston. I have an appointment." She glanced at the stark white walls with bland unassuming prints on the walls. Boring.

The receptionist looked more than uncomfortable chewing on her bottom lip. "I'm so sorry. I meant to call you. The position has been filled."

Banji stared at the woman letting the stunned-into-silence effect wear off and finally mumbled, "Yeah, okay." She turned, adjusted her grip on her briefcase and walked out.

Thinking it was probably for the best, she flopped onto the seat in her crap-car and stared out the cracked windshield. As soon as Santiago got the Trans Am running, this thing was going away. It didn't matter where, just gone. Over a cliff would be good.

She turned the key and the four worn out cylinders clattered to life. Hallelujah. On the way to the mall she let her mind wander searching for a new and better plan. She was done trying to make all the usual choices work. It was time for something unusual.

She parked, walked into the first big department store she came to and called Alena. "Hey, I'm going to do some shopping. You need anything while I'm trolling the mall?"

"No, I'm good. How did the interview go?"

Banji slid the hangers on the rack making it easier to see the colorful top that had caught her eye. "The position was already filled. They forgot to call me."

"You've got to be kidding." Alena exhaled loudly. "That's so rude."

"Not kidding. But don't worry. I've got a plan B." Banji walked a few steps over to the next rack.

"Like what?"

"Pirate treasure." Banji snickered.

"You're going to become a pirate?" Alena giggled. "Sounds like something you'd do."

"Not exactly. I'll tell you about it when I get home."

"Don't stay too late or you'll get caught in rush hour traffic." Alena giggled. "You'll be stuck on the freeway all night, all alone. *Papi* will not be happy."

"I'm going to get a room." Banji bit her upper lip, let go and ran her tongue over her front teeth. She wanted to go home but she wasn't ready to face Santiago. Their relationship was complicated, and this was not the time to go and say something stupid because she was reliving every insecurity she'd ever had.

"Why? It's not that far." Alena's voice lost its teasing quality.

"I want to shop and go to dinner." Banji inhaled. "It's not like I have to get home to feed the pets I don't have."

"What about *Papi*?"

"He's a better cook than I am. He can feed himself."

94

Alena's voice deepened. "That's not the point. He's been irritable all day since you didn't let him come over last night. What's up with that?"

"You said it yourself. I'm a distraction. He'll be able to get back to concentrating on business. The peace and quiet will be a nice change."

"You're not a distraction. We can talk about this when you get here."

"A little breathing room never hurt anybody. You know I've always had this terrible tendency to always be in the wrong place at the worst possible time." Banji used her free hand to sort through some vibrant holiday blouses. She didn't need any but they were pretty for the upcoming gatherings and parties. Alena had mentioned doing something for New Years. It didn't hurt to look. "He might be better off with someone who understands racing and knows when to make herself scarce."

Alena's exasperated huff filtered through the speaker. "Slow down. I distinctly heard you say he was perfect for you."

"That doesn't mean I'm perfect for him." Banji walked over to the next rack of holiday sweaters. "Are you giving a Christmas party or doing something for New Years. They have some really nice blouses for the season."

"New Years and don't try changing the subject. Get a pretty new top and be ready to celebrate with *Papi*. He's a Christmas Eve baby. Get yourself some sexy little thing he can get you out of without too much trouble."

"What size are you these days? I'll get you one. Gabriel can have fun unwrapping his Christmas present." She chuckled. "He'll like that."

"Medium and you're being a pain in the ass. Come home and talk to *Papi*. Whatever is bothering you, he can fix it."

"If I was fixable, I'm sure somebody would have let me know a long time ago. I'm not going to be responsible for some fiery crash that kills someone. I don't need that one added to my list of disasters."

Alena whined, "Nobody's crashing. These last couple of months he's been a whole new man. He's happier than I've ever seen him."

"I have to go. I need new shoes and to check out the bookstore before it gets too late. Text me if you think of something you want me to bring you. Bye." Banji disconnected.

That conversation was going nowhere.

Alena and Santiago had their lives all mapped out. Banji didn't own a map and wasn't sure how to fit into their world. She did, however, fit her feet into a pair of gold designer sandals. Wearing them could make any girl feel super special. They'd go with everything. Looking at them wrapped around her insteps and ankles in the mirror brought a smile to her lips and reminded her she needed a pedicure.

Next stop, lingerie department. Something pretty and comfortable. Her current choices only brought back memories of chilly San Francisco nights and lonely faraway places.

Considering she didn't have an office to go to, or clients to meet with, she didn't need much besides her stone-washed jeans. Working from home definitely had its benefits. She needed nighties, pretty ones, yoga pants, soft t-shirts and athletic shoes to keep her feet protected from spiders when she cleaned out the back room and the shed.

Her phone clicked. Santiago texted: *Are you angry with me, Carida?*

Banji: *No, shopping at the mall since I'm in town.*

She wandered thru the men's department. Something loose and comfortable for Santiago might come in handy. Getting him to wear the navy-blue jersey knit lounging pants was going to be tricky. It would be nice not to fight with his buttons and zippers every time things got amorous. The thought of all that easily accessible yumminess was enticing enough to convince her that buying two pairs was a good idea.

Then on to the bedding and linens. Something smooth and luxurious for him to lie on while she helped him relax after a long day at work.

He definitely needed to relax more. Beach living was supposed to be easy-going. With a little time and patience things would work themselves out.

Timing was everything. Ritter's letters kept referring to waiting for the right time. Right time for what? She needed to get to the bottom of that mystery. Curiosity had always been her biggest failing. But what if she turned it around. Could it be her ticket to success? People always harped on doing what you're good at, what comes naturally to you. Okay, she was good at being curious and poking her nose in where it didn't belong. There had to be a book for that.

Digging into the past required organization. She would see if the bookstore had anything about investigating and researching lost princesses, pirate treasures and curses. A little something different to read. And a spiral note book, a nice big one would be perfect, two would be better along with an organizer and beautiful pens in lots of cheerful colors. She wanted her new office to be authentically hers.

She tucked her shopping bags away in the trunk and drove to her favorite restaurant. The small and out of the way place had the best home cooked catfish, shrimp and hush puppies on the California coast. She ordered the Texas Seafood Platter and a Texas beer to wash it all down.

She missed the Gulf Coast and the hush puppies. Those were little miracles of flavor that never failed to remind her of a happy time spent with Gram.

For Banji's sixteenth birthday they'd driven through Arizona, Louisiana, Mississippi and Texas. The heat, the humidity, and the mosquitos had been miserable but the food and music had made up for all of it. A smile spread across her face. Her fingers itched at the thought of gripping the Trans Am's steering wheel. She curled her fingers into her palms and squeezed tight before releasing her grip on the past.

Alena knew people in Texas. When they went there for races, Banji could tag along. That would take care of several things. Banji could eat her fill of hush puppies, drink plenty of local beer, watch a few races and maybe get a better understanding of what the big deal was. Driving in circles seemed kind of boring to her.

If things were going really well, she could get fitted for a wedding dress from Madame Belinsky's shop in Galveston. Gram had physically dragged Banji away from the window. The store was still there. She'd checked.

Someday she'd take a road trip. Pack up the Trans Am and hit the highway. Timing. She was getting ahead of herself but it felt good having things to look forward to.

CHAPTER SIXTEEN

SANTIAGO'S VOICE rumbled from deep in his chest. "What do you mean she is not coming home tonight? Why not?"

Alena cringed. "She's shopping for some holiday clothes. She also mentioned going to the bookstore. That alone could take hours. It'll be really late by the time she gets done with dinner."

He crossed his arms over his chest. "No."

"Yes." Alena rubbed the back of her neck. "And she might be a little upset."

"Why?" His eyes narrowed and his lips pressed tightly together flattening into a straight line of displeasure.

Alena muttered, "She didn't get the job and she might have gotten the idea she shouldn't bother you when you're working." She inhaled slowly. "I mentioned you didn't like to be interrupted at work."

"She can come to me anytime." His hands clenched into loose fists and then slowly relaxed at his sides.

"Since when? Carmen told me she never interrupted you. Your work was too important for her to disturb you. If it wasn't an emergency, it could wait until you got home."

"There are things about me and Carmen that you do not know."

"I know she slept in a separate room after she found out she couldn't have children." Alena frowned. "I didn't think anything of it. My parents didn't even sleep in the same house."

"We were married. We had taken vows to stay together and take care of each other."

"I'm so sorry." She rubbed her forehead. "I had no idea. I remember when she moved into her own room she told me you were a respectful man who would not ask more of her than she could give. I thought she was sad she couldn't have kids."

"She was my wife. Without children to raise, she abandoned our marriage. I have been alone a long time. But now I have a chance to try again." He ran his fingers through his hair. "Banji did not turn away from me, from my past. I have to explain to her. I cannot let this come between us."

"This isn't all on you. I had my part in it. I'll talk to her. She'll come home." Alena grimaced. "She has nowhere else to go."

Santiago wasn't so sure about that. Banji was resourceful and smart and he'd known two seconds after the door closed behind her that he'd made a mistake. Her smile had disappeared and she'd left without kissing him goodbye. He'd gotten used to being kissed when they parted in the mornings, when he came in after work and any other time she took a notion. He liked it, a lot.

He'd noticed the loss of intimacy immediately and missed that small show of affection. Drifting apart started slowly, he knew that from experience. He could not let that happen, not again, not ever and not with Banji.

Damn, he wanted a deep and lasting relationship, he wanted more, but what? He was more than a boyfriend but he didn't know if he could bring himself to marry again.

Could he become a real husband this time? Could he risk the pain of failure? He wasn't getting any younger. There were too many questions, and he had too few answers.

Tonight, he'd be sleeping alone. He made the short walk from the garage to his house like he'd done thousands of times before but never with such heaviness in his steps. Banji had spoiled him, made him crave her closeness, the feel of her body moving with his when they slow-danced and the affection in her touch late at night when she thought he was asleep.

He flipped on the lights and sat down at the 1960's kitchen table. It was time to make some changes. He'd get some boxes and clean out all the old reminders of his past. They had no place in his future. Something deep inside had changed. He pulled out his phone and pressed Banji's contact.

She yawned. "Hello."

"*Carida*, you must come home soon."

"It's late and I'm tired. I've got a nice room for the night. I'll see you tomorrow."

"We have to talk when you get here. I am not used to anyone but Alena coming to me in the shop. I did not know what to say."

"You didn't do anything wrong and it turned out for the best. I was going to tell you I had an interview today but I didn't get the job. It would have been wasting your time."

"There will be something better. You can come to me anytime you feel like it."

She stifled another yawn. "You shouldn't say things like that. I'll believe you and then what happens when you change your mind?"

"I do not change my mind. We will talk about this also."

"Great." She inhaled deeply and exhaled loudly. "Hmm, I think I'm going to work for myself. Work from home. I'll have to fix up the back room for my office."

"I will help you. What are you going to do?"

"I'm not sure but I'll figure it out as I go along. I only have bits and pieces but they'll come together. I'm following the signs. Antique jewelry, pirate treasures, mysteries, investigating curses; the answer is in there somewhere. I'm still working on it."

"Alena told me you are getting new clothes for the New Year's party."

"I got a few things for the house. It's time for me to do something different. New Year's is a good time to celebrate change and I'm going to dress for the occasion." She snickered. "I got some pretty things to wear to bed."

"*Ay, Carida*, you torture me with this." He gathered his courage and said, "I do not like this staying away overnight. It does not feel right."

"No, it doesn't but I don't like driving the coast road in the dark."

He grumbled, "It can be dangerous. There is fog tonight. I will be here when you get home."

"Don't work too hard tomorrow. You're going to need your energy when the lights go out."

CHAPTER SEVENTEEN

BANJI PULLED up and parked alongside her cottage hideaway. The fresh paint brightened the old place up and welcomed her home. That was a first. Even when she'd lived in her renovated San Francisco, Knob Hill apartment, she hadn't looked forward to getting home in the evenings. It was only a place to sleep. This was where she lived with Santiago.

She liked the idea of them living there together, and needed to talk to him about that. Opening the trunk, she picked up her bags. Cheerful holiday blouses and nighties for herself and Alena along with a couple new pairs of shoes would take care of the upcoming festivities.

She fumbled for the keys and got the front door open. The faint aroma of her scented candles filled the air. It smelled of night blooming jasmine. With her hands full, she elbowed the door shut, carried her things across the living room, and dropped them on the couch. She wanted to sort the new kitchen towels and decorator pillows from the rest of the purchases.

The back door rustled open.

"*Carida*!" Santiago's shout filled the cottage.

What in the world? He was supposed to be at work. She shouted back, "I'm in the living room."

He came around the corner wide-eyed and breathing heavily. "You are home." His arms encircled her holding her snugly against his chest.

"Of course, I'm home." She hugged him back.

He released the bear hug and took her hand. "Come, sit, we must talk."

"Is something wrong?" Something she didn't know about? "Why are you all out of breath?"

"I hurried to get here. I need to talk to you." His hands rested on her shoulders.

"Your ankle is barely healed. You need to take care of it."

"You were upset with me when you left the garage. You did not want me that night and last night you stayed away. Have you forgiven me?" His downcast eyes didn't meet hers.

The sad tone of his voice sank like a knife to her heart. She'd hurt him. Again.

Her hand cupped his cheek. "We already settled this last night. We're fine."

"There is more I must tell you."

She toed off her pumps. "Later. My feet are killing me. I can't think when I'm in pain." She made a pouty face.

Santiago chuckled. "You are a very bad liar."

"I'm not lying. My feet do hurt." She reached back and rubbed her neck. "And my back and my butt. I hate that wretched little car." She wasn't ready for a heart-to-heart talk.

"The Trans Am will be ready soon. I have ordered the last of the parts."

"Oh, thank you. You're the best."

He sat back and patted his thigh. "Here, put your feet up and I will rub them."

"No. They've been in my shoes all day. You're not rubbing my smelly feet. Not happening."

He rose up, putting a knee on the couch, he leaned over her. "We will not argue. I will kiss you until you agree." His lips found hers and his body descended slowly pushing her down onto the cushions.

The screech filling the room hurt Banji's ears. *What the hell?*

"Get off my sister!" Madison swung her purse hitting Santiago between the shoulders. "Get off." She grabbed the back of his shirt and pulled.

"*Ay, Madonna.* Who is this crazy woman?" He raised his arm, protecting himself and Banji from another hit.

Banji peered over his shoulder. What in the world was wrong with Madison? Her sister had never been one to interfere in anything that involved raised voices, never mind raising her own voice.

Banji frowned and said, "Madison, quit hitting my boyfriend."

"Oh, uh, sorry." She shrugged. "He's so big and rough looking. I thought maybe he was attacking you."

Santiago sat up and glared at Madison, who took a step back.

"This crazy girl is my half-sister." Banji sat up and attempted to brush her clothes back into some semblance of order. She looked at Madison. "What are you doing here? Did you even knock?"

"I did but you didn't answer and I heard voices." She winced. "I was afraid you were being mugged or something. He sounded kind of mean."

Santiago rose from the couch in one swift motion and leaned over Madison. "I am not mean to Banji."

"Good lord. Can you two take a step back and let's get to the bottom of what's going on?"

Santiago straightened, squared his shoulders. His eyes followed Madison's every move.

Banji asked, "Why are you here? I told you not to come back."

"It's kind of an emergency." She wrinkled her nose and pursed her lips. "When I told Dad I wasn't going to marry Bennett, he threw me out." She inhaled. "I went to a hotel but they said my credit cards were refused. When I called the card companies, they said he'd closed the accounts."

Banji asked, "Don't you have any of your own?"

"No. Dad said I didn't need them."

"Why didn't you get your own cards? Don't you see, that's another way for him to keep control. You're stuck depending on him for everything."

"I've always been too afraid to argue with him. He gets so mean." Madison bit her bottom lip and stared at the floor.

"Yeah, tell me about it." Banji chuckled softly. "Look, I appreciate you trying to save me but I'm fine. You still haven't told me why you're here."

"I have no place to go. No credit cards, and only the cash in my purse from the ATM. I need a place to stay till I can get on my feet."

"What about your job?"

"When I went in this morning, my supervisor told me Dad had called and told them to let me go." She sank onto the chair by the bookcase. "I called Aunt Marlene and she said I couldn't stay with her because it might make her brother mad."

Banji raked her fingers through her hair. "I told you not to work for Dad." She settled back against the couch cushions. "And what about your Mom?"

"She's locked in her room and won't speak to me." Madison stared out the picture window toward the ocean. "I called her cell phone but it went straight to voicemail."

"Don't say I didn't warn you," Banji huffed and inhaled. "You sound like you're still fourteen years old. It's time to grow up."

"I'm trying but it's not that easy with Mom and Dad watching every move I make. I don't even get to pick out my clothes." She turned her attention back to Banji bypassing Santiago.

"Well, you're going to have to adjust." Banji shrugged. "Hmm, I guess you can camp on the beach."

Santiago turned her direction. "*Carida?*"

"What?" Banji scrunched her nose at him.

"This is your sister."

"No, she's not. She's only a half-sister and not a very good one." Banji scowled in Madison's direction.

Chuckling, Santiago said, "She tried to protect you from me. That has to count for something."

"It only means she's a fool on top of everything else."

"*Carida.*" The warning tone wasn't lost on Banji. "You have a guest room."

"Oh fine." She glared at Madison. "You can stay in the guest room for two weeks. That will give you time to make a survival plan."

"Thanks, I was afraid I was going to have to sleep in the Mustang."

106

"Is the car registered in your name?" Banji looked at Madison and raised her eyebrows.

"I don't know. I never get the registration renewal and Dad carries the insurance."

"You are so screwed. It's probably in his name or the company's. He'll send a repo guy after it. Unless you want to lose whatever's in it, get all your stuff, everything, out of it and sleep in the guest room." She looked at Santiago. "I don't know much about repossessing vehicles. What should we do?"

"They will look here first. If they do not see it, they will wait for Madison to drive it somewhere and park it. They will tow it when she gets out. As long as they have the title they can take it." He looked at Madison. "What do you want to do?"

"Dad can have it. I don't want anyone to get in trouble trying to help me. It's only a car."

He nodded. "I will take Banji where she needs to go." He raised an eyebrow in her direction. "Perhaps she will let you buy her car."

"My car! Why would I do that?" Banji ran her hand through her hair brushing it out of her eyes.

"Because you have the Trans Am."

"I guess." She focused on Madison. "I'll let you have it real cheap. Like twenty-dollars cheap."

"Really? That would be great. Thanks."

"Don't thank me. Thank Santiago."

"Thank you, Mister Santiago."

"Oh, my god, you're impossible. His name is Santiago Cordova. Mister Cordova."

Madison's face puckered up, giant tears pooled in her eyes, spilled out and ran down her cheeks. "I'm sorry," she sniveled.

Banji inhaled and exhaled slowly. "Madison, go empty out your car. If the repo man doesn't show up tonight, he will tomorrow for sure. Dad never comes here but he has the address.

Banji leaned back against the couch cushions and listened for the door to close. "I don't know what's wrong with that girl sometimes. She's too smart to be in this situation. She knows better."

He shrugged one shoulder. "She is a little naïve. People will take advantage of her."

"It's not all her fault. Her mother kept a real tight rein on her. Didn't let her do much of anything on her own. They didn't want her to turn out like me."

"That is their mistake. We will have to watch out for her while she's here." He offered Banji a small smile. "You can help her learn to take care of herself."

"And why would I do that?"

"Because she is your younger sister. She did not have the advantage of knowing Missus Lori. She must learn to take care of herself."

Banji crossed her arms over her chest. "I tried to help her when we were younger but she wouldn't listen. I finally gave up. We were never close. She was their perfect child. They couldn't shove me out the door fast enough."

"She probably did not think your father would treat her this way."

"Why not? He had no trouble treating me like trash." She leaned settled against the couch back.

"I am sure he gave her many excuses for his behavior." He sat down next to Banji. "You are stronger than she is, but she did try to save you from me."

He leaned over and pressed his lips to hers. She wrapped her arms around his neck and kissed him back. Her fingers tangled in his hair. Their lips separated. She whispered, "I missed you so much."

It was after midnight and the house was quiet. Banji sat at the kitchen table reading another one of Ritter's love letters. Santiago slept in their king-sized bed with one of the new pairs of lounge pants hanging on the bedside chair next to his nightstand. Since they had company, he'd agreed to wear them. It was a small win, but she'd take it.

Ritter wrote how beautiful Hawaii was and someday they would see it together. They would go from island to island until they'd seen them all. Banji folded the letter when she heard a rustling noise behind her.

"I couldn't sleep," Madison mumbled.

She had finally stopped whining after dinner. But she'd started crying again halfway through the movie. Okay, so there was a sad part but it had a happy ending.

Banji muttered, "I don't have any sleeping pills. You'll have to tough it out unless you want to warm up some milk. I've heard that it helps." She followed Madison's movements. "The cups are in the cabinet next to the sink."

Madison retrieved the milk carton from the refrigerator. "Thank you for letting me stay here."

"You already said that a half-dozen times at dinner."

"I know but it doesn't hurt to say it again." She put the cup of milk in the microwave. When it binged, she took it out and stepped over to the table. "Do you mind if I sit here to drink it?" She held out the cup.

"No. It's fine. You can sit."

Madison's eyes drifted to the letters in the shoe box. Banji turned them away. "Don't worry about those. They're nothing to do with you." Banji's eyes narrowed. "Did Dad send you here to snoop?"

"No. I told you the truth about what happened."

"That doesn't mean I have to believe you."

Madison's lips trembled.

Banji grumbled, "Don't cry. It'll give you wrinkles."

"Can I ask you something?" Madison sniffled and exhaled.

Banji crossed her arms over her chest. "Yeah, I guess. What?"

"When Bennett would kiss me, I didn't like it. He tasted weird." Her mouth puckered into a yuk wrinkle. "Is that normal?"

"No. It's a sign you're not into him at all. Why would you agree to marry him if that's your reaction to him?"

"Because it was what I was supposed to do. Everyone kept saying how wonderful he was and how happy we'd be." She sipped her warm milk.

"Well, he's behind you now, so go out and find someone who steals your breath away when he kisses you."

"I used to get all tingly when Garth kissed me. We had such a good time at the prom. But he went away to the university and then law school. Dad said I needed to find someone fast, before I got too old and ugly."

"Stop worrying about it. You're not going to lose your good looks anytime soon." Banji tipped her head to one side, her neck cracked and she straightened up again. "You can get a job and start meeting new people. Maybe Alena will let you tag along when she goes to the race track. There's always lot of guys there."

"I guess I could do that." Madison's mouth turned up in a tentative smile.

"Perfect." Banji shifted in her chair. "Get some sleep. Things will look better in the morning."

When Madison disappeared down the hall, Banji opened Ritter's letter. *My girls will look beautiful wearing Hawaiian flower leis. We will go to a luau and watch the hula dancers on the beach at sunset.*

Did Gram have another daughter besides Banji's Mom, Genevieve? Was Ritter her lover before she met Grandpa Bancroft?

She folded the letter up the way she'd found it and returned it to its envelope. It was mailed from Honolulu. She checked the postmark. The date didn't fit the timeline. Gram would have been too old to have children. Something wasn't adding up.

She carried the box to her bedroom, put it in the bottom drawer of her nightstand and slipped into bed.

Santiago rolled over until he bumped into Banji. "*Carida.*"

Her hand drifted over his abdomen and slipped lower. "Did you miss me?" She palmed his length.

"It was terrible." His hips moved pushing his erection against her hand.

"Would you like me to kiss it and make it better?"

"Yes. Please."

Her fingers curled around his shaft and slipped down to the base and up to the crown. "So soft and so hard. Velvet over steel. We have this nice big bed. I'd like you to share it with me all the time." She squeezed him a fraction tighter. "Some days you could come home for lunch."

She slid down taking the blankets with her exposing him. The cool air engulfed him relieving some of the heat radiating from his core. He repositioned himself onto his back with his legs spread. "I am yours."

"I'm going to take very good care of you." Her tongue licked the center groove of his crown starting underneath and moving slowly over the tip. A gentle brush of her lips and momentary warm breath skimming over the sensitive skin brought a groan from deep inside. "Shhh, we have company."

"I do not care." His hands fisted in the sheet.

The slow slide of her mouth over his throbbing crown was enough to drive him over the edge. He'd been too long without her, too long without the warmth. His hands gripped her shoulders. "*Carida*, I need more tonight." He guided her off to the side and situated himself between her legs.

∾

In the morning, Madison sat staring into her coffee cup. "I want what you have."

Banji weighed the stoneware plates in her hands. She'd been about to put Madison's breakfast on the table, but smashing the plate over her head seemed like a better alternative.

"*Carida*, let her explain."

A soft snort and chuckle sounded behind her. Had Santiago somehow sensed her murderous intentions?

"You've got my car and you're sleeping in my house. What more could you possibly want?"

Madison sniffled. "I want to be happy."

Banji put their plates on the table and sank onto her chair. Santiago took his seat on her right and placed his hand over hers. Great. She couldn't hit as hard with her left hand. She was tempted to bite him. So much for happiness.

"You got yourself into this mess. I warned you the last time you were here. Why didn't you make an escape plan? Everyone knows you have to get your money and place to go all lined up before you walk out."

"I wasn't planning on leaving. I thought Mom would back me up." She swiped at her nose with a napkin. "But she looked at me and wished me good luck on the street."

"No surprise there. Look, here's what you can do. Get a job and a place to live, save some money so you can get a decent car and open one credit card account." She scowled. "Is your phone in your name?"

Madison shook her head and pursed her lips to one side. "I don't think so. It's one of those get three lines with unlimited everything deals."

"Then get your own phone. It's time to grow up, pull up your big girl panties and stand on your own two feet." Banji stabbed her fork into the scrambled eggs and took a bite.

Santiago grinned. "*Carida*, if I live here with you, Madison could stay in my house."

Banji stopped chewing and her left eyelid twitched. "It's your house, you can do what you want with it." She put down her fork before she stabbed them both to death with it. "Call Alena and asked her to get us some boxes. She can help us pack up your things and move them over here."

Madison's face lit up. "That would be so great. I could live here close to you."

"And what would be so great about that?" Banji did her best not to gnash her teeth and snarl.

Madison looked down and murmured, "I wouldn't have to be scared all the time."

Banji glimpsed Santiago's clenched jaw and turned her attention back to Madison. "Scared of what?"

"Dad." She inhaled without looking up. "I think he killed your Mom."

Banji's hands fisted on both sides of her plate.

"*Ay, Carida.*" Santiago put his hand over her nearest fist and turned his gaze on Madison. "What makes you say that?"

"I heard him fighting with my Mom. She said she wasn't going out on O'Connor's boat so he could throw her overboard like Genevieve."

The fog in Banji's brain slowly cleared. "When did you hear this fight?"

"About a year ago. That's when things between them started getting really bad." Madison slumped farther, practically shrinking under the table. "Then Bennett asked me to marry him and I thought I'd be able to get away, but now I have nowhere to go, if you throw me out."

Santiago squeezed Banji's hand. "You will stay here in my house. You will be safe but you must not tell your parents where you are."

"I won't. I promise."

Banji turned to Santiago. "I guess this means you're living with me."

CHAPTER EIGHTEEN

BANJI GRINNED AT ALENA. "I appreciate you helping move Santiago to my place." Banji's smirk reached all the way to her eyes. "He said we could leave the kitchen things here for Madison along with the sheets and blankets. All he wants are the black towels and his clothes."

Alena frowned, taped another box closed and put down the roll of package tape. "He'll need his shaving kit." She rubbed the small of her back. "You do know I wouldn't do this for anyone else on earth, right?"

"I get it. You never did like packing and moving. It's a miracle you came back from Texas."

"My Dad and *Papi* needed me. It was time for me to step up and take care of my responsibilities."

"What about Gabriel? Did he mind moving?"

"He'd outgrown his hometown. Becoming a Marine changed him." She stretched from side to side. "I was lucky he was ready to make the move."

"Do you ever think about going back?"

"Not really. We'll see our friends when we're there for the races but I'm not moving again." She looked around. "What's next for you?"

"Besides getting my office set up, I'm going to get to the bottom of Ritter Davis."

Alena's eyebrows quirked together. "And then what?"

Banji's eyes lit up. "Pirate treasure." She picked up the box Alena had finished taping and put it on the pile next to the back door.

"What are you talking about? This is the second time you've mentioned it." Alena pulled out a kitchen chair and sat down.

"It all came from somewhere. Somebody made it and somebody bought it, or stole it. Either way it went from one person to another. I'm going to figure it out."

Alena shook her head. "You're going to get yourself killed. You go digging up something that should be left buried and somebody could decide to bury you." She leaned forward putting her hands on the table. "I have a better idea." She looked over the table at Banji. "Work for Betmunn Racing. Design the best collectable accessories and posters. Work with our publicity team."

"I'm not a designer." Banji's nose crinkled up and her forehead wrinkled. "I've never done anything like that."

"Exactly, so our stuff won't look like everyone else's." She stood up. "You're a great artist. Try it and if you don't like it you can go back to terrorizing pirates."

"I can't terrorize the dead. But I do kind of like the idea."

"Which one? Pirates or Betmunn racing."

"Both." Banji giggled. "This could work."

Alena exhaled and picked up an empty box. "What's next?"

"I guess the bedrooms."

They walked down the hall to the first door on the left. Alena wrapped her fingers around the knob. "This was Carmen's room." She opened the door and stepped inside.

"She didn't sleep with Santiago?" Banji's brow furrowed as she looked around the room and took in the full-size bed.

"No, not for a long time. Once she found out they couldn't have children she moved in here."

"I don't think I should be in her room. I didn't know her and she wouldn't appreciate some stranger going through her things." Banji looked around the room and did her best to suppress a shiver. The religious wall decorations were a little overdone for her tastes. "I'll go work on packing Santiago's room."

Alena reached out and took Banji's upper arm. "Santiago doesn't run from his responsibilities. He took care of her."

"That's a good thing but it doesn't explain why he hasn't let me in here until now. He's hiding something."

Their eyes met.

"If that's what you think, go dig around in his room." Alena pointed at a door across the hall. "Look through his stuff, under the mattress, whatever it takes to satisfy your curiosity. See what you can find."

Banji walked over, opened the door to Santiago's room and looked around. It looked normal, neat and tidy which might be considered odd for a man's room but some men like things orderly. She opened his closet. Well, nothing incriminating there. His shirts were hung with the blue ones grouped together, then the white dress shirts—all three of them, and a couple black ones. Minimalist. That was enough to send a shiver down her spine. She didn't do minimalist anything.

His dresser held his work pants and jeans folded neatly. They were bulky. And then there were his white t-shirts. She was going to need more than one box. Good thing she'd gotten two dressers to match the king-size bed. He could have one all to himself.

She sat down on the edge of his bed and stared at the black, Daytona souvenir t-shirt in her hands. She needed to have a heart-to-heart talk with him.

"*Carida*, you look very serious. What are you thinking about?"

She looked up. "What are you doing here? We're not done packing."

"I came to see how it is going? Do you need help?"

"Not really but I want to ask you something." She put the t-shirt on the bed next to her hip.

"Okay." He lingered in the doorway.

"What don't you want me to see? Every time I said anything about coming over here, you didn't want me to."

He walked over and sat next to her. "I did not want you to see the way I lived."

"Even when Carmen was alive, you were all but alone. For years and years, you slept here by yourself. Why?"

"We were married."

"Didn't she love you anymore?"

"I loved Carmen but she was never in love with me. I had to get over it and make the best life I could for us." He reached over, took her hand and threaded his fingers through hers. "She could not love a man like me. If you found out, I was afraid you would not want me either."

"I'm not Carmen."

"No, you are my *Carida*." He looked at the open doorway.

"Okay, now that we've got that straightened out, let's get you out of here, but it's going to cost you." She kissed his cheek. "You're going to have to dance with me in the moonlight under a string of blue lights on the back porch."

"It will be my pleasure."

She patted his thigh. "You'll have to put up the lights." Before Banji had time to say another word, she was interrupted by Alena yelling from the other room.

"Banji, somebody is towing your sister's car!"

"Here we go." She hung her head and inhaled deeply. She shouted, "Don't worry about it."

Alena dashed into the room. "What do you mean don't worry about it? It's her car."

"No, it's not." Their eyes met. "Dad didn't put it in her name. It's probably leased. Just another one of his lies." She shrugged. "He gave me a piece of junk but at least it was mine. I have the title to it."

"What do you mean, it was yours?"

"I sold it to Madison last night. I'm going to drive Gram's Trans Am once it's running."

"Oh, great. I guess. So, is that why Madison took your car to go shopping?"

"Yeah. I can only imagine the hysterics if she came out of the store and the Mustang was gone."

Alena leaned against the doorjamb. "Your Dad has always been such a dick." She looked at the floor and shook her head slowly. "Good thing Madison has you."

"No, she lost me a long time ago." Glancing at Santiago, she said, "If it weren't for your *Papi*, she'd be camping on the beach."

117

"Right. Until your conscience got the better of you. I know for a fact you used to send her all sorts of little things from your travels in Europe." Alena grinned. "Take some time to get to know her."

"I only sent those things because I felt sorry for her on birthdays and Christmas."

"Right." Alena straightened up and moved out into the hall. "Okay, I've got Carmen's room packed up. What do you want me to do with the boxes?"

Santiago's grip tightened on Banji's hand. "Put them in the truck. I will take them to the donation store."

"You got it. I'm on it." She disappeared down the hall.

Banji caught his eye. "Are you sure? Don't you want to look through them in case there's something you want to keep?"

"That part of my life has been over for many years. There is nothing there for me."

They carried the last of his boxes into what was now their bedroom and put them down on the floor next to his dresser.

He looked at Banji. "Is this truly what you want, *Carida?*"

"Yes." She looked at the stack of boxes.

He took her in his arms. "I will fix our dinner tonight." He leaned down and spoke softly in her ear. "Then we will dance in the moonlight before I carry you off to bed."

"That'll be nice. We'll have the house to ourselves." She snickered. "We can make all the noise we want."

"I think I would like to make love to you on the beach in the moonlight."

"That sounds perfect." She stretched up and kissed him gently. "How about in the spring when it's warmer."

118

CHAPTER NINETEEN

BANJI PULLED her hair back and fastened it into a messy ponytail. What a difference a couple of weeks could make. There was no time like the present to get started on cleaning out the back room. The sun energized the day and she had the cottage to herself.

Madison had made herself comfortable in Santiago's house and was busy scribbling her new life's plan into the organizer Banji had given her. Santiago was busy putting together Betmunn's new engine that would make them worldwide contenders.

Banji opened the door to the small room at the end of the hall. It was dusty and the musty odor hit her nose. She opened the blinds to let in the light and cracked the window to get some fresh air. She scrutinized the boxes and piles of old clothes trying to decide where to start.

There were bound to be spiders in there somewhere. Yeah, better to leave them undisturbed for a few more minutes. She backed out and walked to the kitchen. The cabinet under the sink held her stash of insecticide spray cans. It would have been nice if there had been a pair of dishwashing gloves left over from the old days, but no. She would have to fight the eight-legged terrors bare-handed.

Fine. She snatched up two large plastic trash bags, a red can of spider death and went back to attack the targeted piles of clothes and boxes. Maybe she should be a mercenary. Spider killer for hire.

Banji dragged the two full bags of old clothes down the hall and left them by the back door, picked up a new bag and went back to the expanding mess in the back room. Once disturbed it kept growing and spreading. She was becoming suspicious that the room was trying to hide something from her. The third bag finally caught the last of the outdated apparel. That stuff had gone out of style thirty years ago.

Next, she pulled out one box at a time and opened them cautiously. Old books, tax returns, newspaper clippings, things she'd have to look through, sort out and shred. Her back ached and her feet were numb. The evening sun cast shadows around the room. She'd lost track of time but she was almost done.

In the very back corner behind the last cardboard box her hand landed on a hard, brass fitted footlocker. She wasn't sure the cracked leather strap would hold if she pulled too hard. She made a space and grabbed the back edge and pulled it away from the wall. The lid would have room to open, if she only had the key. A key like the one she'd dropped in the shoe box along with Ritter's letters.

She limped to her room and dug the shoe box out from the bottom drawer of her nightstand. Her fingers ran around the bottom corners till they touched the cool metal. She scooped it up and hustled back to the footlocker where she knelt down and slipped the key in the lock.

She inhaled, held her breath, and gingerly turned the pitted metal key. If it broke off, she'd have to get a locksmith to open it. Her luck held and the lock released. She lifted the lid. A man's dark blue jacket and cap were on top. She brushed her hand over the coarse wool. The label on the manila envelope was addressed to Ritter Davis in care of Genevieve Bancroft.

Banji put the jacket aside. His life was reduced to these few things. Her hands shook as she picked up the envelope and opened it.

The accident report was vague and didn't provide much in the way of answers. He'd eaten his dinner and gone to stand watch. When the next man on duty went to relieve him, Ritter wasn't there. After searching the ship and not finding him, they believed he must have been washed overboard during the storm. It was too late to turn around and search for him. They called in to the nearest ports to keep watch for their missing crewman but there was no trace of him.

She put the pages aside and reached for the next envelope. The life insurance company was researching the incident. Envelope after envelope of settlement information payable to Banji's mother not Gram. Banji, his daughter, was the alternate beneficiary.

Banji pushed his clothes aside. Letters, several stacks neatly tied and lined up filled the bottom. She recognized her mother's handwriting on the envelope's return address to Sand Dollar Cottage. Starting before her mother's wedding day and ending the day after he went missing. Genevieve hadn't known she was writing to a dead man.

Santiago stepped into the kitchen and immediately noticed the silence. The stereo wasn't on. That wasn't like Banji. She liked playing the old records in the afternoon. He'd come home and she'd be there with a hug and a kiss for him. Today there was nothing.

He called out, "*Carida.*"

Silence.

He walked down the hall checking the rooms along the way. The open door at the end of the hall caught his eye. It was usually closed. He pushed it open a few inches wider and peered inside.

"*Carida*, what is wrong?" He crossed the room and went to his knees beside her.

She rubbed her hand under her nose. "It's him. It's Ritter. All this is his." She clutched a seaman's classic pea coat to her chest.

He peered inside the footlocker. "The company must have sent it after he died."

"Yeah. It's been in here for years." She sniffled. "Gram never told me."

Santiago reached for the papers lying on top. "May I?"

"Sure, no point in trying to hide the truth. Ritter Davis is my father. He was in love with my mother. Those letters are from her to him. He saved them."

"I do not understand." His brow wrinkled as he read the paper in his hand. "This is from the shipping company. They sent his belongings here to his family."

"He put my Mom on his employment application." Banji inhaled a shuddering breath. "I've always believed that she walked out into the ocean three weeks after he went missing. She never saw this stuff." She sniffled. "Madison told me Lloyd Preston borrowed a boat and threw my Mom overboard. He must have drugged her first so she couldn't fight back. Gram let me read the coroner's report when I was old enough to understand it. Mom had overdose levels of anti-depressants in her blood." She swiped at the tears running down her cheeks. "I need to read every one of her letters to him. I have to know what happened."

"Yes, but not tonight." He looked at the room she'd emptied out except for Ritter's belongings. "I will paint this room and get you a good desk."

She stared at him with red-rimmed eyes. "You don't have to do that." She glanced at the open footlocker. "I'll take that thing out to the living room where I can sit on the couch and read the story of my mother's tragic love affair."

"No." He scooped her up still clinging to Ritter's coat and carried her to the living room where he sat down with her on his lap. "We will sit here together."

"Something tells me I'm going to need lots of tissues. I'll go to the store tomorrow." She buried her face in the coat. "This is all I have of my real father."

"You have his letters to your mother and the rest of his things." He tucked the loose hairs that hung in tendrils around her face behind her ears. "I can sit with you while you look through it." He kissed the top of her head. "He must have been a very good man. I would like to know more about him. Will you let me read his letters?"

"Sure, you can read his while I'm reading my Mom's." She shifted, curling into his chest. "I don't know who I am anymore."

"You are Missus Lori's granddaughter, my *Carida,* and Alena's friend. You belong here with us."

She sniffled. "The cards were right. I'm starting a new life but I never expected this." She clutched the jacket tighter.

"I will call Alena to come fix dinner and we will talk about this discovery."

Banji watched Alena put the platter of chicken fried steaks on the table. "Santiago should be out of the shower any minute." She craned her neck and looked down the hall. "Should I change my last name to Davis?"

"Hell yeah, you should change your name." She walked back to the stove. "That louse Preston could never have been your Dad. He's always been a sneaky little creep."

"Why didn't Gram tell me? It would have explained so much." Banji rubbed her temples.

"And it could have complicated things worse than they already were." Alena carried the bowl of mashed potatoes to the table. "Are you going to tell Madison you're not sisters?"

Banji shook her head. "No, that news can wait. It's bad enough she had to hear her Dad accused of killing my Mom." She glanced down the hall. "It happened so long ago. I've thought about it and there's no way to prove it. But at least I understand why things were the way they were." She looked pointedly at Alena. "What do you think Santiago will do now? I'm not the person he thought I was. He'd have every right to leave me."

Alena's butt hit the chair to the right of Banji's. "Not in this lifetime." She reached out and put her calloused hands over Banji's. "He's in love with you, even if he won't admit it. He's not going anywhere." She glanced toward the hall. "He's afraid to remarry, but give him time."

"He's never said he loves me." Banji looked at Alena's hand resting on hers and scowled. "You need to get some hand lotion for those claws of yours. They feel like sandpaper."

"Hey, I'm a working girl these days. I have a race car to build."

"Yeah, but if you grab Gabriel with those, we'll be able to hear him screaming all the way over here." Banji giggled. "It will not feel good on his sensitive male parts."

The corners of Banji's mouth turned up in a teasing grin and they broke out laughing.

"Give *Papi* time to say what's in his heart. Don't give up on him."

Alena got up and pulled the pot of green beans off the burner. "Let's get dinner on the table, then we can sit back and watch the tide roll in."

"I've got some Texas beer and wine in the refrigerator. We can drink to starting over."

CHAPTER TWENTY

Late in the night, Santiago rolled over and didn't bump into Banji. His eyes popped open and he checked the room. She wasn't there and the bathroom door across the hall was open. The bedside clock glowed two in the morning. He sat up and pulled on his jersey pants. He wasn't alone anymore and there was no telling what he might run into in the dark.

He padded out into the hall. The door to the back room was closed. He turned toward the living room and kitchen. The kitchen was empty. He moved into the living room relieved to see her shadowed figure sitting in a chair in front of the large picture window.

He walked up and put his hand on her shoulder. "I woke up and you were not next to me."

"I'm sorry. I couldn't sleep and didn't want to disturb you." She reached up and rested her hand over his. "You need to rest. You have to work in the morning."

The footlocker sitting on the far side of her chair caught his eye. "I will stay home and paint your office." She wasn't going to read the letters until she was good and ready. He would stay home, paint, and give her time to decide.

"Alena needs you at the garage."

He kept his voice firm and quiet. "I want to get your office ready."

"My god, you are so stubborn." She looked up. "I don't need a babysitter. I can do this."

He stepped to the side of the chair. "We will go to the store and you will choose the paint for your office in the morning." He took her hand and brought it to his lips. "I will do this for you." He pressed a kiss to the back of her hand.

"Why are you so good to me?"

"Unlike that unfortunate corsair, I will take care of what I have been lucky enough to find."

Banji stood up, wrapped her arms around Santiago's neck, and rested her head on his chest over his heart. "They never had a chance, did they?"

His arms encircled her, molding her soft curves firmly against his body. He swayed her to the music playing softly in his head. "They risked their lives to be together but greed and vengeance followed them."

"But it didn't have to be that way."

Santiago skimmed one hand to the small of her back. His lips pressed to the crook of her neck and he eased closer.

Her foot brushed against his. She murmured, "Your feet are like icebergs. Let's get in bed so I can warm them up for you."

"What about the rest of me?" He smiled and pressed a kiss to the top of her head.

"I can start with your toes and work my way up." She took his nipple between her teeth and flicked her tongue over it.

"*Ay, Carida.* I think you like torturing me."

"Only a little." Her hand slipped between his legs and gently massaged his testicles and growing erection through the soft jersey material. "I think you like it."

"Yes, very much."

In the morning, they drove to town and Banji chose a pale peach so light it was almost white but it would look open and airy behind the pale blue seascapes she would hang on the walls. She helped Santiago prepare the walls and spread the drop cloths they'd remembered to buy.

He kissed her and said, "Go fix our lunch while I put the painter's tape around the window trim."

"It'll be sandwiches and chips like before." She tried not to wince thinking back to the first cold-cut lunch she'd fixed him. She really needed to get Alena to give her some easy-to-fix cooking lessons.

He smiled. "My favorite."

Who was he trying to kid? "Okay, I'll let you know when they're ready."

She strolled down the hall to the kitchen. It wouldn't kill her to make a couple of sandwiches. Her head was still in the refrigerator looking for the lettuce when she heard the back door open. She straightened up, banged her head and yowled, "Ouch!" Holding her head, she stepped back and scowled at her intruder.

Alena stifled a giggle. "Sorry. I thought I'd come help you fix lunch."

"How'd you know?"

"*Papi* called me. He wants to talk about the new car while we eat."

Banji rubbed the sore spot on her head. "I can't keep letting him do all the cooking. Can you show me how to make some really super-easy meals so he can have a break?"

"Sure. We'll get you a crock pot to start with. You put all the ingredients in and let it cook for a few hours. That way you can work and not worry about having it all go up in flames." Alena snickered. "Please, I'm begging you, never go near the barbeque grill. We don't want the fire department coming out here for flaming hot dogs."

"Stop laughing. It's not funny." Banji dropped the sandwich ingredients on the counter. "You can look in the pantry. Gram had some old appliances in there. Maybe there's a crock pot."

"What have we got for sandwiches?" Alena sorted through the packages on the counter.

"I'm not sure. Santiago does most of the shopping. I pulled out everything I could find that might go between two slices of bread."

"How did you survive living alone?"

"Deli, take-out, cheap restaurants, peanut butter and jelly." Banji shrugged. "I had a toaster oven and a microwave."

"Okay, well, let's get started." Alena picked up the bread and took out six slices. "Butter both sides of these while I look for a square griddle."

"I think I saw something like that in the lower cabinet by the stove."

Alena dug out the pan and put it on the burner. "We're good. So, how's the new office coming?"

"I picked out the paint and wall décor. The rest will have to wait. I started looking through Ritter's things and there are a bunch of letters from my mom to him. I'm going to read them and find out what the deal was." She continued buttering the bread slices.

"Are you ready to know the details? It's going to change the way you've thought about your mother."

"Ritter Aloysius Davis is my father, not Lloyd Preston. That makes up for a lot. The mystery of how I ended up with my middle name has been solved."

"How can you be sure?"

"I saw it on the birth certificate in Ritter's things. Mom sent it to him."

"But you've been filling out everything as Banji Preston all these years."

"My name got changed somewhere along the way after I was born and before they got my Social Security card. It'll take some back tracking to find out exactly what happened and when. I've got my first unofficial mystery to solve."

Alena leaned over and whispered, "I like the sound of Banji Cordova."

"Shut up!" Banji hissed. "He hasn't even hinted about that kind of permanent. We're okay. Don't go starting trouble."

"No trouble. We'd be related for real is all." Alena giggled. "You'd be my stepmom."

"There's something seriously wrong with that picture."

"But you're thinking about it, right?" Alena glanced at Banji. "Right?"

"I'm good with the way things are for now."

"He's a little on the old-fashioned side in case you haven't noticed. Eventually, he'll want more."

Banji stared at the counter top. "I don't want to make him uncomfortable and scare him away. Guys don't like serious talks about long-term commitment. They get to feeling trapped or something. It's in all the magazines. You need to read more."

"I don't have time to read those stories. I have cars to build and a husband to take care of. With the holidays coming up, things tend to get sentimental and *Papi* might start feeling romantic. We could encourage him a little."

Banji stared at the jar in her hands. "Unless you want a mayonnaise facial, you'll keep all that to yourself. He can make up his own mind when he's ready without any interference from you."

Taking the jar, Alena said, "Mayonnaise is nothing. When we were kids you dumped a bucket of wet sand over my head."

"You knocked over my sandcastle."

"It was already falling down."

Banji frowned. Alena would remember that detail. "This thing with Ritter and my mom has been waiting to come out for years and I can't think of a better time than now. It's not like I have anything better to do with my time."

Santiago walked up behind her and wrapped his arms around her middle. "*Sí, Carida*, this is the perfect time. You can solve the puzzle of what happened to them and make a new life for yourself here with me." He nuzzled the side of her neck before kissing her cheek. "Your office will be beautiful."

How much had he heard? Banji was afraid to even think about it. Ever since she'd arrived at Gram's, fate had taken control of her life. She was definitely going in the direction the cards had predicted even if the road was a little bumpy.

She turned in his arms and hugged him. "That's because you're amazing with a paint brush."

From the corner of her eye she caught Alena's raised eyebrow. Santiago was amazing at everything he did but they weren't having that discussion over lunch.

Alena carefully placed the sandwiches on the griddle. "Okay, everyone grab what you want to drink, food will be ready in about ten minutes."

~

Santiago ate his sandwich, watched and listened to Banji and Alena talk about the upcoming holidays. He would help put up the lights and decorations. Banji wanted blue lights on the back porch. He could do that. The soft glow would be perfect for dancing to something slow. They would cuddle and kiss while sitting on the swing he was getting her for Christmas.

A small smirk teased the corner of his mouth. He didn't need Alena's encouragement. He had romantic plans of his own. The idea of a permanent relationship would take some getting used to. Getting married was forever and he wasn't sure he could make that kind of commitment. At least not yet.

He lived in her house, slept in her bed, and wore the pants she'd bought him. Today she'd asked Alena to teach her to cook so she could feed him something other than rotisserie chicken from the deli. He was satisfied with the life he had. For now.

The antique roll-top desk he'd bought her would be delivered in two days. The Trans Am would be ready in another week. He liked the man he was becoming, the man he'd always wanted to be.

His thoughts were interrupted by a loud clamp of thunder.

Alena's head snapped toward the picture window. "Damn, there's a storm coming in fast. I better get home." She pushed back from the table. "Sorry to stick you with the dishes, but I left the windows open in the breakfast room."

"No problem. I'm good with doing dishes." Banji snickered. "There's something relaxing about hot water and slippery soap suds." She grinned at Santiago.

Alena opened the back door and glanced over her shoulder. "I don't want to know."

Santiago put his hand over Banji's. "I know you like to take a nap when it storms. The dishes can wait."

CHAPTER TWENTY-ONE

IT STORMED FOR TWO DAYS. The best two days of her life. Banji had Santiago all to herself. She rolled with him in the sheets, danced with him in the dark, and cuddled with him on the couch watching old movies. And then the sun came out. What a revolting development! Life returned to normal.

The paint in her office dried perfectly and the seascapes decorated the walls. The house was quieter than usual since Santiago had gone to the garage that morning. She turned on the stereo to break the silence.

She settled on the couch and opened Ritter's footlocker. Before she could pick up the first packet of letters the backdoor opened and Santiago call out, "*Carida*, I have a surprise."

Catching a movement out of the corner of her eye, Banji shrieked and scrambled to get her feet under her and stand on the couch with her back against the wall. "There's something in here. I saw it run under that chair." She pointed across the room.

Santiago planted his hands on his hips and laughed.

Banji wailed, "It's under there staring at me. It looks like a rat!"

"*Carida*, it is a kitten. I named him Aloysius. He will keep you company when I am not home."

"Are you sure? It has big yellow eyes and whiskers."

Santiago got down on his knees and reached under the chair.

"No, it'll bite you. It might have rabies." She pressed her back tighter against the wall.

He scooped the small ball of grey fur into his hand, sat back and held it to his chest. "See, it is only a kitty." He looked over at her with a smirk plastered to his lips. "Come down from there. You are frightening Aloysius."

"No, and what's that dog doing in my house?" She stared at the small ball of wet black and white fur next to Santiago's leg.

"Star is still a puppy. I found them huddled together in the doorway of the garage. We do not have anything there to feed them." He petted the small puppy. "Their ribs are poking out. They need food."

She sank down onto her knees on the couch cushions. "What if they have fleas?"

Santiago grinned. "We will wash them so they do not."

"I've never had a pet. I don't know anything about taking care of dogs and cats."

"It is not hard. I will show you."

"You can't name that kitten Aloysius. I won't know if you are yelling at me or the cat."

"I do not yell." He quirked an eyebrow in her direction. The kitten blinked.

Banji grumbled, "Right. We can call him Wishes. That's a good name for a cat."

"Wishes and Star." He cradled the shivering kitten against his chest. "What do you think? Are you Wishes?" He looked at Banji. "He is not objecting so it must be okay."

She settled deeper into the cushion. "What are we going to feed them? I don't have any pet food."

"You have bread and milk. There is left over hamburger from last night."

She protested, "But the milk is for my coffee."

"You've had your coffee this morning. I fixed it for you."

"Oh, right. I can go to the store and get more."

He chuckled. "And stop at the pet store. They need beds, kitten and puppy food and water bowls."

"How will I know which food is the best?"

"The clerk at the pet store can tell you about the different brands."

She bit her bottom lip. "I don't know."

"You will need puppy papers for house training Star and a litter box and litter for Wishes."

"Me? What about you. You're the one who found them."

"Do you want them to wait till I get off work this afternoon?"

"No." She crawled across the couch moving closer to get a better look at the kitten. It was kind of cute.

"Then you must go to the store."

Banji gave up and huffed, "Fine."

Banji hauled load after load of groceries and pet supplies into the kitchen. She'd finally lost her mind. She was jobless, living in her grandmother's house, sleeping with an older man, and now she had pets. She didn't do pets!

Alena came through the back door all cheerful and giggles. "Hey, *Papi* told me you got a new kitten." She stopped abruptly and stared at the shopping bags strewn around the kitchen on every available surface. "What in the world?"

"Yeah, and a puppy."

"I got the impression the puppy was his."

Banji stuck her hand on her hip and grumped, "Well, since they're all living with me, I guess that makes them mine. The whole bunch of them."

"What's wrong?" Alena opened one of the bags and peeked inside.

"I've never had pets. I don't know anything about taking care of animals." She inhaled and held her breath for a count of five and exhaled. "What if I can't do it? What if I mess up?"

"It's not that hard. You give them food, water, shelter and get them their shots once a year. That's about it."

"That won't work on Santiago. You try sticking him with a needle and see what happens."

Alena tamped down a giggle, pulled out a chair and sat down. "Back up and tell me the whole story. What's up?"

"He should be gone by now. Everyone leaves. They don't cook my breakfast and bring me pets." Banji flopped down on a chair opposite Alena. "I don't know what I'm doing."

"You're settling down." A smug grin spread across Alena's face.

"Why is this happening to me?"

"Because you've already seen the Eiffel Tower, the Spanish Steps, the Trevi Fountain, the Tower of London and ridden in a gondola under the Bridge of Sighs in Venice." Alena tipped her head to one side. "You could always go back to Europe and look for a job. The Maritime Museum might hire you."

Banji leaned back in her chair, crossed her arms over her stomach and smiled. "I do love pirate treasure."

"Don't forget, *Papi* is very attached to you."

"He won't go with me." Banji uncrossed her arms and leaned forward resting them on the kitchen table. "And I couldn't take Wishes."

"Exactly." Alena raised an eyebrow and focused her gaze on Banji. "Have you considered the possibility that you're right where you're supposed to be? You've got the one thing money can't buy."

Banji quirked an eyebrow. "Really, and what's that?"

"Family."

"Have you been watching TV romance movies again?" Banji leaned forward shortening the distance between herself and Alena. "None of those girls have to deal with anything close to this mess."

"It's not that bad. Do you mind telling me how my nomad friend has decided that my *Papi* is the right man for her?"

"I saw it in the cards. That's all I can tell you."

"And what else?"

Alena crossed her arms under her breasts which pushed them up resembling an overstuffed balconette bra.

Banji nodded toward Alena's chest. "That is not a good look on you. Your boobs look like over inflated pool floats."

"Stop changing the subject. *Papi* is seriously involved with you."

"And? What's the problem?"

"You've never been in love with any man that I know of. Not even seriously infatuated for more than two weeks."

"Well, you sleep with him and it'll all make sense."

Alena broke out laughing, snorted, reined it in and choked it down. "Not happening. Worst idea ever."

Banji's eyes grew wide. "No. I mean you can't do that. Um, okay, fine. He fits; he's what's been missing from my life."

"Try again."

"He's strong and steady, someone I can count on. He does so much for me just because he wants to." Banji chewed on her bottom lip. She softly said, "I trust him."

"Really? He's very intimidating until you get to know him."

Banji shook her head. "I guess I missed that part."

"Okay, if you're happy, I'm happy." She tipped her head toward Banji's pile of bags on the counter. "And you're getting along with Aloysius."

"Ah, his name is Wishes." Banji's brow wrinkled and her eyes narrowed. "I should have known you had something to do with all this."

"Not really. I got the call when *Papi* found them and I thought you could use the company." She uncrossed her arms. "When the racing season starts, we'll be on the road. I thought you might not get so lonely back here at home if you had some company."

"About that, I'd like to go to Galveston with Santiago."

"Sure, but what about Star and Wishes? Who's going to watch them while you're in Texas?" Alena glanced around the room. "What have you done with them?"

"They're in the guestroom. I didn't want them roaming the house while I was gone." She got up and went over to the packages on the counter. "I need to wash their bowls and put out some food and water for them." She reached in and pulled out the first bowl she came to. "I'll get a pet sitter or ask Madison to come over and check on them. It wouldn't hurt her to learn a little responsibility."

"Has she found a job yet?"

"Not that I've heard, but she did get her own phone. She changed the address on her driver's license and we put my old car in her name while we were at the county offices."

"What about the insurance?"

"I paid for the first six months. Can't have her driving around uninsured looking for a job." Banji washed the bowls and put them in the dishrack to dry.

"How does she like living at *Papi's*?"

"Loves it. She's made herself right at home. Not sure what's up with that. It's kind of scary."

Alena shifted in her chair. "I thought I'd invite her to the New Year's party."

"Wouldn't hurt. No point in leaving her alone while we're having fun."

Their conversation was interrupted by a knock on the front door.

Banji glanced at the door and looked back at Alena. "I'm not expecting anyone."

"Do you want me to answer it?"

Banji muttered, "No, I've got it." She walked over, opened the door and stared at the man wearing a dark green work uniform. "Can I help you?"

"I have a delivery for Banji Preston." What the hell? "What is it?"

He tapped the clipboard. "A roll-top desk."

She turned to look at Alena. "Did you know about this?"

"Yeah, *Papi* got it for your office. We found it at a warehouse sale. It belonged to a nineteen-fifties private investigator, very old-school. It's got history and will bring you good luck."

"Something tells me I'm going to need more than luck." Banji took the clipboard and signed for the delivery. "It goes in the back room."

Alena held the back door open while three large pieces were wheeled in. She looked over at Banji. "You'll have to show them where you want it. It'll be too heavy for you to move after it's put together."

"Why would Santiago do this?"

"You said you wanted to work from home and you needed an office."

"What if nobody hires me?"

"Ah, you still have my offer."

"Well, sure, I'm going to do your jewelry designs and posters but that won't take all my time."

"How about you roll with this and see what happens?"

CHAPTER TWENTY-TWO

AFTER ALENA LEFT, Banji got out her orange scented furniture polish and wiped down the solid oak desk and matching chair. The chair would definitely need a pad for the seat. No way she could sit for hours on that hard, wooden surface without her tailbone complaining. No wonder old-time investigators were always portrayed as grumpy, ornery men. Their butts hurt from sitting on chairs like hers. She eyed the thing and ran the cleaning cloth over the contours one more time.

The seventeen small and two deep file drawers would be great for organizing her projects. Seven letter slots would keep her correspondence in order. She sat on the chair and rolled it up to the desk. It didn't feel as bad as she'd expected. She wiggled a little and giggled. Her butt fit. She spread her hands out on the desktop feeling the grain of the wood. "I love this desk."

"I am glad." Santiago chuckled.

"Ah!" Banji screeched and stood up, only to bang the tops of her thighs against the lap drawer and smack back down onto her chair. She glared over her shoulder at a smirking Santiago. "You scared me."

"The desk suits you." He stepped further into the room.

She pushed back from the desk, swiveled around and got up.

"I love it. Thank you."

"You are welcome, *Carida*."

She met him in the middle of the room, put her hands on his shoulders, stretched up and kissed him soft and slow. When she was done, she brushed his hair back from his forehead. "You're a gift from the sea. I don't know what I did to deserve you but I'm glad I did it."

His fingers tightened their hold on her waist. "You told me you did not regret kissing me."

"Right. And I still don't." She grinned. "I think I'll do it again to be sure." She pressed her lips against his in a more sensual kiss. His lips parted and her tongue danced with his. So indulgent, warm and inviting. "Still perfect."

"I must go back to work." He gently swiped his thumb across her lips. "We will continue this later."

"I'll be right here settling into my new desk." She watched him walk down the hall until he was out of sight. The sight of him still tugged at her heart. Yes, she had it bad for the big guy.

Well, back to work.

She spent the next hour organizing her desk and tucking away her new office supplies. Banji's antique jewelry research and appraisal service had a cheerful work space. She was moving on with her life and career.

She glanced down the hall. Her mother's letters were waiting patiently to be read. It wouldn't hurt to take a quick peek at her tarot cards to be sure everything was still headed in the right direction. Gram's papers would have to wait.

After a quick shuffle, Banji stared at The Wheel of Fortune: New hope prevails, order has been brought back to your life, solitude has come to an end and you are able to look forward to life as a couple. Realize that you must take on the responsibilities of a harmonious life together.

She had the afternoon to herself. It was a good time to call Barcelona Starze and find out what happened to Alessia's locket. She needed more information about the curse and the pirate.

Princess Alessia had to have been out of her mind to fall for a corsair, a nasty filthy pirate. He probably had a half-dozen diseases and fleas or lice, maybe both. Running away with him reeked of mystery and begged the question of what was she running away from? It had to be something really bad to make Salvatore look like the answer to her problem.

Her fingers pressed the numbers for Miss Starze. Hopefully, she hadn't changed her phone number.

"Hello."

"Miss Starze, this is Banji Preston, the appraiser from the Maritime Museum. Do you have a minute to talk?"

"Sure. What can I do for you?"

"I'd like to ask you about the locket and the curse." Banji held her breath and silently prayed Barcelona didn't hang up on her.

"Wow, Salvatore's heart. That thing really works. Anyone who touches it finds their true love." Barcelona hummed, inhaled and exhaled loudly. "But there's a catch."

Banji's brow wrinkled and her eyes narrowed to slits. "What catch?"

"Let me try to explain this as best I can. My sister, Sahara, came across the story of the runaway princess of Genoa and she went looking for the pirate ship *El Anochecer*. She followed the clues to the Bahamas and found Alessia's diary in a church. Alessia was betrothed to a brutal man, the Count De Balboa. When she fell in love with Salvatore, she left everything behind to marry him."

"She had to be desperate to put her life on the line for a pirate." Banji settled down in her office chair and put her phone on speaker.

"Exactly. Balboa followed them and she was afraid they would never be safe. She wrote it all down the best she could and left the diary with a priest in Governor's Harbor." Barcelona didn't hide the sounds of drinking from a bottle. "Sorry, I'm thirsty. It's another hot day in Texas. Gotta stay hydrated."

"No problem." Banji opened her notebook and pulled a pen out of the holder. "So, what's in the diary?"

"Alessia couldn't understand why her father and Balboa wouldn't leave her and Salvatore alone. She put a curse on them. They would die alone and unloved without the locket."

"Okay, sounds fair. But I get the feeling there's a part two coming."

"Oh, yeah." Barcelona snickered. "Whoever holds the locket will find their true love." She inhaled deeply. "Alessia wrapped it up, stuck it in a chest and it literally went down with the ship."

"But your sister found it." Banji tapped her pen on the pad. "So, what's the deal with it now?"

"Whoever holds the locket will find their true love. Hmm…"

"What aren't you telling me?"

"Where he goes, you must follow."

Banji wailed, "Are you kidding me?"

"No. *El Anochecer* sank. Salvatore was fatally wounded and died in Alessia's arms. She shot herself so they wouldn't be parted."

"How do you know?"

"Sahara got the ending from the priest's journal. He cared for the survivors from *El Anochecer*. The cabin boy swam to shore and hid in the church along with a few others."

"And if I don't follow him, then what?" Banji pressed her pen to the paper scribbling with shaking fingers.

"I don't know. There are parts of the diary we can't figure out. But I'm pretty sure you'll lose your true love."

"No! That's not in the cards. I would have seen it."

"Well, how's your eighteenth-century Age of Enlightenment Italian? If you can translate the parts we can't, maybe the answers you're looking for are in the diary."

"Great. Where are you and where's the diary?"

"Right here in Galveston. Sahara is here with Boris, I'm here with Misha, and Cami is here with Lyev."

"Cami, as in Cami Fiero?"

"Yeah. Do you know her?"

"Cami Fiero went to high-school with me. Last time I talked to her she was living in Galveston and married to a Russian sailor of some kind."

"Sounds like the same girl. Cami came here a couple years ago from California."

Banji shook her head. "Small world." She inhaled a shaky breath. "I'm going to be in Galveston for the opening of the new race track."

"If you want to take a look at the diary, I'll let Sahara know."

"Oh, I absolutely want to take a look at it."

141

"Does this mean you've met someone?"

"That's exactly what it means. But I only touched the locket for a few minutes and I was wearing cotton gloves to protect it. As a professional appraiser, I don't want to get any oil or chemicals from my hands onto precious metals I don't own. That curse shouldn't have affected me."

"Not true. Cami only held it for a couple minutes at Sahara's wedding reception and it got her Lyev. It brought him all the way from Saint Petersburg to Galveston. It's not a matter of how long you have it or if you own it. We've already figured out that much."

"So, what happens if I don't follow this guy wherever he goes?"

"I don't know. You'd have to try it and find out."

Banji paced and screeched, "It's true. The curse is real."

Santiago grasped her shoulder, stopping her pacing and pressed his hand against her forehead. "You are having a fever. Alena is coming to check on you."

Banji swatted his hands away. "I don't need Alena. I'm doomed. Doomed as doomed can be." She turned her eyes on him. "What have I done to you?"

"Nothing bad." He chuckled. "I am fine." He reached for her again.

She stepped back and wailed, "I'm not sick."

"You must not worry. There could be a way to break the curse."

Would she fall out of love with Santiago if they broke the curse? Banji yowled, "No! We can't break the curse. Not until we know more."

Alena shut the back door, gasped and asked, "Know more about what?"

Santiago bit out. "She has a fever. She does not know what she is saying."

Banji grabbed Alena's arm. "We need to call Cami now before it gets any worse. She knows Barcelona Starze, the lady who brought the locket into the Maritime Museum."

"Let me take a look at you." Alena gently placed her finger under

Banji's eye and pulled down the lower lid. "Um, looks okay." She placed the back of her hand against Banji's forehead. "Maybe a little warmer than normal." She grasped Banji chin and tugged. "You look okay."

Banji bared her teeth. "Let go."

"Don't you dare bite me."

Santiago quietly watched the goings on and asked, "Would she do that?"

Alena glanced in his direction. "You have no idea." She looked back at Banji and grinned. "I've had years to find out just what an uncouth, little savage she really is."

Banji plopped onto the nearest kitchen chair. "I'm not a savage. I'm what you'd call a free-spirit." She wrinkled her nose at Alena. "It's not my fault that creep got in the way of my teeth."

Alena looked at *Papi*. "Give her two fever reducers with a nice warm cup of tea and let her rest. She'll be fine. We'll call Cami this evening and see what we can find out."

"Come back here! We need to talk to Cami now." Banji sprang to her feet.

Alena trotted off the back porch and back to the main house with Banji and Santiago trailing after her. She left the kitchen door open for them and dashed into her office.

Alena's husband, Gabriel, looked up from the computer screen on the desk when she burst through the door. "What's up?"

Alena snickered. "Banji's been accosted by the curse on the pirate treasure that made her miss my wedding."

"What? Are you sure?" He followed her movements as she grabbed a book on sunken treasures from the shelf behind the desk. "If those old movies are right, there's always a way to break the curse."

Alena slapped the book on the desk and started flipping pages. "There's got to be something we can do."

Gabriel leaned back in the executive office chair and laughed. "Oh, man. I feel sorry for *Papi*."

Alena nodded. "Cami might know. We're going to call her. It's an emergency. We need to fix this before Banji does something dumb." She glanced over at Gabriel. "What time is it in Texas?"

143

Gabriel chuckled. "It's a couple hours later in Galveston. If she's married, she's probably home fixing dinner." He raised an eyebrow at Alena. "Like a good wife."

Alena grabbed her phone out of her pocket. "You're a Marine, go shoot something or go down to the beach and catch something. Cook has the holidays off but there's crackers and cheese in the kitchen if you're really desperate."

~

Santiago took a seat on the over-stuffed couch and pulled Banji onto his lap. "Stop wiggling. I will not let you go until I find out what this is all about."

Banji's head flopped back like she'd been shot. "I hate my life."

Gabriel chuckled. "This is great." He shot a look at Banji. "You're not getting out of this. It's a done deal. And about time if you ask me." He rocked back in his office chair and put his feet up on the mahogany executive desk.

"Clue, nobody asked you." Banji squinted and glared at Gabriel. "And get your feet off Alena's desk."

That only made him laugh louder.

Banji grumbled, "You're impossible."

Alena giggled. "He's complicated." Her eyes lit up. "Hey, Cami! Banji's here with me and we need to talk to you. I'm going to put you on speaker." She moved the phone away from her ear and pressed the speaker icon. "The curse on Barcelona's pirate locket has cast its spell on Banji."

"How do you know?" Cami's voice came through loud and clear with a hint of amused concern. "Is she okay?"

"No, I'm not okay," Banji wailed.

Alena grinned. "She's fine. My *Papi's* got her."

Cami giggled. "No. Are you kidding me? She has a man in her life, amazing."

"Not kidding. He found her on the beach a few weeks ago."

"Oh, my, god! What happened?"

Banji muttered, "Wouldn't you like to know?"

"Well, actually I would," Cami's faint snicker came through clearly.

Banji frowned and grumbled, "It's that damned locket from hell. The one I appraised in London. Barcelona Starze told me you know all about it."

Cami said, "I had no idea you were the appraiser. What a coincidence."

"Pay attention. There's no such thing as coincidences. The museum called and asked for an appraiser. Technically, I didn't touch it. I wore my best cotton gloves." She inhaled noisily. "I was making a drawing of the engraving. It's such delicate work. I've never seen anything so fine."

"And?"

Banji hiccupped. "And I finished and put it away in the safe so Barcelona could pick it up."

"Then what happened?"

"I came home, went to work at Nerbert's, got fired, moved to Gram's and Santiago found me."

Cami asked, "He found you or you found him?"

"I don't know. I looked up and there he was walking along the beach." Banji stared into Santiago's amused eyes. There was a twinkle in them she'd never seen before. "We started talking and there's something about him that really works for me."

Cami's next words did nothing to fix the issue. "Oh, wow. Well, that's it then. You're one of the lucky ones."

"Don't say that. There's got to be a way to fix this."

"There's nothing to fix. It's wonderful." Cami giggled. "You've found your true love."

"That can't be right." Banji sniffled and rubbed her nose.

"Why not? Doesn't he like you?"

Santiago looked down and met Banji's stare. "Answer her, *Carida*."

"I love it when he talks South American." Cami sighed heavily. "It's so romantic."

Banji wailed, "Then you shouldn't have married a Russian."

Alena snickered. "It's okay, Russian accents can be pretty romantic when they set their minds to it."

Gabriel's eyebrows drew together and he asked, "How would you know?"

"I watch movies and hear things." Alena broke out laughing. "This is priceless. I wish I had a recording of it." She looked at *Papi* and tamped down her laughter. "I'm thinking you're fond of Banji?"

Gabriel held up his hands in surrender and looked at Santiago. "Don't look at me. I've never even seen the locket. This is the first I've heard about it."

"I do not need to see it or touch it." Santiago looked at the phone in Alena's hand. "*Mi Carida* is perfect for me."

Cami snickered. "Well, there you have it. The locket is still working. Alessia's diary isn't clear on the details, but so far everyone that's touched it since Sahara brought it up from the wreck has found their perfect mate."

"Then I will hold it and we will know it is true." Santiago nodded.

"That's a good idea." Alena stood up straighter and grinned. "I like it."

Banji groused, "It's not a good idea. It needs to be dropped back in the ocean pronto!"

"I am not afraid. It will not change the way I feel. But I will do it so Banji can be sure we are meant to be together." Santiago hugged her a little tighter and kissed the top of her head.

"When I held it, I could hear something rattling inside of it. It might be the answer to solving the curse." Cami asked, "Do you want me to try to open it? It seems wrong somehow but I could try to do it if you think it's important."

"No. Leave it alone. Opening it might break the curse and then nobody else will be able to find their true love. I don't want to be responsible for that." Banji leaned into Santiago. "I'm good the way I am."

Santiago smiled over the top of Banji's head. "Leave it alone."

Banji grumbled, "We're coming to Galveston for the opening races at the new resort. We can go out to dinner when we get there."

"Great." Cami cleared her throat. "Lyev is working on the

construction crew's evening shift and tells me the track is going to be fast."

Alena said, "Can't wait. I've got a fast car."

Santiago adjusted his hold on Banji. "We have reserved rooms at the resort hotel for the grand opening."

Banji sniffled. "I like Texas fried catfish and hush puppies."

Chuckling, Cami said, "We have lots of fried shrimp and hush puppies here on Galveston Island, and we have a beach."

"Well, okay, I can make do with shrimp."

Gabriel opened his mouth and shut it when Alena fixed him with her warning glare and shook her head. She said, "Great. Sounds like a party to me."

Santiago released Banji so she could stand up and locked looks with Alena. "I will take her home if you are sure she is not sick."

Alena smiled knowingly. "She's not sick, only cursed. She'll be fine."

"Stop saying that." Banji hissed at Alena. "You're making things worse."

Cami added, "It's going to be okay. I promise. The locket knows what it's doing. I'll talk to you later." She disconnected the call.

Banji drew a finger across her throat and glared at Alena.

Alena winced. "Sorry but he'd find out eventually."

"Find out what?" Santiago's brow wrinkled.

"That Banji's already fallen for you."

Banji grumbled, "Shut up. I haven't told him yet. You're ruining everything."

"All right. Fine. Go home and feed the cat. I'm sure Aloysius is hungry."

"Wishes, his name is Wishes, and I wish you'd hush up." Banji glared at Alena. "And stay out of my love life. I can make a perfectly fine mess of it without any help from you."

CHAPTER TWENTY-THREE

SANTIAGO OPENED the door and followed Banji out into the evening air. The sunset was almost gone below the horizon. He took her hand and paced his strides to match her smaller ones. He'd waited his whole life to be walking hand in hand with his true love.

He was curious to know more about the mysterious cursed locket. It could explain the reason he'd been contemplating changing his mind about remarrying. He stopped and tugged her around to face him. "I am yours, *Carida*. Only yours."

Her eyes filled with tears and she stuttered, "I'm so sorry. I wanted to take you for a romantic walk on the beach and say everything perfectly. Now, Alena's gone and blabbed. That stupid locket ruined everything."

Santiago couldn't hide his satisfied grin. "It is not a problem. We are walking home on the beach and you can kiss me. It will be very romantic with the sun sinking on the horizon." He brushed a loose strand of her hair away from her face. "And I will kiss you."

"That would be really nice."

~

Banji took his hand and wove her fingers through his. She loved his big hands. His warm touch never failed to thrill her. She'd waited her whole life for this man. And she had no clue how to tell him that wouldn't make her sound pitiful.

She didn't do pitiful, ever, never. Her boisterous persona was her shield. She might sink to feeling down and shed a few tears in private but never where anyone could see it. No one but Santiago. She hadn't been ready for that. And the fact that he was still standing next to her and not running away was a first.

She tugged on his hand. "Come on, let's go home. I want to talk to you about something important."

"And I want to talk to you." The subtle smile under his moustache wasn't lost on her.

They walked hand-in-hand along the beach trail. The ocean waves washing ashore and their footsteps in the soft sand were the only sounds floating on the evening breeze. Before they reached the trail below the cottage Banji slowed and pulled Santiago's hand and turned toward him. Facing toward the sea and setting sun, she said, "It's almost dark and I want to see your face when I say this officially for the first time.

He turned toward her and their eyes met.

"Santiago, I thank the moon, the sun, the stars and the sea for bringing us together. And if that curse is to be believed, you are the man for me."

"*Carida*, I have waited a lifetime for you and I would do it all again." He gathered her in his arms and kissed her with everything in his heart. She sensed it, even if he couldn't bring himself to say the words. Her fingers were still tangled in his hair when their lips parted.

Banji caught her breath and said, "There's going to be good days and not so good days, but I'm in this for wherever it takes us."

"Tonight, it is taking us home for dinner, then we will listen to our favorite songs on the stereo and I will ask you to dance with me." His fingers trailed from her temple to her chin.

His touch always amazed her. For such a rough looking man with a manual labor-intensive job, his hands were always gentle with her. She leaned into his touch.

"Slow dancing with you is my second favorite thing in the world." She stretched up and whispered in his ear, "Making love to you is my all-time favorite thing. So, get ready. When the music stops, your clothes come off."

"*Ay, Carida*, you are going to make me wait so long. I thought we might dance very close without our clothes."

"Oh, my god. You are so naughty. I love it." She snaked her arm around his waist. "Come on, stop wasting time. We've got someplace to be. We'd better put Wishes and Star in the guest room for the night. We wouldn't want to scare them with our, um, dancing."

With the stereo playing, he held her tenderly as they slowly swayed to the gentle notes drifting on the night. He let the love for his *Carida* flow from his heart. Her body brushed like velvet against him. These were things he'd only dreamed could be his. Her softness, the warmth of her breaths whispering over his heated skin. She touched a long dormant place in his soul.

Her love made him strong. His love for her gave his life meaning. He still hadn't said the words but he'd come close. Soon he'd have to confess his deepest feelings for her.

How many years had he longed for the genuine love of a woman? "*Carida*, you are my heart."

"I'm afraid it's the cursed locket that's making you say that." She rested her head on his chest below his chin. "I'm glad I held it. I had no idea I could feel this close to someone, not until I held you."

"I would not change it." He stroked her back. "I do not want this between us." His hands followed the sash on her silk robe to the loose tie in the front. One gentle tug and it slipped free. His hands roamed over her supple skin.

"There's a reason I bought these lounging pants for you." Her fingers latched around the elastic waist band and slid them over his hips and down his thighs. They pooled on the floor at around his feet. "Um, that's much better."

He kicked them out of his way.

Her warm hand found his cock. One gentle stroke and it was cocooned between their bodies. One soft hand squeezed his butt cheek and other gently roamed over his hip to the small of his back. Long overlooked nerves tingled and sent erotic signals to all the starving parts of his body.

"*Carida*, tell me, tell me again. I need to hear you say we are lovers forever."

"Santiago, the cursed love for a pirate brought us together. I'm with you wherever this life takes us." It wasn't exactly the way Alessia wrote it but it was close enough. She snuggled tighter against his chest, licked his peaked nipple then kissed it. "I think I'll lick you all over tonight. Would you like that?"

"*Ay, Carida*, you should not say these things to me." He inhaled sharply.

"Why not?" She licked his nipple again and gently teased it with her teeth. "You taste so good."

"Alena was right. You are a little savage. Are you going to bite me next?" Her head bounced against his chest when he chuckled.

"Only a little." She nipped the other nipple. "You'll think about me all day tomorrow when your shirt rubs your nipples."

Taking advantage of the curse might not be fair but it was good for now. When she got to Galveston she'd get with Cami, go find this Sahara woman who was responsible for bringing the cursed locket to the surface and learn the details.

CHAPTER TWENTY-FOUR

BANJI'S NAME had been changed from Davis to Preston at some point. Finding out why before she changed it back might be a good idea. And if she took Alena's advice she might be able to skip it altogether. After last night, it was looking like Santiago had no intention of leaving, ever. But that might only be the curse working its magic.

She loved him too much to trap him into staying with her. She'd feel better about the whole thing once he held the locket.

She made a cup of tea and took it to the living room. Opening the footlocker was easy. Picking up her mother's letters was hard. They were personal and they held secrets that had long since been buried. She put them in chronological order and opened the oldest one first.

Dearest Ritter,

My father is calling in favors to get you fired. He's dead set against my marrying you. I'm worried he'll do worse when he finds out we're having a baby...

The afternoon slipped away and Santiago breathed a sigh of relief as he flipped off the garage lights and locked the doors anxious to get home. Banji hadn't said anything about her mother's letters or the footlocker that sat untouched lurking in the living room's shadows for the last several days. It wasn't like his *Carida* to be restless and put off tackling a project. He knew of one sure way to ensure she rested but they were running out of condoms. He'd have to go to the store again soon.

His determined stride carried him down the path to the beach. His heart stopped when he cleared the dunes. Banji sat at the edge of the tide line with her arms wrapped around her bent knees staring at the dull gray waves washing ashore.

His long strides ate up the distance. He knelt beside her, the cold sand sending a chill up his legs. "*Carida*, what are you doing out here?"

"They're out there." She turned her head toward him. Their eyes met. "This is as close as I'll ever get to them." She sniffled.

He took her hand in his. "You are home. I am here." He searched her eyes for some sign that she believed him.

"I don't understand why it had to be this way." She sniffled and scanned the open sea. "I get it that Ritter had to go away to keep Mom safe from Grandpa, Ellis Bancroft wasn't a nice man, but why did Lloyd have to kill her? She wanted a divorce."

"He is the only one that knows the answer to that."

"There could be something in one of the boxes I haven't looked through. It's always about money with him."

"Missus Lori would have kept anything that was important. If there is evidence he murdered your mother, the police would have to investigate."

"It took a couple of days but they found her. The ocean ruins most evidence." She inhaled and held her breath before saying, "We had a closed casket funeral."

"How did they decide it was suicide if there was no note?"

She frowned and her brow wrinkled. "I don't know. Lloyd always said she was depressed and she'd killed herself." Banji blinked. "I was a kid. I didn't ask how he knew. I accepted what he said because he was my dad."

"I think we should look through your grandmother's things. Missus Lori did not seem like the kind of woman to accept anything less than the truth."

She looked steadily into his eyes. "Gram told me to always keep very good records. That sometimes what you knew and what you could prove were two different things. One piece of paper could make all the difference."

"She was very smart. We must look through her things carefully." He stood up and reached his hand out to Banji. "Come *Carida*, we will go home."

Home, where he could take care of her. The sight of her sitting on the beach in direct line of the next huge wave had scared him damn near to death. What would have happened if he hadn't seen her?

She slid an arm around his waist and gripped his shirt. He matched his stride to hers and walked her non-stop all the way to the bathroom.

Banji was too cold to argue when Santiago picked her up and sat her on the bathroom counter. He bent down and took ahold of her shoe and slipped it off. She scooted back until she was securely seated on the tile counter. He said, "I will fix a warm bath for you."

Her butt was freezing. "Why are you doing this?"

"Because I like taking care of you." He opened the bathtub faucet and stuck his hand under the water. "It will be warm soon."

Banji looked at the floor. "I'm cold."

He bent down and removed her socks. Then he lifted her off the counter as easily as he'd placed her on it. Next stop, her bare feet landed on the rug next to the ancient, titanic version of a claw-footed bathtub.

He was fast and surprisingly precise for a man with such large hands. Her clothes disappeared in a flash. She was already chilled to the bone and being naked didn't help. She wrapped her arms around herself and shivered. He checked the water temp, picked her up and put her in the tub.

She sank under the sudsy bubbles and hot water. He handed her a wash cloth and a bottle of bath soap. She opened the cap and sniffed. Oranges? She looked at him. Naw, couldn't be. She held it up. "What is this?"

"I thought you would like it. You said you liked bubble baths." He shrugged. "I will warm some soup. It will make you feel better."

She watched him walk away. She didn't think she'd ever get tired of looking at Santiago coming, going, lying flat on his back, bent over an engine compartment, it was all good. After pouring soap onto the thick, bright pink wash cloth she got busy scrubbing the salt spray off her skin and out of her hair. Once she was clean and warm, she'd be able to figure out what to do next.

She swished the cloth through the water and watched the suds swirl. She would look into using a similar design for Betmunn Racing. The best designs came from nature and sometimes from unexpected sources, like foaming soap suds.

She looked up and met Santiago's dark, hooded eyes. He stood in the doorway staring at her. "The soup is ready."

"Okay. Thanks." She gripped the edge of the tub and stood up.

Before she could step out onto the bathmat, a large towel engulfed her and she was once again wrapped in Santiago's arms and lifted out of the tub.

He rubbed and patted her dry like he'd done it a hundred times. Then he picked up one of his white t-shirts and slipped it over her head. It hung to her knees and smelled like him. She ran her hands over the petal-soft material. "This makes me feel better."

She followed him to the warm kitchen filled with the enticing aroma of herbs and spices bubbling on the stove. Comfort food on a cold rainy day was second only to being with him. She snuck a glance at his downcast eyes and frowning lips.

Her stomach growled. "This looks good."

He grumbled, "You should eat before it gets cold."

The medley of flavors spurred her appetite and it didn't take long to finish eating. She could live on his savory beef and vegetable soup along with a few crackers. She eyed the doorway to the living room. Her tummy was full and it was time to deal with the mess she'd made earlier. The pages of her parent's tragic ending were right where she'd left them. After a good night's sleep things would look better in the morning.

She could tell herself that and a couple more cliché lies to make everything peachy. Crying time was over.

"I need to pick up the papers in the living room before Star and Wishes get to them."

"I have already fed them. I will take Star out for a short walk in a minute. Wishes is good. They are fine in the guest room for now."

"Are they mad at me?"

Santiago stood up without saying a word, took her hand and led her to the living room. They sat on the couch with her tucked to his side. He brushed her hair away from her eyes. "They are not mad, only worried like me. We can feel your sadness and do not know how to fix it."

"It's not your fault." She glanced at the letters scattered on the coffee table. "Grandpa Bancroft ruined everything for Mom and Ritter. His international import business was growing and getting Preston Auction to handle the sales and distribution would increase his profit. The Preston's needed the money. Mom marrying Lloyd kept the business and the money in the family. Gram was so angry; she came here to get away from him and never went back."

"I often wondered why Missus Lori lived here alone. She was a kind woman. She could have found someone else to share her life with."

"She refused to divorce Grandpa Bancroft. She wanted him to die alone." Banji leaned her head against Santiago's shoulder. "She stayed here to be close to Mom and Ritter. I wish she would have told me about them."

His hand closed around hers. "What would you have done?"

"I wouldn't have wasted years wondering why Lloyd Preston didn't like me and I sure wouldn't have tried so hard to please him."

"That is likely why she did not tell you. You grew up independent, strong and smart. She knew that would be important after she passed away."

"Well, it's all out in the open now." She leaned her head back and looked at the ceiling. "Go walk Star. I'll be right here when you get back."

"I will not be gone long." He moved forward and stood up.

"Get going. I'm not in the mood to clean up pee puddles." She made a shooing motion with her hand. "Go on. Star's doing better with the puppy papers but sometimes he misses. I think he gets his front feet on the pad but the back feet don't make it."

When she heard the back door close, she inhaled, held her breath and exhaled. She was okay. She had a roof over her head and food in the refrigerator. Alena had offered her a job and Santiago was, well, Santiago, her everything thanks to a certain piece of cursed jewelry.

She wiggled onto her side, lifted her feet onto the couch and rested her head against the soft pillows. The yellowed sheets of stationary were right where she'd left them. They had filled in some of the missing pieces of her history. In some ways solving mysteries was not turning out to be the best idea she'd ever had but it wasn't the worst. At least now she could put the past to rest and move on.

Gram had told her a dozen times that experience was the best teacher. If she could take this experience and use it to build her new career and help others, it would be worth it.

She closed her eyes. It didn't help. She opened them and stared out the window. From that angle all she could see was the fading light in the evening sky. She mumbled to herself, "Well, that's depressing." She sat up and looked around. How long did it take to walk a puppy?

She reached out and picked up the letter on the top of the pile, folded it carefully and put it back in its envelope, then the next and one after that. The last one was the worst. Her Mom was leaving Lloyd Preston, taking Banji and filing for a divorce. She'd meet Ritter in Honolulu when his ship docked.

What would it feel like to lose the love of your life? For a fleeting moment Banji tried to imagine her world without Santiago. The crushing pain in the vicinity of her heart put an end to that thought real fast. She'd live in the moment until she solved the mystery of the cursed locket.

If anything got in her way she'd mash it flat and kick it to the curb. It wasn't the same as throwing it off a cliff but it would work. Oh, my god, how likely was it that an experienced seaman would fall overboard right before he was about to be reunited with Genevieve?

Banji rolled off the couch, staggered over to the footlocker, sank to her knees and started digging. The insurance claim, she wanted to read it again carefully, she might have missed something earlier. They'd done an investigation to explain how Ritter had gone missing. Experienced seamen didn't fall overboard on a regular basis. Something unusual had to have happened. She needed a list of who was on the crew. Did Grandpa Bancroft have Ritter pushed overboard? Did Lloyd Preston know Genevieve was leaving him?

Santiago walked along slowly letting Star sniff and explore the weeds and reeds lining the trail to the beach. He glanced back at the cottage. For a thoughtful woman like Missus Lori to get so angry, the man must have done something terrible. Something horrifying enough that she couldn't stand the sight of him and wanted him to face death abandoned and alone.

He walked a little farther and stopped. Star had found something of particular interest. His paws dug at the sand and sent it flying. If life was only that simple.

Carmen had left him alone in their room. She hadn't moved out of the house but she wasn't really there either. The coffee was made when he got up in the morning and they sat at the same table for dinner. He worked in the garage all day. She kept the house, did their laundry and planted a few herbs and peppers in the small garden next to the house. In the evenings, she watched a few shows on TV then disappeared into her room. If they had something to say to each other, they said it during dinner. He never wanted to live like that again.

He tilted his head and looked up at the heavens. The first stars of the evening winked into view. It was time to go back. Back to Banji and the life he'd started building with her. He didn't need some long-lost trinket to know he was in love. Love like nothing he'd ever imagined. It wrapped around his heart and comforted his soul. The thought of losing it terrified him.

Star beat him to the back porch wagging his tail and waiting for Santiago to open the door. They were home. He stepped inside and hung Star's leash on the peg next to the rain slickers.

Banji called out, "You need to look at this."

"What is it, *Carida*?" A few steps later he stood looking over her shoulder.

She handed a fistful of papers to him. "It's the insurance accident reports for Ritter. Only I don't think it was an accident. They say the cause is undetermined."

"We will show these to Alena tomorrow. Betmunn Racing has a security department and a couple lawyers. They can look at these. I will stay home and help you look in Missus Lori's boxes."

"You can't do that. You have your cars to build and races to win. This is my project. I'll do it. You already got me the desk. Some of that old gumshoe's luck might rub off on me. I have to try."

"All right, if that is what you want. But you must tell me if you need my help."

She took his hand and got to her feet. "I will, I promise." She stretched up on her tiptoes, pulled him down for a kiss and then whispered, "Let's cuddle up in bed and keep each other warm."

CHAPTER TWENTY-FIVE

THE NEXT MORNING, Banji walked to the garage with Santiago and then on to the main house. She'd called ahead so Alena and Gabriel wouldn't be caught in a compromising position or something equally embarrassing. Not that Banji cared but still it seemed like the polite thing to do. Gabriel was big on manners. He still had that Marine training thing going on. Once a Marine always a Marine.

She shouted, "Hey Alena, I'm here and have I got news for you."

Alena yelled back, "I'm on the phone. Grab a cup of coffee and sit down."

The coffee pot sitting on the tile counter was full with a trail of steam rising from the center opening. Alena always had the best coffee. Medium roasted beans from exotic places. Talk about spoiled. She'd probably used it to seduce Gabriel. Banji poured herself a steaming mug, plopped down at the table and took a tiny tentative sip.

Hot, hot, hot. She put the mug down and leaned back in her chair. She'd comfortably settled in when Alena hurried into the kitchen. "What's up? You said it was super important."

"I think Mom and Ritter were murdered." No point in beating around the bush. "And I think Grandpa Bancroft and Lloyd Preston are responsible."

Alena fixed herself a fresh mug with vanilla creamer and sank into the chair opposite Banji. "Why would they do that?"

"To stop my Mom from divorcing Lloyd and marrying Ritter. Lloyd was having an affair with Leanne and Mom had the pictures to prove it. Mom would have gotten a nice settlement and Grandpa Bancroft would have lost his distribution network."

Alena stirred her coffee. "Your grandpa is dead and can't be prosecuted."

"Lloyd isn't dead, yet." Banji raised her mug and took a small sip. Blew on it and sipped again. "If he had anything to do with their deaths, I want him held responsible." She put her mug down and wrapped her hands around it. "Madison told me she heard her Mom fighting with Lloyd and Leanne told him she wasn't going to be thrown overboard like Genevieve. If Leanne has evidence, it might get some justice for my Mom."

"All right. I'll call my security chief and see what we can do." Alena caught Banji's eye. "He knows people. Some seriously effective people."

Banji shoved copies of the reports across the flowery stenciled surface of the table to Alena. "I'll bet somebody on the crew got paid for pushing Ritter overboard." She sat back. "Lloyd used to brag about going out fishing on George O'Connor's boat. He could have used it to get rid of my Mom's body."

Alena spread the papers out on the table. "There's no statute of limitations on murder. We only need enough to get the police to open a case." She tapped on the insurance claim. "What happened to this payment?" She looked directly at Banji. "This is a significant amount of money payable to your Mom and you're the secondary."

"I don't know. It's not in Gram's personal bank statements. I don't think Lloyd got it either. I remember him having a fit that something was missing. He was supposed to have gotten more." Banji shook her head. "I was the beneficiary of my Mom's will. She kept her finances separate from Lloyd." She raised her mug and took a long swallow. "But after Mom's estate was settled, he sent me to stay with Gram. When I got home from the first visit, my room had been moved to the other end of the house away from everyone. Madison wasn't even born yet and I thought Dad and Leanne just wanted their privacy. It didn't dawn on me that they didn't want me to hear what they were talking about."

"Well, looks like we've got a mystery to solve." Alena's mouth turned down at the corners. "I don't want you going near this mess. *Papi* will never forgive me if anything happens to you." She shuffled the papers into a neat pile. "Promise me you'll stay far away from this until we have the bad guys under lock and key."

Banji swallowed hard and cleared her throat. "About that. I've been thinking that until I get to talk to Cami's friend Sahara, I need to lighten up on this thing with Santiago. It's not right to stick him with a cursed love affair after everything he's been through."

Alena leaned forward and rested her arms on the table over the stenciled strawberries. "You can't be serious. Do you have any idea how badly this idiotic plan of yours will hurt him? You pull away from him and it'll be a repeat of Carmen. Don't do it."

"I thought of that. That's why I'm telling you. You know him better than anyone. What happens when he holds the locket and it turns out that I'm not his true love? What if it's all been a terrible mistake? I don't want to keep his hopes up if it's not real."

The kitchen chair screeched over the floor as Alena came to her feet. "That's it. Come with me. We're calling Cami and getting to the bottom of Neptune's curse now."

Banji refilled her mug and trailed after Alena to the library. "It's Salvatore's curse, not Neptune's.

"I don't care whose curse it is. It ends now."

Banji settled in one of the overstuffed easy chairs across from Alena's desk. "I like this room. It smells like old-time pipe smoke."

"That's because my Granddad smoked in here every evening, rain or shine, win or lose." Alena flopped into the executive chair behind the desk. "His meerschaum pipes are over there in that old smoking cabinet."

"You're so lucky. Everybody loves you. They always did." Banji sighed and wiggled herself deeper into the soft seat back.

Alena pressed the buttons on the desk phone and muttered, "Not everybody. Only the important people." She focused on Banji. "Same as you. The important people in your life love you. The rest of them don't matter." She looked down at the top of her desk. "Hey Cami, It's Alena and I've got a problem here. Can I put you on speaker?" She chewed her bottom lip and grumbled, "Thanks. Here's the thing. Banji is worried that when *Papi* touches that miserable locket she won't be his true love."

"I suppose it's a possibility but it hasn't happened that way yet. Everyone here finds their one-and-only when they hold the locket and it's a perfect match."

"You're sure?" Banji leaned forward. "It's important. I don't want Santiago to feel pressured into staying with me over this silly curse."

"There's nothing silly about it. I only held it for maybe a minute at Sahara's wedding reception and then I caught the bride's bouquet. Next thing I knew, Lyev was on his way to America. And the rest is history. You'll see when you get here. Sahara and Boris, Misha and Lona, me and Lyev." She sighed. "It's so romantic. You and Santiago. I can't wait to meet him."

"He wants to hold the locket. Can you arrange that? Then we'll know for sure."

"Of course, I can. It's in Misha's safe." Cami giggled. "Misha is so in love, I like watching him blush when we talk about the locket."

"Sounds good." Alena smiled at Banji. "There, see it's going to be fine."

Cami's voice lost its giggle quality. "It's for real, Banji. You've found the right guy. Love never comes easy but it's worth the sacrifice. You'll understand it better when you read Alessia's diary. It's all in there. You studied in Italy and can probably do a better job translating it."

"Barcelona told me about the diary." Banji glanced at Alena. "We already agreed I'll take a shot at translating it when I get there." Every time she turned around there was another reason to go to Galveston. Banji was sure the answers to a lot of things were waiting to be found on the island. "Since I spent a lot of time in the museums reading old documents related to their art, we thought I might be able to figure out the meaning of the old phrases."

"That's wonderful." Cami giggled softly. "Sahara has done her best and Boris helped her but there are parts of it that don't make sense to us."

Banji flopped against the back of the chair. She closed her eyes, took a deep breath and counted to five. Ten would take too long. "I need to know if he loves me for real before I go see Madame Belinsky." Damn, she hadn't meant to let that cat out of the bag.

Cami squealed. "Oh, my god. Are you really thinking about getting married? I'm going to tell Lulu. She'll be so excited. She's the wedding planner for Crystal's chapel at the new resort. She does all our family weddings. You can get married there. This is wonderful but you have to come early. There's a seventy-two-hour waiting period between the time you get your marriage license and can have your ceremony."

"No, no, and no. I'm not getting married on a racetrack in Galveston. No." Banji crossed her arms over her chest. "Besides I'm not part of the family."

"That's not true. You're part of my family. You and I went to highschool together. Remember the Convent of the Sacred Heart. It's closed now but we were there together. We promised each other we'd be friends forever. That's family in my book."

Banji groused, "You always were too smart for your own good. You remember everything."

"*Papi* will love it. It's perfect." Alena looked at Banji and then glanced at the phone. "Who's Lulu?"

"Niko's wife." Cami made it sound like everyone knew that. "He's Boris's brother. Don't worry, you'll meet everyone when you get here. I already told Lyev you're all coming."

Alena's tone went serious. "Banji is part of my family, too. Maybe you should mention that to the folks at your end."

"Of course, but I'm sure it'll be fine. You'll see."

The ensuing silence was a dead giveaway that something wasn't right on Cami's end of the conversation. There was something bothering her that was going unsaid. Banji swallowed hard and asked, "What aren't you telling me?"

"Zala's missing."

"Exactly how is she missing? You don't simply misplace a yacht the size of *CaliGirl*." Banji crossed her ankle over her knee and grabbed it with one hand hitching it higher on her thigh.

"When we went out to observe the underwater earthquakes and Caribbean tectonic plate movement last summer I got some pictures of things that we weren't expecting. I think she went back to get a better look."

"What things?"

"Old stuff that shouldn't be disturbed. Even Sahara says to forget about it and treasure salvaging was her living."

Prying the details out of a reluctant Cami would take too long. There were only so many things that could be of interest to Zala. "And she didn't want to forget it."

"No, I asked the guys to listen for any radio chatter about *CaliGirl* but there's been nothing so far."

"She'll turn up and probably be a little worse for wear. *CaliGirl* will need repairs and Zala will be alive and kicking ass." Banji exhaled noisily. "You can count on her to have an amazing story to go with her voyage to the far end of the ocean."

Silence hung over the room for several long seconds. Cami quietly said, "I'm really afraid this time. The *Siren's Song* was never meant to be found."

Banji exhaled loudly and grumped, "I don't even know what that is but Zala will be fine. She's always fine." Banji tilted her head back and stared at the ceiling. "If she's not back by the time we get there, we'll go find her."

"Okay, I'll tell Boris so he can have everything ready if we need it."

"Perfect. Talk to you soon. Bye, Chameleon." Banji snickered.

"Bye, Banjingles." Cami disconnected the call.

Alena waited a few seconds before saying, "After *Papi* holds the locket and doesn't run screaming down the seawall looking for some mysterious woman we've never heard of, this will be settled once and for all. I don't know this Lulu, but I get the impression we don't want to piss her off."

"You're probably right about that. I've heard wedding planners can be temperamental. At least the ones in San Francisco are."

"Who and what is Madame Belinsky?" Alena quirked the side of her mouth.

"She's a dressmaker. Very old school. The most beautiful dresses you've ever seen in your life." Banji sighed. "It takes months to make one of her dresses from start to finish."

"How long have you been planning this?"

"Since I was sixteen. Gram took me on a road trip for my birthday. I saw a dress in the window and had to stop and look. Even I could tell it was handmade, a true work of art. I've been saving up to get one ever since."

"Since you're sleeping with *Papi*, it seems to me you're going to have to do the right thing and marry him." Alena grinned. "He'll look handsome all dressed up in a tuxedo standing next to you in your princess dress."

Banji nodded and grumped, "I'm not getting married at a race track and I'm not wearing white."

"Cami said something about a wedding chapel. We can ask about that." Alena's eyes narrowed. "We probably need to call and find out what dates are available."

Banji commented, "No problem. Why don't you get right on it?"

"Me!" Alena squealed. "What about you? It's your wedding."

"You're the matron of honor," Banji bit back and grinned. "I think you need to give the groom away."

"Since when?"

"Since now. It's your job since you're my friend and his daughter. I'm asking him to marry me so you need to walk him down the aisle and give him away. And knowing Cami, she's probably on the phone with Lulu right now." Banji's lips turned up at the corners. "You want your *Papi* to have the best, right?"

Alena picked up a pen and tapped it on a note pad. "I have a race to win. I don't have time to organize a wedding."

"Let Cami help you."

"Let's hear the real deal." Alena's eyes narrowed and speared Banji with a no-nonsense look. "Why are you waiting until we're in Galveston to propose?"

"Because he needs to hold the locket first. If that goes okay, we'll go for a romantic walk on the beach in the moonlight. I'll ask Santiago to marry me and he'll accept." Banji smiled like she'd won the lottery.

Alena exhaled and leaned back in her chair. "Okay, you get him to say yes and we'll all go eat shrimp, catfish and hush puppies. I'm buying."

"Great." Not great. How was she supposed to go to the dressmaker with everyone tagging along? "I need to make a stop at Madame Belinsky's as soon as we get there for the final touches. She'll only have a week to finish my dress before the ceremony."

Alena sat straight up coming to attention like she'd been struck by a bolt of lightning. "Right. I'll go with you. I'm going to need a dress to walk down the aisle and give away *Papi* to my best friend."

"And?"

Alena clapped her hands and laughed. "I want to be there when you ask him. I gotta see this." She clasped her hands together. "Please, let me be there?"

"No. I want it to be a surprise." Banji shook her head and pointed at the desk phone. "Call Cami, have her get with Lulu. We can celebrate your winning and my wedding with one big party after the race." Banji stood and walked toward the door. "What are we doing for Thanksgiving? It's only three weeks away and I should put in my order at the bakery unless you want tiny charcoal-flavored meteorites enbrochette for a side dish."

"Figure it out," Alena barked. "I've got to make a list of what we're going to need and call Cami back this afternoon." She snickered. "I love it. I'm giving the groom away."

CHAPTER TWENTY-SIX

THE FOLLOWING days dragged by waiting for word from Betmunn's investigator. Banji spent hours sorting every page of Gram's papers and reading them carefully. It was way more complicated than she'd ever imagined. She did however find the title to the Trans Am mixed in with some Christmas cards and slips for Certificates of Deposit.

Gram had not believed in filing cabinets. They made it too easy for people to snoop in her business. She had believed in money. And from the looks of things she'd had plenty of it. Still had plenty of it if the reports from the executor were correct.

"Hey, where are you?" Alena's shout drowned out the stereo.

Banji's reply faltered. "Ah, in my office." Finding out she was better off than she'd ever suspected was a nerve rattling experience. Gram had lectured endlessly on the merits of girls needing to be self-sufficient financially.

Alena stopped and leaned against the doorjamb. "What's all this?"

"More of Gram's stuff. I found the deed to the cottage and the title to the Trans Am. She pushed aside a pile of bank statements and poked at a blue sheet of paper. "This says I get access to her bank accounts on my thirtieth birthday. Until then I get the trust payments she left me."

"Okay, so nothing new since her attorney read you the will."

"There's this." Banji pulled a folded page from one of the small

168

slots on her desk. "This is the insurance payment. Since Mom was deceased when the insurance company settled the claim, it went to me as the secondary beneficiary. And since I was a minor Gram handled it for me."

"So, where is it?" Alena pushed herself off the doorjamb and stood up straight.

"Gram put it in my money market account."

Sauntering across the room, Alena asked, "Don't you check your bank statements?"

Banji shrugged. "Not that one. She set it up when I was a kid. It was like a savings account she'd put money in for my college education, so I didn't pay any attention to it. Living in Paris and Rome wasn't cheap. It's probably pretty empty by now. My financial advisor gets them. He said it wasn't a big deal. I only look at my checking and credit card balances."

Alena's head dipped forward as she looked down studying the toes of her boots. "Not a big deal. How big does it need to be before you pay attention to it?" She shook her head. "You are insane. Yep, that's it, certifiably nuts."

"It's not my money. It's Gram's and my Mom's."

"Hello, earth to Banji. They left it all to you."

"They didn't want Grandpa Bancroft or Lloyd to get it. I'm keeping it safe from Lloyd-the-leech-Preston. Besides I don't need it. I made a good living as an appraiser."

Alena scoffed. "And now you're working for Betmunn Racing and doing jewelry appraisals on the side."

"Yeah, so? I'm not broke." Banji leaned back in her chair. "This place is paid for. I've got a roof over my head. I don't see what you're worried about."

"You need to pay attention to your finances." Alena straightened up and ran her fingers through her curly hair, moving it out of her eyes. "You don't have to live like this. You could move back to the city, get a nice place, eat all the high-end deli take-out food you want. You could have it delivered."

Banji grumbled under her breath. "I don't like money. It always comes with something bad attached to it." She focused a steady gaze on Alena. "I like it here. I'm not going anywhere. I can live off of chips and dip if I have to."

Alena burst out laughing. "I hear corn flakes are good."

Banji picked up the bank statement and held it out to Alena. "I think I can afford the dress."

"Holy, mother..." Alena's eyes widened and she gasped. "You can get all the dresses you want."

"You've got nothing to gripe about. You got yours from A. Crystal Foxz." Banji smirked. "That's like the Grand Prix of dresses."

"After you dropped the wedding bomb on me, I looked up Belinsky's dress shop. Her dresses are too elegant to wear. They belong in museums." She grimaced. "She wanted to know what color I wanted."

"I knew it." Banji tapped her index finger to the side of her head. "You couldn't resist. We're going to be beautiful on the day I marry Santiago."

Alena frowned and her brow crinkled. "What if *Papi* turns you down?"

"He won't. I checked. It's in the cards."

"You never cease to amaze me." Alena shook her head. "And here I was beginning to think you invented flying by the seat of your pants." She inhaled. "Remember you have to get him to the courthouse three days before the race?"

Banji lifted her chin and sighed. "It's going to be fine, unless that stupid curse trumps my cards."

"So, while *Papi* and Gabriel are choking on smoking tires and burning fuel doing time trials, we're going shopping. Have I got that right?"

"Yes, and can you please keep it to yourself. There's a lot of time and miles between here and there." Banji shifted in her chair. "Santiago doesn't need to know anything about it."

Santiago backed silently down the hall. He didn't need to know about what? He slipped out the back door and retraced his steps to the beach. Being too trusting had cost him twenty years of his life that he couldn't get back, couldn't do over. He couldn't make that mistake again.

He stopped to watch a seagull skim over the ocean's surface searching for its next meal. Win or lose, it was all about trying. If he didn't get to the bottom of what they weren't telling him, it would eat at him and his suspicions would grow until it choked the life out of his relationship with Banji.

Mind made up, he turned prepared to walk back to the cottage and face the situation head on.

Alena waved and called out, "Hey *Papi*, are you on the way home for lunch?" She was still laughing when she reached him. "A little afternoon delight?"

"What?"

She rolled her eyes. "You know."

"No, I do not know."

"Oh, honestly. It's an old song. It means having sex in the afternoon. You know, like go home for lunch, roll around in bed for some fun before going back to work."

He put his hands on his hips. "Then just say that. Go home for sex."

"Are you kidding? Nobody says that. It's more fun saying it the other way. Like it's a secret." She chuckled and asked, "Okay, what's wrong? If you were headed to the cottage, you'd be there already not standing here staring out to sea."

He was no good at lying so he blurted out the truth. "Banji is hiding things from me. I heard you talking."

Alena inhaled and muttered, "Oops." She glanced away. "Well, damn." She shoved her hands in her back pockets. "Have you reconsidered getting married?"

"Why do you ask?"

"Just answer the question." She pulled her hands out of her pockets.

He straightened his shoulders. "I have thought about it."

She clapped her hands together. "Great, and what did you decide."

"I have not decided." He nodded curtly.

"Don't make it sound like you're agreeing to be executed. It's not

171

very romantic." She giggled. "Everything is going to be okay. You're going to be surprised, so take a deep breath and relax. Trust me. It's all good."

"What is all good?" His brow furrowed. "What are you talking about?"

"You're going to have a great time in Galveston." She laughed, stepped past him and jogged toward the trail leading to her house. She raised her arms over her head and yipped, "Yes, this is going to be the best party ever."

He yelled, "What party?"

He watched Alena disappear into the dunes.

A smile slowly crept across his face. He was definitely in the mood to make love to his *Carida* and it would certainly take all afternoon.

CHAPTER TWENTY-SEVEN

A WEEK LATER, Thanksgiving arrived on schedule. It wasn't as if it could be late and Banji was ready. She eyed the bakery boxes sitting on the kitchen counter. She'd placed her order early to be sure she had the coveted apricot pie along with the pecan pie that Alena and Gabriel loved.

Madison came through the back door holding her contribution to the feast. She'd gotten two loaves of San Francisco sourdough French bread. She held out her hand with the bagged loaves dangling from her fingers. "Aren't these French string market bags great? So old fashioned. Did you see they're coming back in style?"

"That one is pretty. Do they come in other colors besides hot pink?"

"Yes, but this one goes with my outfit."

Banji eyed Madison's dress and sweater. Finally, something with more color. "Did you get that in town?" It reminded her of something she'd seen in the boutique window a few doors down from the bakery. "It looks great on you."

"Yes, thanks. Dani's Drawers is the cutest shop. I talked to the owner. She's going to let me work there on the weekends." Madison looked around the kitchen and back at Banji. "I really like it here. Do you think Santiago will let me stay on in his house? I could pay rent."

"You'll have to ask him. He needs to use the garage and the shop for his work."

"That's okay. My car can stay outside. That's easier for me."

Banji tried not to wince. "You'll get a better car eventually, then what?"

"I'll worry about that when it happens. I'm perfectly happy driving Little Rusty. Santiago has it running like new."

"You gave it a name?" She eyed Madison, looking for signs of increasing lunacy.

"Sure. Why not? It fits me and it's mine."

"You've got that right." Banji scoffed. "If you're happy with it, that's all that matters."

Madison stepped closer to Banji and rested one hand on the counter. "I can help you advertise your business."

"Why would you do that?" She glanced at Madison from the corner of her eye.

"Because my degree is in business marketing and I'm good at it."

"Are you going to do that for the boutique?"

"I thought I'd try it along with sales. I already told Dani I'd start with something small. If it gets busier, I'll get more hours."

"I don't have any customers yet. I'm not sure I'm ready for any. I'll let you know if I need a marketing plan." She reached for the bakery boxes. "We need to get going. Alena's got the turkey ready. She was candying the sweet potatoes when I talked to her. That should give us enough time to walk over there without having to run."

"Okay." Madison bit her bottom lip. "I like it here. I want to stay. Do you mind if I ask Santiago about renting his house?"

"That's fine." Banji noticed Madison didn't smile or make some silly chirping comment. "Really, I don't mind. It's kind of nice having you around."

Madison perked up. "Great." She practically danced out the back door.

Banji rolled her eyes and closed the door following Madison across the porch. She needed to get Alena alone for a few minutes and have a talk. Santiago had been acting oddly since the afternoon Alena visited. That was the first time he'd made love to her in the middle of the afternoon but it wasn't the last. Okay, so he'd discovered sex wasn't something that had to be done under cover of darkness or hidden by rainy-day shadows. He'd finished working on the Trans Am, brought it home and stuck a big red bow on the roof. That was weird and Banji didn't believe in coincidences.

～

Alena looked over her shoulder at Gabriel. "I told you the holidays would be small affairs."

"I'm not worried." He wrapped his arms around her waist and hugged her back to his front. "This is perfect. Our family is growing. We have Santiago, Banji, and Madison."

"I think Madison is inviting her old high-school boyfriend for the New Year's party."

"Is she thinking about staying here or going back to San Francisco?"

"I'm not sure. We'll have to wait and see." She turned, went up on her tip toes and kissed his cheek.

Santiago walked in from the dining room. "I have put the turkey on the table. What else do you want me to do?"

"The casserole is ready to go along with the covered vegetable bowls. These sweet potatoes will be ready in a few more minutes." She spooned the brown sugar and butter sauce over the slices. "Have you talked to Madison? How's she doing?"

Santiago shrugged one shoulder. "She is fine but my house is covered in flowers. Flower pots everywhere." He shook his head. "She should work at a flower shop or a plant nursery."

"That would be a waste of her education. I talked to her about hiring on with us in our marketing department." Alena turned off the burner. "She said she'd think about it. She's never done anything with cars or racing."

"If she worked for you, she could stay here. I do not think she wants to move out of my house. She has put lace curtains up in the kitchen."

"Uh-oh. That's a sure sign she's turning it into her own place." Alena giggled. "It's a good thing you like it at Banji's."

Santiago grunted, picked up the casserole and said, "I will come back for the other bowls."

Alena spooned the sweet potatoes into a serving bowl. "It's working. He didn't even try to deny it."

"He more than likes living with Banji." Gabriel stepped aside and picked up a bowl of creamed corn. "I recognize the look. It's the same one I had when I moved in with you."

Alena grinned. "You know our Galveston trip is coming up in a couple months. That could do it. A walk on the beach, a margarita on the pier, the locket does its thing and he pops the question."

"We'll be lucky if he makes it through dinner." Gabriel turned away from the window. "Trouble is on approach carrying apricot pie. He's going down."

She snickered. "Don't say that. It'll take more than pie to convince him."

"I'll have to take your word for that."

Alena stretched over the sink and peeked out the window. "How do you know it is apricot?"

"Banji asked me what kind of pie we wanted to go with the apricot pie she was ordering. I told her pecan."

"Oh, yum. I love pecan pie."

"I know."He swooped in for a quick kiss. "And I love you."

～

Madison flitted through Alena's kitchen door and chirped, "Hi! Thank you for inviting me." She held up her hot pink net shopping bag. "I've got the sour dough French bread."

Banji followed close behind and closed the door keeping out the chilly November breeze. The fall leaves were blowing away and the Christmas music was already playing on the radio.

All her worrying while she packed up her Knob Hill apartment had been for nothing. From the minute she'd arrived at Sand Dollar Cottage her life had taken on a new direction. She looked around the kitchen and smiled. This was her life now and these people were her family.

For all the years she'd spent being angry and wishing Madison wasn't her half-sister, she still hadn't gotten around to telling her that they were not related. Somehow that knowledge had lost its charm. It was probably all his fault. Banji glanced at Santiago who was standing in the doorway leading to the dining room looking inscrutable. That thought tickled her and she had to tamp down a giggle. He was definitely a good influence on her, not that she'd ever admit it.

Banji held out the bakery boxes. "I've got the desserts."

"Great. I'll butter the bread and put it under the broiler." Alena reached for a crusty loaf.

"Your house is amazing." Madison beamed a genuine smile at Alena. "Classic. So graceful and iconic."

"Thanks, it's been in the family forever." Alena slipped the first loaf out of the paper sleeve.

"It would work wonderfully for a marketing strategy built around the long racing history of your family."

Banji's head snapped to the side and she stared over her shoulder at Madison. "What are you talking about?"

"Alena asked me if I'd like to work in Betmunn Racing's marketing department. It's an idea I've been playing with." Madison shrugged. "I was thinking some models wearing cute clothes from the boutique and the pretty cars arranged on the lawn would be colorful and eye-catching."

The bread knife sliced the loaf horizontally with a minimum of effort. Alena laid the two halves open and started spreading butter from one end to the other. "It would be good advertising for the boutique. They have tops that look good with tight jeans and cargo pants. Women who like racing are usually there for the fast cars and guys. It's a long afternoon in the sun. I've seen a few in sundresses or shorts but that's inviting sunburn."

"I can work with that." Madison snickered and blushed. "The guys are there for the fast cars and sexy women. I watched a race on my laptop. I really should go to one and see it for myself. Getting a feeling for the crowd and atmosphere would help me develop a spot-on marketing plan."

"No problem. I can get you in." Alena turned toward Banji. "This could really work. You design the new line of jewelry, accessories and posters while Madison does the marketing."

Banji unlocked her jaw and sniped, "You've lost your mind. The gasoline fumes have warped your brain."

Madison clapped her hands. "That's great. I can't wait to get started."

Banji shook her head and muttered, "I need to call the Devil and find out if Hell has frozen over."

Alena countered, "It's going to be fine. Give it a chance."

"I love how the family business keeps growing." Gabriel hugged Alena.

"*Carida*, did you bring the apricot pie?" Santiago walked across the kitchen directly to Banji and put his hands on her shoulders. "Everyone is looking forward to our first Thanksgiving together."

He knew darn good and well she'd brought it, and she received his unspoken message. She shouldn't be mean to her used-to-be half-sister on Thanksgiving.

"I love apricots." Madison's smiling lit up her face. "This is going to be the best Thanksgiving." She looked around the room meeting everyone's eyes. "What can I do to help?"

Banji caught herself and clamped her mouth shut. She studied her sister from across the room. The delighted smile on Madison's face couldn't be faked. She was settling in to her new-found family. It was time to take a page out of Santiago's book and let the girl have a home with them. Unless Lloyd Preston had a major personality change, Madison was going to need a safe home and a family, even if it was an unconventional one.

Alena leaned back against the counter. "There's a pitcher in the refrigerator. You can fill the water glasses on the dining room table while Gabriel opens the wine."

Once Madison was safely out of the room, Banji slid closer to Alena and whispered, "I haven't said anything to Madison. She still thinks were half-sisters."

"No worries. It's Thanksgiving and we're family."

"Thanks." Banji breathed a sigh of relief.

After dinner Santiago and Banji walked Madison home while they listened to her endless chatter. She loved the fresh air, the ocean, the fog horns, Santiago's precious house. Madison didn't miss San Francisco and had settled in to their circle. He knew better than to say anything to Banji about the possibility of her sister being a permanent fixture in their lives, but he could see it happening bit by bit.

He had more than he deserved and he feared the day it would all be snatched away without warning. Each day with Banji was a gift he treasured. An honorable man would propose to the woman he loved. There was commitment that came with marriage vows but that commitment could be a trap. When he'd promised to never marry again, he hadn't met Banji.

His heart pounded faster and he gripped her hand a little tighter. He should go ahead and get it over with, but he'd promised Alena he'd wait until they got to Galveston.

Banji interrupted his thoughts. "Did you like the pie? I think it was almost as good as Gram's but her crust was flakier."

"It was very good with the vanilla ice cream. It brought back many good memories. Thank you for remembering it." The moment for proposing passed and his bout of impatience with the situation evaporated.

"Gram always made it for the holidays. It was the one thing I could count on. The world might end but Gram's apricot pie would be on the table for Thanksgiving."

"Alena will save me a piece for tomorrow." Santiago chuckled, "She will have to hide it from Gabriel. He had never tasted apricots before today."

"I think the bakery is going to get another order for one real soon." Banji hazarded a guess. "I'm not sure but I think I heard him making growling noises when she took the pie off the table."

Santiago asked, "Do you think we could find Missus Lori's recipe?"

"It's probably in one of her old cookbooks. Why?"

"If we find it and give it to Alena, she could make them for us." He muffled a grunt. "And Gabriel."

"Right and some cookies would be good."

CHAPTER TWENTY-EIGHT

THE FOLLOWING MORNING, Banji stared at the top shelf where Gram's favorite cook books were neatly lined up. Being able to reach them required her to move the ancient step stool into position. The book for pies, cakes, and cookies was sandwiched between casseroles and classic favorites, whatever those were.

How hard could it be to find a pie recipe? She pried the worn-ragged dessert cookbook out of the lineup and prayed it was the right one as she carried it to the kitchen table.

The worn and stained cover had seen better days. A vague memory of Gram standing at the counter making cookies stirred within her. The book and its memories were precious to Banji and a familiar sense of rightness settled over her. She could do this and anything else she set her mind to.

Her favorite chocolate chip cookie recipe was in it. She and Gram practiced making them every summer. Banji taste tested the chocolate chips and Gram did the mixing and baking.

Sitting at the table, she flipped to the page for apricot filled cookies and copied the recipe onto an index card from her office supplies. When she finished that, she moved on to the pie recipe. Santiago could deliver them to Alena when he picked up their lunch plates of left-over turkey and trimmings.

She closed the book at the same time Santiago bent over her shoulder and nuzzled her neck.

"Alena wants us to come eat with them." He tucked his phone into his back pocket.

"That works. I have the recipes ready for her." She stood and moved toward the door. "I'm sure hers will be at least as good as Gram's."

Santiago followed her out. "It will save trips to town."

Banji raised her face toward the sun and inhaled deeply. The warm rays and the brisk ocean breeze accompanied her and Santiago as they strolled to Alena's. Winter was closing in along with Christmas Eve, but there would still be mild temperature days ahead.

She drifted closer to Santiago and threaded her fingers through his. "What would you like for your birthday?"

He looked out at the horizon. "I do not need anything."

The quietness of his voice and the faraway look on his face contradicted the words. She wasn't about to let him get away with that answer.

"Okay, but there must be something you would like? If I have to guess, you might end up with a thong. Do you prefer red or black?" She squeezed his hand. "How about bright blue with sequins?"

His eyes went wide. "No."

"All righty then, think of something." Banji turned her head away to hide her smug grin. Teasing him was so easy and so much fun. He'd only have to wear it long enough for her to get him out of it. She was already a pro at getting him out of his twill work pants and jeans.

Getting him to ask her for anything wasn't likely to happen, but she'd given him the opportunity to speak up. She'd wait a few days and ask Alena. If there was some gadget or tool he would like, Alena would know and Banji would get it for him. Problem solved.

Santiago's mind whirled with visions of him trying to squeeze himself into a thong. No, it would not work and he wasn't going to try. He would look silly. Why would Banji even think such a thing?

The breeze caught her hair and he glimpsed the crinkle at the outer corner of her eye. The barely perceptible laugh line gave away her glee at his response. He wasn't used to being teased.

There had been very little laughter except for the times he and Alena found something funny. There had definitely been no teasing, and no flirting. People were too afraid of him for any of that, and his relationship with Carmen had been about survival and duty.

He brushed his hand over his moustache and hid his grin. It was time for him to change his ways.

They walked in Alena's kitchen door. Santiago looked from Alena to Gabriel, inhaled and said, "I am not a male stripper. I will not wear a thong." He crossed his arms over his chest.

Alena's cheeks puffed out, her eyes got big and she burst out laughing. "Oh, my, god, I can't even begin to imagine that." She glanced at Gabriel. "Don't even think about it. I like you fine the way you are. No thongs for you either."

"I'm disappointed." Gabriel pouted and then smiled broadly. "I always wanted to try one."

Banji flopped onto a chair. "Don't pay any attention to these two clowns." She gazed at Alena. "I threatened to buy Santiago a thong if he doesn't tell me what he wants for his birthday."

Gabriel nodded. "Threatening a man with torture if he doesn't confess sounds serious." He met Santiago's stare. "You'd better come up with an answer before she thinks up something worse than a thong."

Banji settled back in her chair. "It wouldn't hurt you boys to get dressed up for the occasion once in a while." She put the recipe cards on the table. "Here, I brought you Gram's recipes for the apricot pie and cookies." She caught Alena's eye. "It'll save time and money running to the bakery."

Alena shrugged and giggled. "Miss Mari will be so disappointed. She keeps hoping Santiago will come to his senses and realize a more mature lady is what he needs."

Santiago's head jerked back and he glared at Alena. "My senses are fine and I have what I need."

Alena's lopsided smile confirmed her satisfaction at hearing him say it.

Banji mumbled, "Guess that's good to know." She looked at Alena. "What's for lunch?"

"Grab the bowls out of the oven. I've been keeping our food warm in there. I'll get the plates."

Gabriel slipped past Santiago. "I'll get the iced tea." He opened the refrigerator and grabbed the pitcher. Turning toward Santiago he quietly said, "You're in so much trouble. I'd sleep with one eye open, if I were you."

Santiago seated himself next to Banji. He leaned over closing the distance between his mouth and her ear. "I will tell you what I want for my birthday when we get home."

"Turkey makes me tired. I'll probably need a nap." Banji snickered. "Madison is helping with Black Friday at the boutique, so we don't have to worry about her barging in and hitting you with her purse."

He winked. "We can rest and talk after your nap."

Alena croaked, "Wait, what? When did Madison hit *Papi*?"

"When she showed up in my living room unannounced." Banji chuckled. "She thought he was attacking me, but she's figured out he's my boyfriend so he's safe now."

Gabriel shook his head and muttered, "And she's still alive. That's got to be some kind of miracle."

"I do not hit women." Santiago frowned. "No, never."

"The miracle is my half-sister is getting herself organized and becoming a functioning adult." Banji fidgeted with the napkin. "I haven't told her the news that we are in no way related. One major life changing event at a time is probably all Madison can handle."

Alena lowered her eyes and folded her hands on the table. "You know she still calls you her sister. She's going to need that connection to get through the next several months."

"I'm not the one who pulled the rug out from under her. That would be her father." Banji rocked back in her chair and stared at the ceiling. "He's evil. He keeps wrecking people's lives with his greed."

"He is not your father. He cannot hurt you anymore." Santiago took her hand. "You are with me." His lips curled up under his moustache. "There is room for Madison."

Gabriel leaned forward and rested his arms on the table. "Damn straight on that. We're family."

Alena exhaled and looked deliberately at each person present. "There's plenty of room at the table for everyone. We've got this."

～

Santiago walked Banji home imagining all the possible ways they could spend the afternoon. Star met them at the kitchen door. Banji leaned down and petted him. "Are you ready to go out?"

"I will take him." Santiago reached for the leash.

"I'm going to lie down. Come join me when you get back."

He clipped the leash to the collar. "Of course." He glanced her way and smiled. "We will not be gone long."

She waved as they crossed the porch and headed down the stairs.

He and Star trundled along the same path they always took. Lunch had gone well with the exception of a couple tense moments. Banji was slowly getting used to the idea of being part of Alena's extended family and he was getting used to the idea of building a new life for himself with her.

He was also getting used to taking naps after lunch. He was eager to get back to the cottage, but Star made a few stops along the way to investigate whatever new discovery caught his attention.

Santiago unclasped the leash and hung it on the peg by the door. They'd been gone long enough for Banji to get settled. He moved quietly down the hall, unbuttoning his shirt as he went. She was lying on her side facing the windows. He slid under the comforter behind her, draped his arm over her ribs and snuggled up to her back.

She murmured, "How was your walk?"

He pressed closer. "*Ay, Carida*, very lonely without you."

"Well, you're here now." She patted his hand.

"Always." His knee nudged the back of her legs.

"Do you mind Madison living in your house? I can tell her she has to find another place if you don't like her staying there."

"I do not mind. A house falls apart if no one lives in it. She can stay."

"I don't know how to tell her we're not sisters anymore. It's like her world is falling apart and I'll be making it worse."

Santiago assured her, "We will be her family. That will help."

"I've only ever had Gram that I could count on. I don't know how to do family."

"We can do this together."

Worry echoed in Banji's voice. "That's a lot to put on you."

"It is not so much. She is doing her best to start over. Alena is helping with work and we will help with family. Madison is not alone."

Banji rolled over facing Santiago. "I never dreamed all this would happen. You don't deserve to have your life turned upside down like this."

"I do not deserve the happiness you have brought me." Santiago swallowed hard and inhaled deeply. "I am grateful every day and every night that you are here with me."

"It does feel good." She skimmed her hand down his side to his hip. "You were made for me." She urged him closer and slipped her leg over his thigh.

"*Carida*, you will not get much rest if you keep doing these things to me." He nudged his erection against the warm space between her legs.

"Resting is over rated." She kissed a trail along his collar bone starting at the soft base of throat. The soft moan and faint vibration of his chest told her she was on the right track. He was a sensual man, loving and kind.

She had all afternoon to make love to him.

CHAPTER TWENTY-NINE

THE NEXT MORNING, Banji swiveled around in her office chair and stared at Alena leaning against the doorjamb with one hand on her hip.

Alena huffed, "Well, what does *Papi* want for his birthday?"

"Have you ever heard of knocking?" Banji tipped her head from side to side and rolled her shoulders. "What if Santiago and I were in the middle of humping each other into the next galaxy and you came barging in? You might get an eyeful of something you'd rather not know about."

Waving her hand in a shooing motion Alena said, "I saw him going into the garage earlier. I knew you weren't rolling around in bed with him." Grinning, she added, "You gotta take it easy on the old man. He's not as young as he used to be."

"He would not appreciate hearing you say that." Banji grinned broadly showing her teeth. "And he's fine the way he is. Smokin' hot as a matter of fact."

"Careful, that's my *Papi* you're taking about." A silly grin spread across Alena's face as she moved away from the door. "Have some respect and quit dodging my question."

"If you wanted to know about his birthday, you could have called." Banji rested her hands on the arms of her chair. "What are you really doing here invading my space this morning?"

Alena grumbled, "Fine. I need you to read the cards for me."

"What's up?" Banji leaned forward. "Did something happen?"

"First things first." Alena sauntered across the office and stopped beside the desk. "What does he want?"

"He wants to drive the Trans Am to Galveston." Banji turned toward her desk, cleared a space, and tucked the yellowed papers into the corner cubby.

"Why?"

"I don't know. It must be a man thing. He rebuilt it, now he gets to drive it." Banji shrugged. "Or he's the man and he does the driving. Pick one."

"That doesn't make a lot of sense. He knows women drive. I drive." Alena ran her fingers through her hair. "I bet he wants to be where you are. He'd never forgive himself if something happened to you on the road. He's very protective when it comes to the people he cares about."

"What could possibly happen? I've got a cell phone and my roadside assistance card. I'm good." She exhaled loudly. "Hell, I made it to Rome and back in one piece."

"That's not the point. What if you got carjacked?" Alena sank onto the straight-backed chair next to the desk.

"What fool would want that old car? Besides we'll be following you and Gabriel."

Alena rolled her eyes. "What if we get separated in traffic? It's a muscle car. It's one of the last few of its kind and it's hard to come by. You have to be careful."

"It sounds like a pain in the ass. Maybe I should get a plain, preowned SUV for everyday driving. You know one of the smaller ones for running errands, getting groceries, taking the pets to the vet for shots."

"That won't fix the Galveston trip." Alena leaned back, slid down and stretched her legs out straight. She rotated her ankles and grumbled, "The Trans Am is on the poster for the classic's exhibition. People will be expecting to see it."

"How the hell did I let you talk me into this?" Banji pivoted to face Alena.

"You want to eat hush puppies and shrimp with Cami."

"Catfish." Banji scrunched her upper lip and nose. "Whatever." She reached in the lap drawer and pulled out her tarot cards. "Okay, here we go. What's the deal? What's got you questioning fate?"

"Nothing specific. I didn't sleep well." Alena scooted to an upright position, picked up the cards, shuffled them 3 times and cut the deck into three piles. "Okay, I'm ready."

"Concentrate on your question." Banji did a simple six-card spread.

She gazed at the cards, her eyes narrowed and her brow knit. "This doesn't make sense."

"What do they say?"

The Ace of Pentacles says he sees himself taking his time in relationships. The Five of Swords reversed says he's been deceived in previous relationships and still suffers from the deception. The Star says deep in his heart he believes his relationship will be successful." Banji looked steadily at Alena and leaned back in her chair. "What was your question?"

"Has *Papi* found his forever love?"

Banji huffed, "You can't do that. It's his future, not yours."

Alena tapped the nearest card. "We saw it in the cards. The Four of Wands says this relationship represents the future for him."

"This is Santiago's life we're talking about. It's bad enough he's the object of a curse I brought on him and now you're messing around in his fate."

"Remember when you got the Four of Cups Reversed?" Alena raised her eyebrows. "You've gotten involved in a new relationship. You've found the courage to show your feelings and change your life. It all happened."

"It's still happening." Banji gathered the cards and put them back in her desk. "You cheated. You can't go poking in other people's destinies."

"*Papi's* life is tied to mine. We're family." She inhaled deeply and let her breath out slowly. "He's all in when it comes to you."

"Yeah, he made that pretty clear yesterday afternoon when we got home." Banji snickered. "Gotta love that man."

"Does that mean you're still planning on making an appointment with Madame Belinsky?"

Banji grinned, "Already taken care of."

"What? When did that happen?" Alena scrambled to move forward and lean into Banji's personal space. "What did she say?"

"I called Cami this morning and she added Lulu on to the call." Banji giggled. "Did you know Lulu was Lulu Cordero before she was Lulu Rustov? She used to do those unusual wedding destination articles for the high-fashion magazines."

Alena scowled. "Do I look like I follow high-fashion?" She plucked at her jeans. "Does this look like any kind of fashion at all?"

Banji's lips puckered. "Um, it's California Saturday casual." She resituated herself in her office chair. "Anyway, Lulu has all the numbers for Madame Belinsky and we called her."

"You're making me dizzy with all this. Who are these people?"

"Pay attention. Lulu is married to Niko, Crystal Foxz is Boris and Niko Rustov's cousin. We're going to get to meet her."

"Stop bouncing in that chair. You're going to break your tailbone and you're giving me a headache to go with the dizzy. Hold still and tell me what's so exciting about that?"

"Well duh, she has the Princess Charlotte jewels." Banji sighed. "They're some of the most beautiful jewels in the world second only to the Imperial jewels of Russia." Banji leaned forward and murmured. "Princess Charlotte left Russia right before the revolution and took everything she had with her to America."

"Yeah, so?"

"She was in love with the captain of her guard, Vasili Rustov." Banji lowered her voice to just above a whisper. "He got her pregnant. She wanted to wait for him in Paris or London but he insisted she go to America."

"I don't like the sound of this. Something tells me it's not going to end well."

"*Carida.*" Santiago's voice boomed through the cottage.

Banji grimaced and put her index finger in front of her lips. "I'll tell you later." She turned her head toward the doorway and called out, "In the office."

Santiago appeared framed in the doorway a moment later. "I have the groceries and I picked up lunch from the deli."

"Thanks, angel. I'll help you put the groceries away." She went to him, stretched up, pulled him down and kissed him. "You're the best."

He glanced toward Alena. "Do you want to eat lunch with us? There is plenty."

"No, I'm good. Gabriel is home and we're going to watch football this afternoon." She blushed. "Well, he's going to watch football and I'm going to watch him."

They walked to the kitchen together. Alena's hand gripped the doorknob. "I'll check with the investigator next week. Remington should have an update for us by then." She let herself out.

Santiago unpacked the groceries while Banji washed her hands. He pulled out the new box of condoms from the last bag, set it on the counter and smiled. He was ready. He had Banji, food, wine and all the necessities for spending the weekend making love to his *Carida*.

His hand stilled and he glanced at her from the corner of his eye. She'd called him an angel. Angels went on top of Christmas trees and decorated churches. He was nobody's angel. Devil, monster, fiend, sure, but not an angel. What did it mean?

"*Carida*, do you want a Christmas tree?" He stared at the counter top.

"That's probably not a great idea this year. Wishes will try to crawl up in it and play with the decorations. Star will be tempted to pee on it. I think we can skip it this time but we'll decorate the living room with other things." She dried her hands and took their plates out of the cabinet.

Okay, so he wasn't the angel on the tree. "Do you want to go to church services?"

"No, I'm not into that, but you can go with Alena and Gabriel." She put their plates on the table and walked to the refrigerator. "What do you want to drink?"

Whiskey, he could use a stiff drink but he said, "Beer." He wasn't working so it was okay and it would calm him enough to think things through. His mother was the only other person who had ever called him an angel and he'd proved her wrong many times over ages ago.

Banji grabbed two cans out of the refrigerator and put them on the table. "These will go perfect with the pizza."

"How did you know that is what I got? I did not tell you."

"I can smell it." She giggled. "Honestly, my nose isn't broken. I lived in Rome and I can smell pizza from a block away." She put a handful of napkins in the middle of the table. "We're going to need these. In southern Italy they put the cheese on top last, that way the other toppings stay nice and moist underneath while it bakes in those big ovens."

He carried the supreme pizza to the table and sat down. "We can make our own next time and you can show me."

"That would be fun." She reached out and pulled a large slice onto her plate. "Gram had a pizza pan. I'm sure it's still around here someplace. I'll find it and we can decorate the house for Christmas and make pizza."

"I will put the blue lights up on the porch for you." He bit into his slice and chewed.

"If the weather cooperates, we can dance under the lights." She took a drink and put it down. "Then I'll kiss you all over and wish you a very happy birthday."

Santiago coughed trying not to choke and grabbed his can of beer. He took a swallow to clear his throat. "You must not say such things to me when I am eating."

"Why not?"

A drop of condensation trickled over his fingers. "Because I picture it and then I forget everything else but the way it feels when you touch me like that."

Banji licked her lips and a couple of her fingers. "Hmm, really. Guess we'll have to do more of it so you can get used to it."

"*Carida*, you are making it impossible for me to eat my lunch."

"Fine. Drink your beer." She smirked around her next bite. "Soon as I'm done eating this, I'll come over there and nibble on you."

He put down his beer and stood up. "Enough."

"What?" Her innocent wide-eyed stare did not fool him. She said those things on purpose knowing it would make him hungry for more than food.

He came around the table, pulled her out of her chair and hoisted her onto his shoulder. "We are going to bed. Now."

She chuckled, "I love it when you get all sexy bossy."

He marched down the hall and rolled her carefully off his shoulder and into the middle of their bed. He loomed over her and straighten to his full height. Unbuttoning his shirt, he asked, "What else do you like?"

Banji held out her arms to him. "You. I like you."

CHAPTER THIRTY

THE WEDNESDAY AFTER THANKSGIVING, Banji plopped into the leather chair across from Alena and asked, "Are you sure you want to do this today?"

"I scanned your documents to Remington the same day you gave them to me. He's had time to get started." Alena's smiled faltered. "What's wrong with today?"

"Nothing's wrong. I want to know what happened but it's scary at the same time. I'm not sure I want a murderer for a grandfather."

"You could find out he's not responsible for Ritter's death." Alena's hand rested next to the desk phone. "Then he'd only be a greedy shit that trashed your Mom's life."

"Great. That makes me feel so much better." Banji eyed the phone and inhaled a deep, deep breath and let it out slowly. "Go ahead."

Alena leaned forward and pushed the button labeled, *Remington.*

A deep, gruff voice barked out of the speaker, "Remington."

"Good morning, I'm here with Banji. How's my favorite investigator?" Alena's eyes glanced briefly at Banji and she grinned.

"Good. Working." A loud exasperated sounding huff and the shuffle of papers came through loud and clear. "Ellis Bancroft was a cut-throat businessman and the undisputed king of wheeler-dealers."

"We already knew he was shady but what about Ritter?"

"Are you sitting down?"

"Yes, as a matter of fact we both are." Alena shot Banji a warning glance and mumbled, "Get ready."

More paper shuffling. "The check to Santino Bosco. I went to see his grandson. He had the old man's ledgers. Can you believe it? He kept track of his contracts. I'll send you the picture of the page. Check your email."

"Great, but what did you find?"

"Bancroft, Preston, Davis, fifty thousand dollars." Remington coughed and cleared his throat. "He didn't do the job himself. He contracted it out to some guy, Harold Svenson, on board Ritter's ship."

Banji raised her voice and asked, "Have you found this Svenson? Can we have him arrested for murdering Ritter?"

"Sorry, he was crushed when a shipping container broke loose during rough seas off the coast of Borneo."

Banji groaned, "Damn and double damn."

"Did you find out anything about Genevieve Preston? Was it suicide or murder?" Alena's eyes flicked to Banji and connected.

Nodding, Banji chimed in, "Yeah, what about my Mom?"

"Two weeks after the coroner filed the death certificate indicating the cause of death was suicide, his mortgage was paid off." Remington grumbled, "Where the hell did I put that report? Ah, here we go. Missus Preston's doctor provided an affidavit stating she was being treated for depression and he'd recently increased her anti-depressant medication dosage."

"Does it say why?" Banji gripped the padded arms of her chair and leaned forward.

"No, but my guess is to cover the levels found in her blood. She was borderline overdose." He cleared his throat again. "That medication comes with a warning for increased suicidal thoughts and tendencies. All Lloyd Preston had to do was give her the pills and let her kill herself. Guess he didn't want to wait."

More paper shuffling. "George O'Connor gave me a notarized affidavit stating Lloyd borrowed his boat for a three-day fishing trip the week Genevieve Preston died."

"Can he be held responsible for any of this?" Banji looked from the window to Alena. "There's got to be something we can do."

"The doctor has retired, the coroner passed away last year from a heart attack. I'm still waiting to receive the copy of the canceled check. Since Lori Bancroft was on the account and Banji is her beneficiary, I was able to get a court order to release the documents. Once you have that you can ask the lawyers if there's enough evidence to get a case to trial."

Banji sniffled and leaned back resting her head against the soft padding of her chair.

Alena said, "Thanks Remington. You're the best of the best. I'm adding a little something to your Christmas bonus."

"Any time, Al."

They disconnected and Alena looked at Banji. "I'm sorry but at least now we know."

"Yeah, we do." Banji's lips thinned to a slim line as her mouth formed a serious scowl. "I'm going to love watching Lloyd lose everything he's ever had."

"What are you going to do?" Alena's brows drew together.

"I don't have to do anything. I pulled an Alena trick and read his cards." She frowned. "He has a very dark and stormy future. The Hangman turned up. Not a good sign."

Alena leaned all the way back in her chair. "Wow, sounds like he's coming to the end. What about Madison's Mom? Did you see anything about her?"

"No, and I didn't ask about Leanne. She's not my problem. Santiago's happiness and our future is my top priority."

"Speaking of the future, Christmas is coming. Have you decided what you're getting *Papi*?"

"Something to show my appreciation." Banji raised her hand and waved as she walked away. "I'm going to the mall. It's pretty this time of year with all the decorations. He needs to relax. I've got something special in mind. He's going to love it."

Alena called out, "Try not to give him a heart attack."

❧

Mission accomplished and she was home before Santiago. She set their take-out dinner on the kitchen counter and hurried past Star to the bedroom where she tucked the pricy bottle of warming massage lotion away in the top drawer of her nightstand. Only the best for Santiago. It wouldn't damage his ink but it would soften his damaged skin and relax the muscles underneath. It was also edible in case something came up that needed more personal attention.

Wishes opened his eyes and followed her movements from his napping place at the head of the bed between their pillows. She felt a light bump against her leg and looked down. "It's okay. Santiago's going to feel so good." She reached down and gently rubbed Star's head. "Let's take you for a quick walk."

She tucked dinner away in the oven to keep semi-warm and grabbed the leash off its hook. She was getting fast at hooking up and getting out the door without tripping or getting tangled up. Walking a puppy that got easily excited and ran in circles took concentration. If she wasn't careful, she'd end up face down in the dunes.

On their way back to the cottage, Santiago caught up to them.

"*Carida*, wait. I will walk with you." He took Star's leash from her hand, bent down and kissed her. "I missed you today." He rubbed his chest with his free hand. "My t-shirt seems rougher today for some reason." He grinned.

"I'll add more fabric softener to the wash next time." She grinned back. "I wouldn't want your nipples getting chafed."

"I do not think fabric softener will help."

The twitch at the corners of his mouth gave him away. She put her hand on his shoulder and pulled him down. Her lips brushed against the shell of his ear. "I'll be glad to kiss them and make them better." She placed her right hand over the center seam of his work pants and pressed his growing erection against his abdomen. Banji closed her eyes and said, "I could kiss this and take your mind off of everything."

His husky bedroom voice floated on the air around them. "I am yours, *Carida*."

Star yipped and pulled against the leash breaking the spell.

Banji opened her eyes and looked into Santiago's. The promise of his devotion sparkled in their dark depths. They held the words he couldn't say and the feelings he couldn't hide.

"It's only fair since you've already got all of me." She pressed her lips against his.

He could destroy her and she'd be powerless to stop him. This was the vulnerability she had avoided like the plague and fate had broken down her defenses with this quiet unassuming man. She wanted to snarl and bite something. This was not supposed to happen to her. She exhaled a resigned sigh. "I guess this means we're a couple now."

His arm slid around her back and he nudged her forward. "Yes, we are together. We must go home now."

Their relationship had evolved to the next level. His confidence had reached a point where he was showing her the vulnerable man hidden inside. The one he'd tucked away for safe keeping.

"You don't have to cook tonight." Banji smiled. "I got us California Carne Asada burritos. They're delicious." She snickered, "But not as delicious as you."

After dinner, Santiago got up from the table and put his plate in the sink. He turned his head and looked at Banji. "Thank you. It was very good."

"I knew you'd like it." Her hands were busy cleaning off the counter. "Go take your shower. Let me know when you're done." She dropped the used wax paper wrappers and paper bag in the trash. "I have a surprise for you."

"What surprise?" His eyebrows drew together wrinkling his forehead.

"If I tell you it won't be a surprise. Take your shower and go lie down."

He frowned. "I think I will watch TV for a while."

"Fine. There's no rush. I've got all night."

He made his way to the living room, sat in the recliner, and turned on the TV. Star settled on the floor next to his chair. Before the first commercial came on, Banji made herself comfortable on the couch. Wishes clawed his way up and onto the cushion next to her.

They looked like the happy families on TV. Mom, dad, dog, cat, the only thing missing were the kids. His eyes widened and his heart rate kicked up. No, he'd given up on having kids. He'd already lived through the disappointment of trying, hoping, and failing. No. He couldn't go through that again. Banji wouldn't want to have children with him. Would she?

Santiago gripped the arms of the recliner and pushed himself to his feet. "Star needs to go out."

Banji eyed the puppy and then focused on Santiago. "Really?"

"Yes. Come, Star. Time for your walk."

The second the back door closed behind him, Santiago brushed his hand over the top of his head and down to the base of his neck. He stepped off the porch and onto the sandy trail leading to the beach. His hand gripped the leash tighter.

When a woman on TV told a man she had a surprise for him, it usually meant she was pregnant. Before he had time to form his next thought, he heard a squawk overhead and something wet splatted on the top of his head. Without thinking he reacted instantly. His hand brushed over the wet spot and came away with bird dropping smeared across his palm. The seagull gliding away on the air current overhead was the guilty culprit.

Santiago swore under his breath. He was tired, sweaty, and covered in bird poop. He turned around and tramped back to the cottage with Star trotting to keep up.

He stomped through the back door, unfastened the leash, hung it on the hook, marched directly to the bathroom and closed the door firmly. He was in the process of divesting himself of his filthy clothes when he heard a knock on the door.

Banji's concerned voice reached his ears. "Are you all right?"

"Yes. I am going to take a shower."

"Okay."

He opened the faucets and stepped under the spray. He needed shampoo and lots of it. After four rounds of scrubbing and rinsing his hair, he finished cleaning up, got out and dried off. More than anything else, he wanted to lie down and close his eyes.

The cottage was quiet when he stepped out into the hall. He walked across to the bedroom and stopped next to the bed. Banji was waiting for him. The sheer baby-blue nightie did absolutely nothing to conceal her from his gaze. The comforter and sheets were turned down.

"What is that?" He pointed to a pillow lying in the middle of the bed.

She crooned, "Come on over here and lie down. The pillow goes under your tummy to keep pressure off your male parts and support your back."

"No." His ass would be in the air. Not a pretty picture to his way of thinking.

"Yes. Don't be so stubborn. You're going to really like this." She leaned forward resting her open hands on the mattress next to the pillow. "Come on. Look at these nice clean sheets. They'll feel so soft and smooth against your skin."

He didn't give a damn about smooth sheets. It was what came next that he didn't like. His mind flashed back to his youth. To a night he'd done his best to forget.

Her nightie did nothing to hide her cleavage. Two beautiful, soft, supple globes with pink nipples drew his attention to the tempting woman waiting for him. He forced his eyes away from her breasts and met her gaze.

He swallowed hard and asked, "Why are you doing this?"

"Doing what?" She straightened up, turned and picked up a bottle from the night stand. "I'm going to give you a massage so you can relax and get a good night's sleep. It'll make your skin feel better."

"My skin is ruined." The scars started at his shoulders and went all the way to his feet.

"No, it's not. It only needs a little help." Still holding the lotion in one hand, she patted the pillow. "Let me get the hard-to-reach places for you."

"You have not seen all of me." He looked away.

"You don't always sleep on your back and sometimes you kick off the covers. I've seen you." She nodded twice. "I know exactly what you look like naked, front and back.

"They tied us down and branded us like cattle." He remembered the searing pain, the smell of his burning flesh and he shuddered.

"I'm not tying you down. You can get up any time you want to." She knelt on the mattress and moved closer to the middle. "Be an angel and let me rub those knots out of your shoulders and back."

"I do not know how to be an angel." He took one hesitant step toward the bed.

"That's all right." She patted the pillow again. "There's more than one kind of angel and you're the right one for me."

"Are you sure?"

"Never been so sure of anything in my life." She rested back on her heels. "Come on." She opened the lotion and poured some into her palm. "Get comfy and let me rub all your worries away." She flashed him a grin. "We're going to make some new memories for you. Good memories."

He relaxed his frown and arranged himself face down, his hands under his cheek and helpless. He didn't like it. He squeezed his eyes closed tight. Was there anything he wouldn't let Banji do to him?

The mattress jiggled and her voice whispered softly in his ear. "I'm going to start with your shoulders and work my way down. If you want me to stop, say so and I will."

His warm breath flowed gently over the top of his hand. "I want to do this for you. You must teach me."

"We can learn together. Tonight, I'm learning how to give you what you need."

The faint scent of eucalyptus, lavender and peppermint teased his nose. "I do not want to smell like a girl."

"Let me take care of you." She chuckled softly. "You can take a shower in the morning but tonight you're mine."

Tonight, and every night for the rest of his life. Her hands moved from the base of his skull out over his shoulders. When she'd finished with the knot under his right shoulder blade she moved on to his back. His first instinct was to tighten his gluteal muscles when her hands skimmed over his butt. Her gentle kneading of the muscles eventually enticed him to let go and enjoy the sensations. Moments later her fingers slipped into the space between his thighs. He didn't recognize the groan coming from his throat. Nothing had ever felt so good. She moved on to his thighs and lower to his calves. When she got to his feet he sighed and moaned softly.

"How's it feeling? Is the tightness easing up? The peppermint is a pain reducer, lavender helps with sleep and eucalyptus helps you breathe easier. The sweet almond oil absorbs quickly and is good for your skin."

"I am falling asleep. You must come lie down next to me."

"But there's still your front to do."

"Not tonight, *Carida*." He rolled to the side, pulled the pillow out from under himself and flung it out of bed. "I need to hold you. Please."

Banji grabbed a hold of the covers at the foot of the bed and pulled them up while Santiago situated himself at the head of the bed.

He held his arms out to her. "Come, we will keep each other warm."

She settled down and tucked in close to his side with her head resting on his shoulder. "Are you okay?" She draped her arm across his chest.

"Very good."

"You still haven't told me what you want for Christmas."

"We will do this again." He kissed the top of her head. "And the front. That is what I want."

Her fingers skimmed around his nipple and teased it to a peak. "I have something special for that."

His hand rested over hers and pressed it tightly to his chest. "Tomorrow, *Carida*."

CHAPTER THIRTY-ONE

Banji fell asleep holding Santiago and being held by him. The soft whisper in her ear and the finger tapping her shoulder interrupted her slumber the next morning. She groaned, "What?"

Madison quietly said, "Get up."

Banji's eyes blinked open and she rolled toward her side of the bed and glared at Madison. "What in the hell are you doing in my bedroom?" She looked around the room. "What time is it and where's Santiago?"

"He's in the shower." Madison glanced toward the hall door.

"What is wrong with you, sneaking in here this early in the morning? Get out. Learn to use the phone."

"I tried but nobody answered." Madison chewed on her lower lip. "Mom called at five o'clock this morning and said Dad is driving her down here to get me. I walked over here at six and sat on your porch. I've been waiting for someone to get up."

"How did they even find you?" Banji sat up and slid her legs over the side of the bed. She nodded to her bedside chair. "Hand me my robe, would ya?"

Madison turned and picked the silk robe off the chair. "This is so pretty. You always have the prettiest clothes."

Banji's left eyelid twitched. She took the robe and shoved her arms into it. "I'm waiting. How did they find out where you are?"

"Dad got it from my supervisor at my old job. I asked her to pack up my desk and send my things to Alena's. They are going to her house." Madison glanced toward the hall. "It sounds like Santiago's through with his shower. Can I help you make his breakfast?"

Calm, Banji needed to stay calm. She dug her fingers into her thighs and reminded herself to breathe slowly, in and out. "Okay, that would be great. There's bacon and eggs in the refrigerator. I'll be there in a minute."

"Okay. I'll go get the bacon started." Madison turned, disappeared out the door and down the hall.

Banji stood up and brushed the covers into place and muttered under her breath, "I don't want to go to jail today. I can't kill her."

"*Carida?*" Santiago stood in the bedroom doorway wearing his dark blue jersey pants tied loosely around his hips.

"What?" She eyed him up and down. So fine. "Madison's in the kitchen fixing breakfast." He had a way of distracting her even when he wasn't trying to.

"I found her on the porch when I took Star out this morning. I let her in to make our coffee. She needs to talk to you." He walked over to his dresser and pulled out a white t-shirt and peeled off the jersey pants.

"Her folks are coming to get her." Banji went to the closet and brought out his work boots, pants and shirt. After laying the clothes on the bed she turned and faced him. "I don't know what to do with her. She's an adult. All she has to do is tell them she's not going anywhere. Lloyd can turn their Mercedes-Benz around and go back to the city."

"She is afraid. She needs our support." He picked up his shirt, put it on and reached for his work pants.

"Alena gave her a job besides the one she has at the boutique, I sold her my car, and she's staying in your house. What more does she need?"

He finished buttoning her shirt and walked over to her. Santiago wrapped his arms around her and hugged her to his chest. "Family. She needs people to stand beside her."

Banji rested the side of her head over his heart and hugged him back. "Fine, I'll hold her hand while she calls her Mom."

They walked to the kitchen together. Banji sat down at the kitchen table while Santiago stepped over to the counter. He looked down at Madison. "I will finish fixing breakfast. You need to talk to Banji."

"Okay." Madison looked from Santiago to Banji. "Did I do something wrong?"

"No, you didn't do anything wrong." Banji wiggled around on her seat getting comfortable. "Come sit down. I want to talk to you about calling your Mom back. If you're not planning on going home with them, they're wasting time and gasoline coming here."

"I don't want to go with them. Santiago said I could stay in his house as long as I want to."

Banji forced herself to smile. Madison had somehow found a way to burrow her way into their lives like a tick on a dog's back. "How about if we go in the living room and you call them and tell them that."

"Daddy always gets so mad if I don't do what he says. I'm scared of him worse than Mom is."

Banji's brow wrinkled. "Are you telling me Leanne is afraid of Lloyd?"

Nodding vigorously, Madison said, "Yes, she's always been afraid. She told me we had to be careful not to make him mad."

"Well, that's too bad, cuz today he's going to be really pissed. He's missing a day at the office and he's on a fool's errand." She looked over at Santiago and back at Madison. "You have a home here with us and Alena. If you want it to stay that way you need to put some boundaries on your folks."

"What do you want me to do?"

"Take out your phone and call your Mom. Tell her you're not going anywhere. They can have breakfast in Los Gatos or Santa Cruz, turn around, and go home."

"They'll be mad at me," Madison whined.

"And what are they going to do about it? They threw you out. All you have to do is stay out. You have a job, a car, and a place to live." Banji sucked in a deep breath. "You have a family here if you want it, but you can't have them and us. It's time to pick one."

Madison got up, walked over to the counter, and picked up her phone. She swiped and pressed the screen. "Hi! Mom, I've decided I'm staying here. You and Dad should go home. There's no point in coming here." She put her phone on speaker.

"You can't be serious." Leanne's voice came through loud and clear.

"I am serious. I like it here at Alena's and I'm staying." She inhaled deeply. "I'm not coming home and I'm not marrying Bennett."

"How are you going to live? Think about the kind of life you're throwing away. You don't want to live like Banji the rest of your life."

Madison's eyebrows drew together as she stared at Banji. "What's wrong with the way Banji lives?"

"Well, um, she has no security. No husband to take care of her. If it wasn't for her grandmother, she wouldn't have a roof over her head. She's probably living in that shack eating oatmeal and corn flakes at this point."

Banji bit her cheek to keep from telling off her used-to-be-step-mother. This wasn't her fight but it pissed her off anyway. She stared at Santiago, who stared back at her. He had an odd look on his face like he'd been severely insulted. Was he thinking about the no husband comment? She'd have to deal with that later.

"Look Mom, I have to go. I have to go to work and I'm going to be late. Please go home and leave me alone."

Leanne squawked and Lloyd's voice boomed out of the phone. "You get your suitcase packed and be ready to get in this car. I'm not putting up with anymore of your nonsense."

Madison's chest puffed up and she defiantly stuck out her chin. "I'm not going with you and I'll tell Alena to lock the gate so you can't get in."

"I'll cut you out of my will. You won't get a single cent," Lloyd threatened.

"I don't care." Madison threw her head back and giggled. "Oh, my god. I really don't care anymore. Bye, Dad." She disconnected the call and looked around the room at Banji and Santiago. "I guess I should call Alena and tell her to lock the gate."

Banji smiled broadly at Madison. "Eat your breakfast and we'll walk over and talk to her.

⁓

Alena looked at Madison and said, "Come on, let's go shopping. You need something spectacular to wear to the New Year's party. You want to look great. There'll be people from the company and the racing industry. It's a good opportunity to network."

"Can I still come if I don't have a date?"

"Sure." Alena grinned, picked up her shoulder bag, and adjusted the strap on her shoulder. "Come on. I could use something new. I don't want Gabriel to get bored looking at me in the same old thing."

Banji grumbled, "I'm calling bullshit. Gabriel's got that look. He'll never get bored."

"Same goes for Santiago." Alena shoulder bumped Banji. "It wouldn't hurt you to get something. *Papi*'s not immune to pretty girls in hot dresses."

"How many party dresses do you think I can buy? It's not like I have a lot of places to wear them these days."

"We have company parties and charity fund raisers. You'll get to wear them more than once." She nudged Banji. "Let's get out of here and go have some fun."

Madison followed them out to Alena's Mustang. "This is going to be the best New Year's party. I've got all the decorations ready to put up." Alena and Banji's gazes met over the roof of the car. They simultaneously said, "Right."

CHAPTER THIRTY-TWO

THE FOLLOWING days passed quietly which only served to add to Banji's worries. It was the calm before the storm. Lloyd Preston didn't like to be contradicted. She had no doubt the sneaky creep was in his office plotting his revenge. She didn't trust him as far as she could throw him.

She didn't believe for one minute that Madison's old high-school flame, Garth, had miraculously thought of her and was available after the Bennett disaster. And he'd somehow found her phone number. Really? How convenient. Banji wrinkled her nose thinking about it. She smelled a big fat rat.

It wouldn't be safe to leave Madison alone on the street. Keeping that in mind, they weren't taking any chances. Either she or Alena drove Madison to work in the mornings and picked her up in the evenings. Santiago accompanied Banji and Madison to the grocery store. Only a complete fool would challenge him.

Banji pulled up in front of the busy boutique. Christmas shopping was in full swing. Madison had decorated the front window with eye-catching holiday outfits that were sure to attract shoppers. From the look of the crowd inside, it was working. The lighted, gold-glittered reindeer in the center of the display added a touch of elegance and whimsy.

The colorful lights and decorations wound around the street lamps added old-fashioned appeal. Banji inhaled the aroma of baked pie crust and vanilla. The Trans Am smelled great. The trunk was full of Christmas presents so the cookies and pies for tonight's treats and tomorrow's dinner rested on the back seat along with two bottles of Napa Valley Moscato.

She glanced at her watch and then at the boutique's door. It was still a few minutes before six o'clock in the evening. A look up the street and a check of the rear-view mirror didn't reveal any cause for concern. Everything looked normal, and that worried her. The only reason for the lack of retaliation would be that Lloyd was too busy trying to keep up appearances.

The auction business slowed this time of year but his import business was busy. He'd always made a big deal out of advertising he was stocking up for the after-Christmas rush. He wanted to get his share of the customers looking to spend their holiday money and gift cards.

The soft tap on the passenger window got her attention. Banji checked to be sure it was Madison before she released the power lock. This was not the time for an unwelcome surprise. She plastered a smile on her face and asked, "How was the last-minute rush?"

Madison settled into the passenger seat, positioned a stuffed shopping bag on the floor between her feet and fastened her seatbelt. "Good. Really good. My marketing plan is paying off." She glanced at the back seat. "Did you get everything for lunch tomorrow?"

"I sure did." Banji did her best to sound cheerful as she pulled away from the curb. Frightening Madison would put a damper on everyone's holiday.

"I'm so excited. I can't wait for everyone to open their presents."

"You do understand this isn't going to be like the Christmases you're used to. This is Alena and Gabriel's home. Letting us share it is a big deal. We can't ruin it with our usual family squabbles." She shot a serious look at Madison from the corner of her eye while keeping her attention on the road.

"Those weren't my fault." Madison rubbed the back of her neck. "I didn't want to go on those trips with Mom and Dad. They fought the whole time. We'd barely get where we were going and Dad would want to leave. I hated it. I wanted to stay home."

"Well, this year you're getting your wish. Santiago and I will meet you at Alena's in the morning to open presents and then we'll have lunch."

"Alena said we could watch Christmas movies after lunch." Madison stared expectantly at Banji.

"Fine. We can stay for one or two but that's all." Banji parked close to Alena's side door near the kitchen. "It's real nice of Alena to let you spend the night at her house. You shouldn't be alone on Christmas Eve and you can help them decorate the tree. You've got a talent for doing that."

"You don't think Dad will do anything weird, do you?"

"He's always busy with shipments this time of year." Banji stared at Madison. "I'd come over and supervise but I want to celebrate Santiago's birthday with him and a great bottle of Moscato." Banji shooed Madison out of the car. "Go have fun." She watched to make sure she got inside before putting the car in reverse and heading home.

Santiago stepped back and surveyed the cedar swing he and Alena had set up on the ocean-side porch. The gentle curves of the seat and back would be welcoming and comfortable for romancing Banji. Alena had picked out the candle holder and candles. He only needed sunset and Banji to make his romantic evening perfect. He glanced overhead and grinned. The string of blue lights went all the way around the porch ceiling. With the flick of a switch he could dance under them with his *Carida* in his arms.

But first they would fix their genuine Italian style pizza dinner. He gazed out at the Pacific Ocean. The tides and winds had brought them together. If believing in the tarot cards or a pirate's cursed locket made it real for Banji, he'd accept that. Who was he to argue with the power of the sea?

He looked forward to celebrating his birthday for the first time since he was a child, before his mother and father were killed. Before he became a monster. He'd never imagined his life could be like this.

Monsters weren't meant to be loved. He suppressed the cold shiver that ran down his spine. Those terrible days were behind him.

Banji saw him differently. Tonight, would be about him and his *Carida*.

At the sound of the Trans Am's engine growling in the driveway, he went to help Banji bring in their holiday provisions.

Banji heard Santiago walk up behind her before she felt his hands curl around her hips. Bent over and squeezed between the front seat and the car's frame, was not the most graceful position to be in. And it was the only way to gather her wine and pastries from the back seat. Judging from the rumble in his voice, solid grip of his hands and the hard bulge nudging her bottom through her jeans, he was good with it. Her man was getting his amorous mood on board early.

She said, "There's my angel come to welcome me home."

He pressed his erection tighter against her. "You make me act like a devil."

"Every angel has a devilish side." She leaned into him. "I like yours. Help me get this stuff inside and I'll show you how much I like it."

Santiago stepped back and let go of her. "Be careful. Do not hit your head."

She backed up slowly and stood up. Here's the wine. She held out the bag. "I'll bring the bakery boxes." She turned back to the car. "I dropped Madison off at Alena's so we shouldn't have any interruptions."

Banji fished the rest of the supplies out of the car. As soon as she stepped out of the way, Santiago pressed the lock and closed the door. He followed her to the kitchen, closed and locked that door also. She glanced his way.

He shrugged and said, "I do not want to be interrupted."

"Interrupted from what? I thought we were going to make pizza for dinner."

His hands gripped her waist and he hoisted her onto the counter. When she was securely seated, he edged himself between her legs and began unbuttoning her blouse. "I want to do this first. We can make dinner later." He brushed the material off her shoulders. His eyes feasted on her breasts encased in the pink lace bra she'd gotten especially for his birthday. It was a little earlier than she'd planned on him seeing it, but it was his birthday after all and if he wanted to play now that was fine.

His fingers traced the top edge before curling around the soft lace and pulling it down exposing her nipples. A second later his lips fastened around one nipple causing it to harden while he palmed the other breast gently squeezing and kneading her soft flesh.

She threaded her fingers through his hair and arched her back. "Yes, that's what I like." The shiver of delight his tongue generated spread throughout her body all the way to her toes. She wiggled closer to the edge of the counter and to him. Some unseen magnetic force pulling her closer to him. This thing between them went bone deep.

Releasing her nipple, he straightened to his full height and took a half-step back forcing her to let go of his hair and rest her hands on his shoulders.

Catching his breath, his eyes met hers. "Tell me what else you like." His fingers brushed the bra straps off her shoulders.

"I like you, everything about you." Her arms tangled in her shirt-sleeves and she shook herself free. She cupped his cheek in her hand and murmured, "You're my everything."

"*Ay, Carida*, no one has ever said these things to me." He lowered his head till his mouth was next to her ear and whispered, "Tell me what you want."

She wrapped her legs around his waist and her arms around his neck. "Let's go to bed. I want to give you your birthday present."

His arms wrapped around her and he lifted her off the counter. Determined strides carried her to their bedroom. He lowered her to the soft comforter on the bed. She watched Santiago kick off his boots and strip out of his clothes.

Keeping her eyes fastened on his, she unhooked her bra and flung it away. She peeled her yoga pants off and gave them a fling, leaving her wearing only the pink stretch-lace panties.

Santiago leaned down and curled his fingers around the elastic band circling her hips. "Is this for me?"

"Yes." She lifted her hips allowing him to slip them down her legs.

He lifted them to his nose and inhaled. "Very nice."

She watched a hungry smile spread across his face. He threw the panties toward his pillow at the head of the bed. His gaze focused on her with an intensity she'd never seen before.

His hands grasped her hips and pulled her to the edge of the bed before sinking to his knees between her legs. "I have not done this before." He leaned over and kissed her abdomen right below her belly button. "Will you allow me this pleasure?"

"Yes." She'd waited a long time for him to get comfortable enough with her to attempt new experiences. "I want you, all of you, any way that makes you feel good."

"You must tell me if I do something wrong."

"There is no wrong way when it comes to us. We'll learn all the best ways to please each other." She chuckled softly. "It'll take years." She hoped it would take the rest of their lives.

He moved back and ran his hands up the inside of her thighs nudging them wider to accommodate his size. This was going to be like trying to ride a Clydesdale. She softly said, "Put your hands under my hips and I'm going to put my legs over your shoulders. We'll both be more comfortable that way."

"I read about this." He slipped his finger down the center of her folds.

"Great, you can read up on it some more later. Right now, you need to get down to doing." She shivered with anticipation and to the heat building in the wake of his touch.

She couldn't be sure but she might have heard him chuckle. She strained to raise her head and look but it was too late. He'd buried his face in the apex of her thighs. Good man. She relaxed and let him proceed.

Santiago moved in close and swiped his tongue up the center of her folds and over her clit. The soft moan and whispered, "Yes, that's perfect," was all he needed to hear. He continued to lick and fastened his attention on her clit. Her body undulated and quivered.

"You have to stop. I want to come with you inside me. Please, angel. I need all of you."

He stood while she simultaneously scooted back into the middle of the bed. His hand rubbed over his moustache while watching every move she made. He'd remember this night forever.

She held her arms out to him. "I need you."

His right knee landed on the mattress first followed by the left. He lowered himself, his body covered hers. His *Carida*, the one he'd waited his whole life for was asking him to make love to her. He braced his arms on either side of her to keep his weight from crushing her while his erection hung heavily between her thighs.

"Tell me, *Carida*. Tell me you want me."

"I do. I want you, I need you." She gazed unflinching into his eyes. "I love you."

Those were the words he'd yearned to hear his whole life and they were finally his. He would treasure them to his dying day. He was a wanted man. He rubbed his erection through her slick folds feeling the heat, the need his woman had for him and positioned the head of his cock at her entrance. One long slow push and he was in, seated to the hilt and on the verge of losing control.

As if she could read his mind, Banji implored, "Let go, give me all of you." She wrapped her legs around his waist with her heels brushing over his butt urging him to move.

"I could hurt you." He hung his head.

"You won't." She rubbed a heel down and up the back of his thigh. Her fingers touched his jaw gently urging him to turn and look her in the eyes.

Her inner walls tightened around his cock and she murmured, "Let go. It's okay."

One slow stroke led to another and the rhythm between their bodies synched. His speed increase with his need. He wouldn't be able to last much longer. He stretched over her, his cock rubbing across her clit. The tingle at the base of his spine and traveling to the small of his back signaled he was nearing his threshold. He was going to come in the next few seconds.

He clenched his jaw, inhaled through his nose and ground out, "Ay, *Carida*, take all of me."

Banji pumped her hips, rubbing her clit over the hair at the base of his cock and wailed. Her orgasm taking over her body. Head thrown back, throat exposed, thighs clenching, toes curling, she wailed and dug her fingers into his sides.

His cock pulsed; he growled and slammed into her, cum pumped through him, filled her tight space and leaked out around his base. He was done. His head hung low and ragged breaths heaved from his chest. He toppled to the side, his powerful thighs unable to hold him up any longer.

He gulped for air and asked, "Are you all right?"

"Best I've ever been." Her hand found his arm and squeezed right before she rolled toward him and threw her arm over his chest. Her leg rested on top of his thigh.

Santiago inhaled a fortifying breath and asked, "*Carida*, you said it would take years for us to learn all the ways to please each other. Do you want me to stay with you that long?"

"Yes, years and years, like forever would be good." She rose up and looked him in the eyes. "What about you? If you don't want to hang around that long, you'd better tell me now."

"I told you, I will never leave you."

She pushed against his chest and levered herself higher looking him in the eyes. "That's not the same thing. Do you want to stay?"

"Forever will not be long enough." He pulled her down and pressed his lips to hers.

She pinched his side. "You had me worried there for a minute. Don't do it again."

He jerked away from the pinch and said, "No, never."

She patted his chest. "That's my angel."

CHAPTER THIRTY-THREE

CHRISTMAS MORNING BANJI woke up wrapped snuggly in Santiago's arms. She stretched her legs and yawned.

His voice, still rough with sleep, mumbled, "Good morning, *Carida.*"

"Good morning, angel." She hugged him and scattered kisses and licks across his chest. "Would you like to take a shower with me this morning?" She peeked up at his face just in time to catch his eyes pop open wide.

"No, yes, I do not know. Not today."

She felt the trembling in his arms and heard the hitch in his voice. "What's the matter?"

"Nothing." He let go of her, rolled to the edge of the bed and got up. "I will make breakfast while you shower. Then I want to show you something." He pulled on his jersey pants and looked over his shoulder at her.

She eyed the bulge behind the center seam. Her man was definitely awake. She didn't think she'd ever completely understand him but that was okay. She had forever to figure him out. She met his gaze, grinned and asked, "Show me what?"

"It is a surprise." Under his moustache his lips turned up in a satisfied smile. She recognized that look.

"Okay, I'll hurry." She threw off the covers and got out of bed. "You need to take Star out. We sort of forgot about that last night."

"I took him out for a quick walk while you were sleeping. I will take him again now."

She watched him walk down the hall. His step had a little more bounce to it this morning. No mystery there. He'd woken her in the early hours before dawn with a raging erection. Someone needed to write a song about moonlight delight. Her man definitely knew how to make it happen. She slipped on her robe, turned and looked at the bed. It was a hopeless mess.

A satisfied smile slowly surfaced.

She trundled across the hall to the bathroom, shut the door and turned on the shower. After breakfast it would be time to have the talk about not using protection.

~

Santiago took Star for a short walk while the coffee brewed. Clear skies and an easy breeze promised a beautiful Christmas day. His *Carida* loved him. He had the only present he needed.

He stood in the kitchen and looked down the hall thinking back on the night. The sound of the shower made him think of the warm water sluicing over her soft skin. He could join her. She had offered. Before he could take his first step in that direction the water shut off.

He opened the refrigerator and removed the ingredients for their breakfast. He was hungry, hungrier than he'd ever been before. He turned on the radio and hummed along to the song, Feliz Navidad, indeed it was.

Lost in the lyrics he didn't hear Banji walk up behind him but he sensed her. "*Carida*, you smell good."

Her arms slipped around his middle. "You smell like musky sex. I might have to take you back to bed. It's too tempting to resist." Her hands skimmed over his stomach and dipped under the elastic waistband of his pants.

"Breakfast first." He looked back over his shoulder and grinned. "I need to eat and regain my strength."

Banji brushed mascara on her eyelashes and smiled at her reflection in the bathroom mirror. Christmas day was back on her list of favorite holidays after spending several on the ignore-it and it-will-go-away list. Ignoring Santiago was not possible. She adored him and loved the swing he'd gotten her. It was really more for them and but he'd put a big gold bow on it, technically making it hers.

She had plans for that swing. There was one bottle of Moscato and half of the apricot cookies still untouched.

Her Christmas-red lipstick went on last and she was ready to walk over to Alena's. Santiago had driven the Trans Am over with the presents. Alena wanted to put them all under the tree and take pictures to send to her Dad in England.

Banji giggled. That morning Wishes had arched his back, his fur standing on end while he hissed at Rock 'n Roll Santa. The gyrating music box figure played and moved on its pedestal while Star yipped and hid behind Santiago.

The walk to Alena's added to her already merry mood. She almost skipped through the kitchen door. Being happy was fun. She shut the door and took in the empty kitchen.

"Hey, where is everybody?" A few steps later she passed the dining room table set for six. That was one too many. Voices drifted from the living room and she headed in that direction.

Alena met her at the doorway. "Garth called last night and Madison invited him to dinner. He drove down early this morning. Isn't that great."

The encouraging smile wasn't lost on Banji. "Sounds good to me. We've got plenty of everything." She took in Alena's outfit. "The Merry Texmas t-shirt looks great with those new jeans."

"Come on in and I'll introduce you." Alena tugged on her arm. "Changing the subject won't work on me. I know all your tricks."

Banji looked past Alena. "Where's Santiago?"

"He's helping Gabriel grill the meat." Alena peered toward the patio door. "How was *Papi's* birthday?"

Banji quirked her mouth the side and rolled her eyes. "Before or after his panic attack?"

"What did you do to him? He never panics." Gripping Banji's arm, Alena pulled her to the edge of the room the farthest way from Madison and Garth. "Is he okay?"

Smirking, Banji said, "Ask him. Did he look okay when he got here with the presents?"

"He looked like a kid who just discovered ice cream." Alena released Banji's arm.

"Well, there you have it." Banji grinned. "I've got to go hug on him for a minute. I'll be back."

Alena softly asked, "Since when do you go around hugging him in front of company? He's always been a very private person."

"In case you didn't notice it back in the day, he didn't get much in the way of hugs and kisses. It's long overdue." Banji's brow wrinkled and then she smiled. "Besides you're not company. You're family so it's allowed."

"I recognize the red and gold sequin top, black jeans and gold sandals, but who are you and what have you done with Banji?" Alena giggled softly.

"I'm the new and improved version."

"Fine, whatever. Go check on the meat in case those two have gotten distracted. Gabriel is usually good with grilling but lately he's been getting more involved with the mechanics of racing. If he gets Papi talking about horsepower, the ribs and brisket could go up in smoke."

"I'm on it." Turning, Banji made her way to the patio door. With a wave at Madison, she opened the French-doors and stepped outside.

She spotted Gabriel and Santiago, each with a bottle of beer in hand. So male, so grill-master-ish. She suppressed a snicker, walked over and slipped her arms around Santiago's back right above the waistband of his jeans. "Hey angel, how's dinner coming? Alena wanted me to come check on the two of you." She tightened her hold effectively hugging him. "It sure smells good."

"The ribs are done and the brisket needs a little more time, maybe half an hour. Go in and enjoy the movies. We will come in soon."

She released him and stepped back. "Okay, I'll deliver the news." Retracing her steps brought her back to the living room and the Christmas movie playing on the huge TV mounted on the wall. Garth and Madison were huddled tightly together on the couch watching it. She looked at Alena. "What do you watch on that thing?"

"Gabriel likes football and I like to watch the race reruns." Alena looked over from her spot on the couch. "Do you still have your Gram's stereo? I got a new turntable for the components Gabriel wanted. We could listen to the oldies."

"I have it and all her albums." Banji plopped down next to Alena in the conversation pit by the bookshelves. "You know vinyl is coming back, right?"

"I heard something about that."

Madison added, "I have some old albums I bought at a garage sale. We could play those."

"Great, we'll have a girls-night." Alena laughed and looked pointedly at Banji.

Banji bared her teeth at Alena in an exaggerated smile and grumbled, "I can hardly wait."

Madison clapped her hands and said, "We can watch old beach party movies and play records."

Banji turned her head away and muttered, "I'm going to be sick."

Alena leaned closer. "It'll be okay. It's not like we got to do any of that stuff when we were kids."

Banji sat up straighter and plastered a smile on her face. "So, Garth, when did you decide to join us for dinner?"

He leaned forward and peered around Madison. "I called Madison last night and she invited me. I didn't want to sit around the table with my brother's kids and explain to my Mom why I don't have any of my own. Madison said I could join her here."

"Wow, that's great." Banji gave Alena the side-eye. The vibe coming off Garth was all wrong. An uncomfortable creepy feeling between her shoulder blades was a sign. Her sixth sense was going off like a four-alarm fire.

She caught Alena's eye. "Let's go check the kitchen."

Alena would probably like to have her house back so she and

Gabriel could do whatever they wanted to celebrate the holiday. Those two were like on a perpetual honeymoon or something.

Keeping Madison safe took precedent.

Alena followed her to the kitchen. Banji stopped in front of the professional chef's ovens. "I have a real bad feeling about Garth. It's no coincidence he's turned up conveniently for the holidays after the breakup with Bennett."

Alena looked over her shoulder toward the dining room doorway and back at Banji. "Okay, so what do you want to do about it? It's not like we can drag him to the basement and torture the truth out of him."

"Why not?" Banji crossed her arms over her chest.

"He hasn't done anything but come to dinner." Alena's chin crinkled with her frown.

"I don't want him seeing her house, getting inside." Banji huffed out a breath. "I don't want her alone with him."

Alena nodded. "Okay, I've got an idea." She rubbed the back of her neck. "There are lots of Christmas movies. We'll keep them here until it's time for him to go."

Santiago missed her warmth the second she stepped away.

Gabriel took a long swallow of his beer, lowered the bottle and grinned. "You've really got it bad for that girl."

He could deny it but that wouldn't fool anyone. He could ignore Gabriel but that would only confirm his statement. "Yes." He crossed his arms over his chest. "I am not sorry."

"Hell, no. There's nothing to be sorry about. She's smart, pretty…" he looked at the grill, "can't cook but that's not the end of the world. You've got something good." He turned the brisket over.

Santiago inhaled, shifted his weight and fastened his eyes on Gabriel.

"Alena's been worrying about you." He finished his bottle and stepped over to the patio refrigerator for another one. "She'd like to see you settled down and married."

"Banji has not asked me yet." Santiago dropped his arms to his sides.

"That's doing things backwards but hey, if it works why not? Are you going to accept?" He held out a cold bottle to Santiago. "Here. Merry Christmas."

They popped the caps off, clinked bottles and drank long pulls swallowing half the contents before taking a breath.

Santiago mumbled, "I do not know. I heard her talking to Alena. I think she is waiting until we go to Galveston to ask."

"Damn. Maybe we can go a few days early. You can take her on a few romantic dates and see what happens." Gabriel winked. "Yeah, and go to dinner upstairs at the restaurant on the pier. That's where I proposed to Alena."

"I should wear something better than this." Santiago plucked at the black button-down shirt. He'd worn one of the few dress shirts he owned for their holiday dinner.

"Yeah, we'll go to town and get you something that'll turn all the ladies' heads."

"No. I do not want them. Only my *Carida*."

Gabriel smirked, "Right, only Banji, got it." He flipped the brisket again. "This is almost done. Grab the platter and let's load up the meat. It's time to eat."

Santiago sat through dinner quietly watching and counting the minutes until he could take Banji home. There was so much he didn't know about making love and the slow burn of the passion they'd ignited earlier was eating him alive. He caught the knowing look Gabriel leveled at him and the questioning look from Alena.

Hoping to hurry things along, he helped carry their dinner dishes to the kitchen making room on the table for coffee and dessert. He carefully stacked the plates next to the sink.

Alena stepped up next to him. "You look different today, happier, maybe even a little younger which is odd considering you're a year older."

"I am happy." He studied the dishes and waited for the second part of the question. He knew the drill. Alena always started snooping with something positive to start the conversation.

"You don't have to say that if it isn't true. You can tell me. You don't have to stay in the relationship if you're not comfortable. You're not going through that again."

"Everything is good."

"Then what's the problem? You keep looking at the door."

He exhaled slowly. "I want to go home."

"Okay." A smirk slowly spread across her face. "Sounds like you've been bitten by the love-bug."

"Nothing has bitten me." He looked at her as his brow wrinkled.

"It's a saying. I'm assuming you and Banji had a very good time celebrating your birthday last night."

"Yes, we had Moscato wine." His knowing smile hidden under his moustache.

"It must have been really amazing wine. I'll have to get the brand from Banji." She reached for the full coffee pot. "Let's get dessert behind us so you can go home and take a nap. I hear old men get tired and need lots of naps." She snickered and walked away with the coffee.

Alena wrapped her arm around Gabriel and leaned against his side "It's good to see *Papi* so happy."

"About time. He deserves this." Gabriel rested his arm across Alena's shoulders and his hand curled around her upper arm. "We need to go to Galveston a couple days earlier than planned." He kissed the top of her head. "We need time to go on some dates."

"Is that what you two were talking about over the grill?"

"Yeah, he's leaning toward getting engaged and that's the best place for setting the mood."

Alena smiled up at him. "Yes, it is." She turned and pressed herself close to him. "I think it's a good time for a nap."

"I don't need a nap." He looked down at her, his breath hitched and his eyes widened. "Do I?"

She winked. "You absolutely do." She let go of his side and took his hand. "You worked so hard on fixing dinner, you really should rest."

"You're right."

"Set the movies up for Madison and Garth. We'll give them some alone time but then we need to keep an eye on things. Banji doesn't trust him."

"She might be right. There's something off about the guy." Gabriel hugged Alena. "Go get things ready for our nap."

CHAPTER THIRTY-FOUR

THE MORNING after the New Year's party, Banji stood in the driveway and waved goodbye as Santiago and Alena pulled out in Gabriel's truck. The New Year's Day race was more for the fans than anything else. The trailer with the car and supplies had left at the first crack of dawn before the vampires had time to make it to their coffins.

She strolled back through the kitchen, grabbed a cup of coffee and carried it to the back porch where she made herself comfortable in their swing. He knew how to make her smile even on the worst days. Her thoughts were interrupted by her phone ringing. Banji looked at the screen and muttered, "What now?" She swiped to answer. "Morning, what's up?"

Madison giggled and chirped, "He asked me to marry him."

He must be Garth. "Well, that's kind of fast isn't it?"

"Not really. We did go steady our junior and senior years. I'm so excited."

"Great. I'm happy for you." She twisted a strand of hair around her fingers. "So, does he still make you feel all tingly when he kisses you?"

"Yes, it's even better than before. He wants to move in here and open a small law office in town."

"Talk about wonderful. It's almost too good to be true."

"I know, but it's got to be fate or the stars. Right?"

"That must be it." Banji left off, *like the ones floating around in your dream world.* "Just be careful. Things aren't always what they seem."

"He's going to put the announcement in the paper."

Banji didn't like the sound of that. "Don't let him push you into anything. Take your time."

"I will. We're going shopping for my engagement ring next week."

"Try the stores here. Don't go to the city. You don't want to run into your Dad." Banji could feel the trap waiting to snap shut.

"Oh, you're right. I hadn't thought of that. I'll tell Garth to come here."

"I can go with you to make sure you're getting a good deal. We can meet him in Carmel." That would keep Garth from getting her in the car and driving her back to San Francisco.

"Thanks, I'll call you back after I talk to him."

Banji disconnected, put her phone down, and picked up her coffee. She stared at the brown liquid. If she added Kahlúa she'd fall asleep and miss her opportunity to go to the races. She looked out at the ocean and sipped the hot brew. She had her own dream world to worry about.

A couple of hours later, she maxed out the speedometer on Gram's Trans Am. The thought made Banji giggle. Mischief was her middle name. Yep, Banji Aloysius Mischief Cordova had a certain ring to it. She was still working on the Cordova part, but it was definitely looking hopeful.

It wasn't that far to Long Beach and she could watch the New Year's exhibition race from the stands. Santiago and Alena would be down in the pit with the crew. She didn't understand racing, all the points and terminology but she did get the part where the first car over the finish line was the winner.

She parked and followed the people walking toward the entrance. How hard could it be to buy a ticket and go sit down? Southern California could have warm days in the winter. The sun beating down on the bleachers radiated up through her jeans. She jumped up and glared down at the offending bleacher. There was nothing to do but put the program magazine down and sit on it.

Without the itinerary she didn't know who was in the race. She'd primarily gotten it for the ads. Seeing what the competition was doing fell under the heading of research for her designing accessories and posters for Betmunn Racing. She'd have to take the program home and study it later. At least she'd be able to say something relevant about the other entries over lunch tomorrow. She peered down at the track. She couldn't see a damn thing.

She pulled her Bushnell mini-binoculars out of her purse and raised them to her eyes. Much better. Or not! Who was that woman staring up at Santiago like he was a Roman god? She fished her phone out of her purse and watched him lean away from the woman dressed like she was a winning horse at the Kentucky Derby. When she patted his chest, Banji damn near levitated off the bleachers. She breathed a small sigh of relief when he didn't look impressed and moved out of arms reach.

Alena was only a phone call away, but then they'd all know she was there. Hmm, not part of the plan. She dropped the phone back into her purse.

Banji shifted on the metal bleacher and made a mental note to bring a stadium cushion if she ever did this again. She took in the crowd and the size of the track. It was a lot bigger than she'd expected. She exhaled and resigned herself to being civilized.

She reached down and dug her sketch pad and colored pencils out of her tote bag. She didn't want to paint but the temptation to draw had been teasing her fingers ever since Alena had mentioned it weeks ago.

She stowed her sky-blue tote under the bench seat between her legs. Planted at the end of a row, her right elbow had open space in the stairway to move without knocking into another spectator.

It took some shifting and wiggling to find a way to sit without being miserable. She wouldn't do this for anyone but Santiago. For him she'd suffer, at least long enough to figure out what all the fuss was about.

Finally, the cars rolled out onto the track and took their positions. Betmunn's car was in the fourth position from the pole. She didn't have a clue what it meant, only that Alena and Santiago weren't thrilled but they were satisfied with it. At the green light the engines roared and whined, tires smoked and Banji cringed. Round and round the cars went. She would have liked to lean forward but it wasn't possible since the row in front of her was jam-packed. Standing up might be iffy. Her legs had gone numb after the third lap. She'd had enough. She packed up her supplies being careful not to bump into anyone.

She stepped out into the aisle and took a few slow and careful steps until the feeling in her legs fully returned and she could confidently make her way down the stairs and out to the parking lot. She sank into the Trans Am's bucket seat grateful for the molded foam support. It would be a fast ride home. She needed a good long soak in a hot bubble bath to ease the aches and pains she'd acquired in her lower back from being perched on the bleachers from Hell.

She made the turn-off onto the two-lane highway along the coast. She needed to get a grip and face facts. Santiago's passion in life was racing engines and hers was…what? Antique jewelry, art, gemology, pirate treasures? He had become a man too soon in life and she still needed to get her act together.

Banji parked, trudged into the house, and dropped her tote on the kitchen table. Star came trotting in from the living room with his tail wagging. He stopped by the back door. She got the hint. "Okay, you've been good and I'll take you for a quick walk."

She clipped on his leash and opened the door. Evening was coming on fast and the air was cool. Star didn't take long to squat and pee. He was still a puppy and lifting his leg would come with time according to Santiago. She had so much to learn. There must be times when he wondered what planet she was from or what rock she'd been living under that she didn't know such simple things. But he would laugh, hug her, kiss her and go on like everything was fine.

She walked Star back to the cottage where she proceeded to put the leash back on its hook, meander to the living room and gracelessly flop onto the couch. Wishes jumped up on the cushion next to her and curled up for a nap. Star stretched out on the floor next to her feet. It was good to be home. She toed off her shoes, leaned over onto the cushy decorator pillows, curled her legs around Wishes and closed her eyes. A quick nap and she'd be good to take a bath and fix dinner.

Santiago walked in and noticed Banji's tote lying on the kitchen table. Star wandered in from the living room and stood looking up at him. He pulled out the nearest chair and sat down. He petted Star with one hand, picked up the loose pencils on the table and placed them back in the tote.

From the look of it, his *Carida* had been busy drawing. Perhaps she had gone down to the beach. He peeked inside the bag. Her sketch pad was there. His curiosity got the better of him and he pulled it out and opened it. What in the world? When had she been to the race track? He put it back and carried the tote to the living room.

Ah, she was asleep. He put the tote on the floor at the end of the couch and sat down. Wishes raised his head and yawned. "Time to wake up." He reached over and picked up the kitten. "You are growing. I think you have had a good nap."

Banji groaned and stretched her legs, her feet pushing against his thigh. "When did you get home? What time is it?"

"We just got in." He put Wishes down and wrapped his big hands around her ankles, massaged them and moved on to her feet. "Are you hungry? I will fix you some dinner."

"I'm okay. What about you?" She stifled a yawn.

"We ate on the way home." His hands moved up her leg.

"You look tired and dirty." She snickered, "I think a bubble bath would help you relax. I'll go fix it for you."

"It is not necessary."

"I think it is." She sat up. "Take off those grimy clothes and meet me in the bathroom. We could both use a good soak."

He sat back and watched her walk away. His *Carida* was going to give him a bath. She'd mentioned it a long time ago. He'd half-heartedly hoped she'd forget about it.

He was a grown man; he did not need to be given a bath. He was capable of doing it himself and a shower would be fine.

He wandered down the hall to the bathroom and stopped dead in his tracks. "What is all this?" She was naked and standing next to the tub. The overhead lights were off and candles burned in holders on the counter releasing their fragrance into the room.

She leaned over and placed her hand under the running water. "We're taking a bath together."

"No."

"Yes." She sprinkled bath beads into the water.

"I cannot." He stepped back.

"Why not?" Her forehead wrinkled.

"I have never done this." His hand gripped the doorjamb.

"Well, there's a first time for everything." She nodded her head up and down aimed at him. "Get the clothes off." She smiled. "Or do you want me to help you?" She winked.

"No."

"No, what? I've undressed you before. I've seen you naked. What's the problem?" She shut off the water and padded barefoot over to him. Resting a hand on his chest, she captured his gaze with hers. "Tell me what's wrong."

"To care for someone like this is very personal. I do these things for myself. It is too much to ask."

"You're not asking. I'm offering. We're together. We've done way more personal things than this. Is there something I'm missing?"

He sucked in a deep breath. "The bathroom is a private place. Carmen would never allow me in there with her. Even at the end she would only let the home care aide help her with personal care."

"This is our house and I'm not Carmen. In this bathroom, you are allowed to get naked and take a bath or a shower with me. Our house, our rules."

The scent of vanilla teased his senses. The steam rising from the white bubbles enticed him. His *Carida* offering him something no one else ever had was his undoing.

"Okay, I will do this." He stared at the bathtub. He couldn't bring himself to unbutton his shirt. "Only for you."

"Thank you." She stretched up, tugged him down and pressed her lips to his while she divested him of his Betmunn Racing shirt.

Another soft, slow kiss and his restraint crumbled. When their kiss ended, her fingers found their way to his belt buckle, the button behind it, and the zipper below.

"*Carida*, I may disappoint you." He stumbled out of the pants and briefs pooled around his feet.

"You won't. I promise." She took his hand and led him the few short steps from the doorway to the tub.

Banji could lead him naked into the fires of Hell and he'd go willingly. He didn't understand the power she had over him. It had never been like this before. Everything was different with her.

Banji couldn't wait to see him up to his neck in bubbles. Gram's oversized, cast-iron claw-footed bathtub was a relic of days gone by. It had been resurfaced with fresh porcelain, repainted and the brass faucets replaced with shiny new ones. Santiago would be able to lean back and recline like a man of leisure.

She stood next to the tub wearing nothing but a smile. "Get in before the water gets cold."

He stepped forward and stopped. "Turn around, do not look."

Banji giggled and turned around. "Okay, it's safe to get in the tub now." She heard the water splash. "Can I turn around yet?"

"Yes."

She turned and stifled a laugh. Only his head and knees stuck out over the white foamy bubbles and his hair floated along the tops of his shoulders. "Oh, I love your knees, so sexy."

He moved and his knees disappeared as his shoulders rose from the suds.

"Hold still while I get in." She inched closer to the edge of the tub. Noticing his deer-in-the-headlights look, she asked, "Are you ready?"

The look on his face was pitiful and it tugged at her conscience. "If we were in bed and I wanted to be on top, you'd be okay with it, right?"

"Yes."

"Okay, this is the same thing; only instead of laying on top of the mattress we're in a nice warm tub of water with silky soft suds to moisturize our skin." She gave him her most reassuring smile. "I'm getting a little cold out here. Can I get in there with you where it's nice and warm?"

"Yes." He nodded once slowly and put his hands on the rim like he was holding on for dear life. "I am ready."

Banji leaned over, grasped the edge of the tub, and stepped in straddling his thighs. She slowly lowered herself into the water being careful not to press her knees too tightly into the sides of his legs. The very last thing she needed was to hurt him.

Leaning forward, she cupped the water and suds in her hands and poured the warm liquid over her shoulders and breasts. Her hands scooped up more suds and rubbed them over her midriff before moving to his upper arms and shoulders.

The apex of her thighs slid slowly over his erection which separated her folds and slipped over her clit. The tantalizing friction elicited a muffled groan from Santiago and a quivering moan from Banji.

She stretched back exposing the full length of her neck, thrust her chest forward and sighed. "Hmm, does that feel good?"

His thumbs brushed across her nipples tempting her to sink into his touch. "*Sí, Carida*, yes, it is wonderful. I did not know it could feel like this."

Banji spread the creamy smooth suds over his shoulders and wrapped her hands around the back of his neck. "I got us the best foaming bath. It makes everything nice and slippery." Tucked securely in her cleft, his erection twitched and grew harder. She asked, "Would you like me to show you how easy it is for me to take you deep inside?" She rose up enough to slip back and forth over his cock.

"I can come like this." He looked away.

"Stop doing that and look at me. I'm here for you." Her fingers pressed his jaw and his head slowly turned in her direction bringing them face to face. "Tell me what you want."

His eyes were open and unguarded when they met hers. "I want us to be together always."

She rested her forehead against his. "I want that, too."

She reached under the bubbles, positioned the head of his cock at her entrance, relaxed and eased down on his length. He slid smooth as velvet inside of her and he didn't disappoint as he found a rhythm that matched hers. The exquisite sensations he generated quickly pushed her toward her climax. She held out as his built.

When he braced his feet against the end of the tub and tensed his thighs, she knew he was on the verge. He groaned loudly, threw his head back, and gripped the rim until his knuckles turned white. She felt him swell and pulse as the cum pumped out of him and flooded her core.

The warm rush of fluid and the last brush of her clit over his base triggered her release. The intense uncontrollable tingle set off a chain reaction beginning with her inner muscles clamping down tight on his shaft, her thighs tightening their grip on his hips and finally the current racing down her legs to her toes. Her wailing echoed off the walls.

Santiago's arms wrapped around her and crushed her to his heaving chest as he struggled to breathe. He stammered, "*Carida.*"

Santiago struggled to slow his breathing. At times it felt like his body was tearing itself apart. He yearned for release and feared it might kill him at the same time. When the telltale tingle started at the base of his spine, he knew the end was inevitable. He'd spill his heart and soul into his *Carida* along with his sperm. He was a man and he wanted his woman, he wanted to be a father and have a house full of children. And he had no idea how he was going to tell that to Banji.

"*Carida*, we did not use protection." It was a place to begin the conversation. If she drowned him in her grandmother's bathtub, it would be what he deserved.

Her head rested on his shoulder and she mumbled, "It's okay unless you don't want kids. Then we're going to have to figure something out. I don't want to take pills."

A slow grin materialized under his moustache. "I want many children with you."

Her eyes popped wide open. What? "How about one or maybe two?"

"Okay." His lips curled up in a satisfied grin. It was a start.

CHAPTER THIRTY-FIVE

A MONTH LATER, Banji sat poolside with Alena enjoying the sun. They were still talking about her first day at the races. It had not been one of Banji's finest moments. Splashing in a sea of bubbles with Santiago had been the best part of the adventure and worth the misery of being hot and cramped.

They stopped laughing when they spotted Lloyd Preston and his wife, Leanne, walking across the patio toward them. They were still a nice-looking couple. Both medium height, slender, well dressed in a California casual sort of way.

Banji ground her back teeth and stopped short of cracking a molar.

Alena uttered, "Stay calm. Let's see what they want before you start a war."

The intruders stopped at the edge of the wooden patio table. Mr. Preston aimed a curt nod at Alena and said, "Banji, we need to talk."

"What are you doing here? This is private property." She glanced from Lloyd to Leanne.

He looked at Alena, "I'm sorry for the intrusion, but it is important. If you'll give me a few minutes to talk with Banji we'll pick up Madison and go. We don't want any trouble."

Banji snapped, "You're not taking Madison anywhere. You can turn around and leave the way you came."

"You owe me. You lived in my house. I bought you a car. If you hadn't screwed up the Flood's appraisal, I wouldn't have to ask you for enough money to pay the mortgage."

"You got my mother's money. That should more than pay for my room and board." Banji tossed her hair over her shoulder.

"We're going to lose the money we spent on Madison's wedding. If you hadn't interfered, everything would have gone ahead on schedule. You owe me."

She drew circles on the tabletop with her index fingertip. "I didn't interfere in anything. Bennett screwed it up all on his own. Go ask him for some money."

"Her boyfriend from high-school has stepped up. Garth isn't anything to brag about, but he's available and a partner in a moderately successful law firm." Mr. Preston inched around to the side of the table into the shade cast by the pergola.

All the dominoes were falling into place. Banji wanted to scream but she tamped it down and asked, "How do you know about Garth?"

"His father called me."

"He called you or you called him?" Banji tipped her head and raised an eyebrow.

"That's not important. He was happy to hear the news and wanted to talk about the wedding plans. He's allergic to shell fish." Lloyd shoved his hands into his front pockets and his upper lip curled into a smirk.

Banji's fingers stilled, she grinned and mentioned, "I love shrimp." Her eyes narrowed and a severe frown took over. "Sorry, can't help you."

"You can get it from your trust." His whining nasal tone filtered through.

The sound irritated her eardrums and grated on her last nerve along with the fact that he knew about Gram's trust. That was none of his business.

"Gram was my mother's mother. I will not give you a single penny of hers."

"I'm broke because of you."

"You're broke because you're a lousy businessman. You squandered the money Grandpa Bancroft gave you on bad investments, cars, and trips." She left off the part about the money Ellis Bancroft paid to get rid of Ritter. The investigator was still trying to connect it to Lloyd.

Lloyd regarded Leanne, dropped his gaze to the ground at his feet and turned back to Banji. "I did what I had to do, what my family needed to survive. I'm trying to save our home."

Banji snarled, "It's not my home. You might be able to claim you're my evil-step-father but you're not my father."

He shifted his weight from one side to the other. "Your mother and I were married when you were born."

"Ritter Davis was my father, not you."

His eyes widened momentarily then returned to their cold stare. "Your mother and I had an agreement. You were never supposed to find out about him."

"Well, I did find out."

Mr. Preston squared his shoulders. "I'll disown you."

"That threat is getting a little old. Especially since you're not my father. Go ahead. I don't want anything from you." Banji stood up casting a shadow across Lloyd Preston.

Alena's head turned to Mr. Preston. "My legal team will be assisting Banji with any legal matters. You can have your attorney's contact them through the main switchboard or mail."

Leanne moved into Banji's path. "You need to see reason. Madison still believes you're her sister; it won't hurt you to pretend a little longer."

Banji stared directly into Leanne's eyes. "Give me my mother's diamond and ruby earrings and I won't tell Madison all the family secrets."

"I don't have them." Leanne looked at Lloyd. "Tell her."

He ran his hand over the top of his head smoothing his thinning mousey-brown hair. "I sold them to catch up the car payments."

Banji shouldered her way past Leanne. "That's too bad. Guess we have nothing left to talk about."

Leanne reached out and grabbed her forearm. "You need to help your sister. It's the least you can do."

"Let go of me." Banji jerked her arm free and watched Leanne lose

236

her balance, stumble sideways, and plunge into the sparkling turquoise pool. "She's not my sister. We barely know each other. You made sure of that."

Behind her, Alena said, "Uh, let me get you a towel Missus Preston."

Leanne flailed, surfaced and gasped for air. Glaring at Banji, she yelled, "My hair is ruined." She got her feet under her and stood up, which put her chest deep in the water. "You wrecked everything." She sloshed her way through the water to the steps while swiping at the water running down her face. "You're a selfish, spoiled brat."

"Go back to the city and leave Madison alone. She's doing fine without you."

Alena grabbed two sunny-yellow, fluffy towels off the nearest lounge chair and wrapped one around Leanne's shoulders. "There, that will help and here's one to put on the car seat." She shoved a folded towel into Leanne's hands and watched her pat at the water running down her face. "Drive safe."

Lloyd stared at his wife and then turned to Banji. "You remind me of your mother." He put his arm around Leanne's shoulders and steered her toward the path leading to the driveway. Looking over his shoulder he said, "Too bad you didn't drown with her."

Alena grabbed Banji's upper arm and held on tight. Keeping her eyes on Lloyd and Leanne, she said, "If you're not gone in five minutes, I'll have you arrested for trespassing."

"We're leaving." They walked slowly up the path with Lloyd supporting a wobbly Leanne.

Alena let go of Banji's arm and laughed, "It's hard to walk in wet shoes. Your feet keep slipping around on the inside."

"Not my problem." Banji rubbed her arm.

"I was afraid you were going to attack Lloyd and end up in jail. I don't want to have to deal with that, ever. Got it?"

"Yeah." Their eyes met. "My arm is going to have bruises thanks to you." Banji glanced at the reddened area on her upper arm. "You really have a gorilla grip going on girlfriend."

"Better bruises than handcuffs." Alena snickered.

That evening sitting on the swing after dinner, Santiago pulled Banji onto his lap. "I heard you pushed your stepmother into the swimming pool." He raised an eyebrow.

"I did not. She tripped." Banji flipped her hair back over her shoulder.

He admonished, "*Carida*?"

"Well, she did. Right over the toe of my gold Gucci sandals."

"Still, it was not necessary."

"Says who? She's lucky I couldn't fling her and Lloyd into Dante's inferno where they belong."

"Leave her to fate." He planted a kiss on her pouting lips. "We have each other. They have what they deserve."

"Well, as long as I have you, I'm good." She kissed him soft and slow, taking her time.

Santiago let go of her hand, enfolded her in his arms and hugged her snuggly to his chest. He whispered in her ear, "I think we are very good together."

"I'm sure of it." She wrapped her arms around him as far as she could reach and squeezed him back. "Alena and I are taking Madison shopping for a wedding dress tomorrow. She still thinks she's marrying Garth."

"She will like that." Her kiss lingered on his lips, his hands slipped under her shirt and glided over her skin. "You go and have fun."

Alena, Banji, and Madison stood in the center of the best wedding shop in Carmel and stared at each other. Madison said, "You're my sister so you need to stand next to me and Alena can stand next to you." She beamed a satisfied smile at them.

Banji chewed on her bottom lip. "You really should ask one of your girlfriends."

Madison made a pouty face. "But it's not the same thing."

"It's close enough." Banji pulled a dress off the rack and studied it front and back. "Here." She held it out to Madison.

Madison sniveled, "I don't have any friends since I broke up with Bennett." She looked at the dress and said, "You can be in my wedding and I'll be in yours someday."

The sales clerk stepped in and took it. "I'll put this in the dressing room and go see if we have some others in similar styles in the back."

"You can't be in my wedding," Banji mumbled softly and watched Alena snap her mouth shut like she had lock jaw.

Tears pooled in Madison's eyes. "If Alena is giving the groom away, I should be able to give my sister away. It's going to be the first wedding at the Nautilus Pearl Chapel." She pointed at Banji. "You can't stand there all alone waiting for them to walk up the aisle."

Banji prayed for patience and kept her tone even. "You can't give me away."

"Why not?" Madison whined adding emphasis to her pout.

"Because you're not my sister!" came out harsher than she'd intended.

"Oh, shit." Alena slapped her hand over her mouth. She lowered it and said, "This isn't the best time to discuss that. How about we go to lunch when we're done here and talk about it?"

Madison ignored the offer and insisted, "I'm your half-sister. That counts. I want to be there when you marry Santiago. We're family." She stomped her little foot on the soft carpet which made absolutely no sound at all.

"No, we're not." Banji looked quickly around the store and caught sight of the clerk standing in the doorway to the back room holding a dress for Madison to try on and lowered her voice. "Damn." She turned her gaze on Madison. "Truth is, Lloyd Preston is not my father. Listen to me. We're not related."

Madison sniffled loudly. "I don't care. You've always been my big-sister. I can't leave you standing there in front of all those people alone. It's not right."

Banji turned desperate eyes on Alena. "Don't just stand there like the statue of Horus, do something. Explain it to her."

The side of Alena's mouth quirked upward. "Well, she does have a point."

"I've been alone my whole life. Why should this be any different?"

Alena shrugged. "Because it's the only wedding you're ever going to have. We're your family and we want it to be perfect."

"You are absolutely no help at all." Banji exhaled loudly. "Can we get on with finding a dress for Madison? Santiago hasn't agreed to marry me. Until he does there's nothing to discuss."

"Did you ask him? He hasn't said anything to me."

"No, I haven't asked him. I told you I'm planning to do that when we get to Galveston. Don't be screwing up my plans."

Madison flopped onto the tiny love seat next to the lighted triple-paneled mirror and gathered her coat and purse into a pile on her lap. "Mom called to talk about the wedding. She made it sound like another one of Dad's schemes. I told her to forget it. I'm not getting married."

Banji jammed her hands on her hips and glared at Madison. "Why in God's name are we in this store looking at wedding dresses?"

"Because I thought we might find a beautiful dress for you." Madison sniffled, dug in her purse and pulled out a tissue. She dabbed at her eyes. "You always get the prettiest clothes. Maybe I can borrow it."

Alena and Banji exchanged glances and turned their attention to Madison.

Banji huffed out an exasperated breath and muttered, "Stop that sniveling. It'll make your eyes red and puffy. We can't go to lunch with you looking like a space alien."

"I'm sorry." Madison hiccupped and rubbed the tissue under her nose.

"It's going to be okay." Alena sat down next to Madison and patted her shoulder. "Why don't you tell us what happened. It might not be as bad as you think." She shot a warning glare at Banji.

"Right. It might be a misunderstanding of some sort." Banji grabbed another dress off the rack and waved the sales lady over. "This dress is gorgeous. You should try it on. We're already here."

"I don't want to be a bargaining chip in some business deal." She swiped the tissue across her cheek. "I'm so stupid. I thought Garth really loved me."

Alena patted Madison's shoulder. "You're not stupid. Your Dad might be taking advantage of the situation. You need to talk to Garth before you make any hasty decisions. Go try on those dresses so we know what's a good fit and style for you. I'll hold your things while you're changing."

They watched Madison meander into the fitting room and close the door.

They turned to each other and Alena hissed, "What in the hell is wrong with Lloyd? Madison just got over the drama with Bennett."

"He's always looking for an angle that will benefit him." Banji tipped her head back and stared at the ceiling. "He never quits interfering. He has to have everything his way." She snapped her attention to Madison's purse laying on the love seat. "Give me her purse. I'm going to call Garth while she's in the dressing room."

"How exactly do you plan to do that?"

"It's easy. She always uses her birthday for everything." Banji dug around and pulled out the new phone. She glanced at the dressing room door. "Go find another dress for her to try on and keep her busy in there."

Alena got up, scurried over to the rack on the opposite wall, picked through the dresses, grabbed two and carried them over the dressing room. "Madison, I found a couple more that might work. Try these." She opened the door wide enough to shove the voluminous dresses inside. Once the door was securely shut she returned to Banji's side and peered at the phone's screen.

After pressing a few symbols, Banji muttered, "Bingo. Got it." She grinned at Alena and poked two more icons. "Hello, Garth. This is Banji. What's the deal with Lloyd?"

Alena leaned in close and Banji tilted the phone so they could both listen.

He gasped. "Excuse me. I'm not sure what you're talking about."

"I heard you have a business arrangement with Lloyd that includes marrying Madison."

"It wasn't my idea but the bottom line is, you heard right."

"Well, Madison has figured it out and the wedding is off." Banji glanced at the dressing room door. "I think you owe Madison an apology."   v

"I'll take care of it." He cleared his throat. "I'm at work. I have to go. I'll call Madison tonight."

Banji grunted. "Good, you do that."

She disconnected the call, deleted it from the recent list and shoved the phone back in Madison's purse.

At the sound of the dressing room door clicking open, Alena and Banji turned simultaneously.

Madison stepped into the center of the room and twirled. "Isn't it beautiful?"

Banji stammered, "You look like the champagne pink version of Belle's ball gown."

"I know." She twirled again. "I love it."

Alena smiled and softly sighed. "It's perfect for a garden wedding in the spring."

"I'll buy it as soon as I find someone to marry." She started to tear up.

Banji hurried forward and took Madison by the shoulder. "Go change and don't worry. I'm sure everything is going to work out. I'll read your cards tonight. I bet there's something wonderful ahead for you."

With Madison tucked away in the dressing room, Banji turned to Alena. "Madison's not giving me away. I already texted and emailed Zala to stand up with me since you're with Santiago. She's in Greece. She found the *Raikou* in Yerakini. She's bringing it home and Chiffon is captaining *Caligirl*. They're on their way to Galveston.

"You can let Madison be like a bridesmaid. That wouldn't be the end of the world." Alena glanced toward the dressing room. "She wants to be your sister and part of our family."

Banji's forehead worry lines relaxed. "Okay, but you're in charge of keeping her out of Lulu's way. I don't want her pissing off Cami's friend. We need to play nice with the Russians."

"That's not a problem. But you owe me. I want to meet this Zala person."

Banji smirked, "I'd think twice about that if I were you."

CHAPTER THIRTY-SIX

BANJI PRAYED for deliverance from Madison's tearful break up from Garth which took the rest of January and most of February. The only thing keeping Banji from duct taping Madison's mouth shut was Santiago. She'd even offered to use the pretty patterned tape, but no. He was adamant that Madison only needed to talk it out and time would heal the hurt.

By the time March blew in, the waterworks had stopped and they were on the road to Galveston. It was a long, long road with Madison switching back and forth between the Trans Am and Gabriel's truck at every rest stop.

Banji sat across the diner's table from Madison while she chattered on about the great marketing plan she'd launched for Betmunn racing team's participation in the opening races at the resort.

She zoned out and refocused when Madison announced, "I can't wait to see the new resort in Galveston."

"We're almost there." Banji rolled her eyes. "Only three-hundred miles to go."

Alena bumped Gabriel's shoulder with hers. "We'll be in Galveston tonight."

He looked at her and smiled. "We'll check in at the resort, but we're spending the night at our special hotel. I've gotten us a room for two nights." He leaned closer so he could whisper in her ear. "I want to get shipwrecked with you."

She squeezed his thigh. "It's a pirate's moon tonight. We can go walking in the surf."

Madison sighed loudly. "Moonlight walks on the beach are so romantic."

"You live on the beach. You can go walking in the moonlight anytime." Banji eyed Madison. "But a tropical beach would be different. Something with palm trees."

Madison giggled. "Somewhere in the Caribbean would be perfect."

Banji tried not to wince. "Lots of islands to choose from, lots of beaches to walk on, you might stub your toe and find a lost treasure."

"Do you really think I could?" Madison's face lit up. "That would be so much fun."

Banji wanted to bang her head on the table. Instead, she said, "You never know until you try."

After lunch they got back in their vehicles. Madison climbed in the truck with Alena and Gabriel. Banji rode shotgun with Santiago behind the wheel of the Trans Am. Staring out the passenger window at the scenery brought back memories. Gram had let her drive on the open stretches.

She looked over at Santiago who held the steering wheel with both hands. "Gram let me drive this piece of road on our trip. Miles of nothing but cactus for me to run over." She snickered. "Fooled her. I loved driving this car. No way was I going to wreck it. Thank you for restoring it."

"It was my pleasure, *Carida*." He glanced her way. "I am glad it makes you happy."

"You make me happy." She reached over and placed her hand on his thigh. "I'm glad we're going to have a few extra days to look around the island. I'm sure it's changed over the years but there was something welcoming about it back then. For the first time in my life I felt free. I could breathe. I'm curious if it will still feel the same."

Santiago's eyes stayed focused on the road. "Alena and I will be timing test runs on the track getting ready for the race, but you and Madison can go sightseeing."

"Yeah, I'll take her around to the tourist places. She'll like that." Banji squeezed his thigh. "Be sure you save some energy for the evenings. We can go to dinner on the seawall. There's a place on the pier that Alena says is very good."

Santiago grinned. "Gabriel told me about it. We will go."

Banji ignored the niggling feeling that he was being entirely too cooperative. She checked her watch. "We're making good time. We'll get there in time for dinner."

Once the Trans Am was unloaded, she was getting something to eat and then going to Sahara's house. Cami would meet her there and entertain Madison while Banji worked on translating the diary. There was no time to waste when it came to the curse.

While Santiago worked at the track she'd be getting the final fittings for her wedding dress. And somewhere in all that, Santiago had to hold the locket and they had to get their marriage license.

Banji texted Cami, *We're on schedule. Can Sahara have the locket at her house this evening? I'll bring Santiago with me."*

Cami: *She'll ask Misha to bring it over after he closes his shop."*

After dinner, Banji stood next to the Trans Am and stared at Santiago over the roof. "I'm going to Sahara's to translate the pirate's diary. This is your chance to see the locket and hold it."

"You should have told me sooner. I should not meet those people looking like this." He shoved his hands into the front pockets of his faded, worn thin jeans.

"You look fine. They understand we've been on the road all day. Get in the car. I have the directions. All you have to do is sit while I do the driving."

"I can put the address in my phone. It will give us directions."

"No. I don't want to listen to that animated voice mispronouncing the Texas street names. It doesn't speak Texan."

Madison opened the driver's door, flipped the front seat forward and climbed in the back seat. It was a small space, even for her. She settled in, tidied her clothes and giggled. "Okay, I'm ready."

Banji planted her hands on her hips. "It's time to go. Misha is bringing the locket for you."

Santiago exhaled loudly and grunted, "Okay." He got in on the passenger side and pulled the door shut. "I should drive."

"Not tonight. You already did enough for one day." She started the car and pulled out of the resort parking lot. "It shouldn't take us long to get there."

Madison prattled away in the backseat while Santiago held on to the shoulder strap of his seatbelt like it was a life preserver. Banji considered putting them both out at the next stop light to get some peace and quiet.

Madison piped up again, "Alena says Sahara's husband has a daughter and she's a tug boat captain. Do you think she'd take me out on her boat so I can see what she does?"

Banji unlocked her jaw to speak. "I think she'll throw you overboard if you get in the way." Banji snuck a peak at Madison in the rearview mirror. She looked disappointed. Damn. "Lulu's husband is a captain, too. Maybe he'll let you go with his crew. You can take your chances with the Russians."

The pout that sprouted on Madison's face was classic. "I don't speak Russian." Her lower lip trembled. "They won't know what I'm saying and I won't understand them either."

"That might not be a bad thing." Banji stifled a snicker. "I can see some advantages to it. I'm going to ask Sahara's husband, Boris, to take you out tomorrow for the day." She gave Santiago a sideways glance. "You don't get seasick, do you?"

"I don't know. I've never been on a boat before."

"Well, there's a first time for everything." Banji smiled all the way to Sahara's house. She was still grinning when she got out of the Trans Am and walked up to the front door followed by Madison with Santiago bringing up the rear.

Banji pressed the doorbell and waited. She had no idea what Sahara looked like, but she suspected the lady was pretty and smart. Smart enough to find lost treasures, strong enough to dive to the ocean floors, brave enough to snoop in old wrecks and crazy enough to marry Boris Rustov.

The door opened and her guess had been correct. The slender built young woman with her sun-streaked hair and blue eyes could easily catch a man's eye. She said, "Hi! You must be Banji. Cami said you were bringing your sister and your boyfriend." She looked past Banji. "I'm Sahara."

Madison waved with one hand and said, "Madison."

"This is Santiago." Banji took his hand and pulled him forward.

An amused smile graced Sahara's face. "Come on in. Cami can't make it. She has to get her son to bed." She stepped back making space for them to pass her in the small entry way and move into the living room. "I cleared off the kitchen table so we can open the diary and have room to take notes."

Banji followed Sahara to the kitchen. "Madison and Santiago came along to see the locket. He's worried about the curse."

"Great. Misha will be here in about a half-hour. He has to lock up his boat repair shop." She looked at Madison and Santiago. "You're welcome to sit in the living room and watch TV until he gets here. My husband is putting our son to bed. He likes to sit and read to him till he falls asleep."

Banji turned to Madison. "We need to be quiet."

Nodding repeatedly, Madison whispered, "I won't make any noise. I promise."

"And don't hit anybody with your purse." Banji smirked.

Madison whined, "I said I was sorry."

Chuckling, Sahara said, "Let's all have a seat." She looked around at her guests. "Can I get anyone some water or iced tea before we start?"

Madison lowered her voice to just above a whisper. "Nothing for me, thanks. I want to know what the diary says. I don't want to risk spilling anything on it."

Santiago looked toward the living room. "Nothing for me. I will sit in the other room and wait for Misha."

"Okay, well let's get started."

The ladies took seats around the kitchen table and Sahara opened the diary. "All right, here we go." She pushed the faded tome toward Banji. "Give it your best shot."

Halfway through Sahara got up, got a paper towel and handed it to Madison who had totally destroyed her tissue purse-pack with non-stop crying and wiping her nose.

Madison looked up and sniffled. "Thanks. It's so sad. That poor girl. All she wanted to do was marry the man she loved."

Before Banji could comment, the front door opened and a huge bear of a man walked in. Santiago came to his feet in an instant and moved toward the kitchen with purpose. He stopped beside Banji's chair.

She looked up at him. "It's okay."

Misha looked at each person taking his time. When he was done looking, he nodded once. "I am Misha."

Boris walked in from the other side of the room. "Misha, stop scaring the guests. These are Cami's friends from California."

He grunted, reached in his pocket and pulled out a small scarlet-cloth bag. "I have the locket."

Madison put her fingers over her mouth and twittered, "Oh, oh, I want to see it. I bet it's beautiful."

Misha's eyelids drooped to his most intimidating look. "It is very beautiful and it will show a man his one true love." He turned his gaze on Santiago. "Are you sure you want to touch this cursed heart?" He held out the bag.

Taking the bag from Misha, Santiago said, "I am not afraid." He carefully untied the silk ribbon and poured the locket and chain into the palm of his left hand.

Madison crowded herself into the space between him and Banji. She reached out with her right index finger and moved the chain away from the locket. She brushed her finger over the engraving. "Look at that. He must have loved her with all his heart." She sniffled, again. "I want somebody to love me like that."

Banji grabbed Madison's arm and pulled her away. "Oh, my, god. You touched it. You're doomed." Her eyes met Madison's. "Why did you do that?"

"I want to be happy." Madison hiccupped. "You found Santiago."

"What if your true love doesn't love you back? What if he's poor and doesn't live in California?"

"He has to love me back. It's in that book." Madison shook her head. "Don't worry. It's going to be wonderful." A weak smile spread across her face. "I just know it is."

"You're hopeless is what you are." Banji let go of Madison and turned to Santiago. "Well, how do you feel? Any changes I should know about?"

He held the locket up by the chain, carefully lowered it into the bag and tied the ribbon. "I do not know. Maybe. I must think about it." Handing the bag back to Misha, he said, "Thank you for letting me hold it." He looked at Boris. "You must all come to the races. There will be a party afterward." He reached in his back pocket and pulled out a thick stack of race day tickets and handed them to Boris. "Let me know if you need more."

Boris nodded curtly. "Thank you. Our cousin, Crystal, is flying in and we will be there." He walked over to Santiago and glanced at Misha. "We should go sit while the women finish reading the diary. It should not take much longer."

Santiago was aware of the two men assessing him, taking in his size, build, scars and the ink on his exposed arms. In turn, he evaluated them. They were warriors, comparable in size, standing a little over six feet and built for strength and stamina. Misha had scars to show and they both had identical ink on their upper arms. He recognized the knowing look in their eyes. They had all done what they had to do.

Boris lowered himself onto his recliner leaving the couch for Misha and Santiago.

Misha sat and turned toward Santiago. "Cami tells us you are mechanic. You build engines." He glanced at Boris and looked back at Santiago. "I build boats. I like good strong engine."

Santiago took the hint. "Come to the track and I will show you."

Boris leaned forward and stared at Santiago. "We will come tomorrow."

"We are running time trials in the morning. I will be there all day."

"We will be there in the afternoon. Then we will take you to the Riptide to meet our people."

Santiago gave a nod, his eyes on Boris. "I look forward to it."

CHAPTER THIRTY-SEVEN

THE RIDE back to the resort was anything but quiet with Madison chattering away in the back seat. Banji was tempted to bang her head on the steering wheel to block out the sound. How could anyone go on and on non-stop?

There was half a second of blessed silence before Madison said, "I have to get up early. Boris is sending Niko to pick me up so I can spend the day on his tug boat. Boris says Niko's used to having a woman on board because of Lulu. I can't wait. I won't sleep a wink."

Banji grit her teeth and forced a smile. Inhaling a calming breath that was marginally successful, she said, "Sure you will. I've got a great herbal tea that will take care of it."

If that failed, she could always bash the chatterbox over the head and knock her out cold but Santiago wouldn't like that. Better stick to the tea. She kept her eyes on the road and her hands on the wheel. "What did you think of the diary?"

Santiago shifted in his seat. "It was very sad. They risked their lives and lost. I do not blame her for cursing her father and the Count De Balboa. They were greedy selfish men. Salvatore should have killed them and then taken Alessia."

Madison bounced on the back seat, grabbed the edge of Banji's seat and pulled herself forward into the space between the bucket seats.

"You're right. That would have been better. Then they could have lived together in the islands and raised a family." She sighed, "Salvatore was so brave. I bet he was handsome, too. I want a man like that." She turned her head toward Banji. "Do you think there are any?"

Banji squeaked, "Excuse me!"

"I mean, do you think there are any that aren't already taken? It's like all the women I know have all the good guys. I'm not sure there's one still out there for me."

Tightening her grip on the steering wheel to keep from strangling Madison, Banji counted to five before giving up and saying, "Stay away from the railing tomorrow. It wouldn't be good if you fell overboard and ended up with a merman."

"What? There's no such thing. Madison looked at Santiago and then back at Banji and asked, "Is there?"

Banji grumbled, "There's everything in the Gulf of Mexico."

A few minutes later they pulled up and parked at the resort. They walked Madison to her room and went on to theirs two doors down the hall.

Banji kept stealing looks at Santiago. If she wasn't his true love, would she be able to see the love that had always shined in his eyes for her fade?

He quirked an eyebrow and asked, "Why do you keep looking at me like I have grown horns?"

"I'm not. You're imagining things."

He peeled off his t-shirt, dropped it on the chair in the sitting area of their room and turned to face her. "I am the same man I have always been."

"Of course, you'd look the same but that doesn't mean you'd feel the same."

"Nothing has changed. Perhaps it takes time." He shrugged and turned away. He opened his duffle bag and took out his kit. "I am going to take a shower." He looked over his shoulder at her. "Do you want to go first?"

"No. Go ahead." Banji picked up the TV remote. "I'm going to see what's on. I need to unwind from the road."

She watched him disappear into the bathroom, clicked on the TV, and scrolled through the guide looking for news. She needed something to take her mind off the curse, the locket, and the man in the shower. The chances of her relaxing were zero. She stretched out on the bed, plumped a couple pillows behind her head, and closed her eyes. He had to be the most exasperating man on the planet.

Banji woke up to the gentle sounds of Santiago breathing peacefully beside her in his sleep. The TV was off. Darkness surrounded her and the waistband of her jeans was rubbing her skin raw. Damn. She got up and shucked off the jeans, t-shirt, and bra. After a bathroom visit, she slipped into bed and cuddled up to Santiago. This might be her last chance.

Santiago opened his eyes and peered at the light streaming through the opening between the curtains. It was morning and he could hear the faint sounds of people talking in the hall. Banji stretched her legs, grumbled something unintelligible, and snaked her arm over his middle.

He'd grown used to her snuggling up to him in the night. The idea of waking up alone was something he pushed from his mind. He did not want to consider the terrible loneliness he would suffer without her. The locket had worked its magic, if that story was to be believed. He was more in love with her than he'd ever been, if that was even possible.

He rolled toward her, aligned their bodies, and snugged her to himself. "Good morning, *Carida*." He pressed his erection solidly against her, nudging his way between her legs. "I am a cursed man."

She wiggled into a receptive position and murmured, "Perfect."

Banji had zero interest in running time trials but she did need to get with Lulu and finalize the wedding details. After kissing Santiago goodbye, she called Lulu and agreed to meet her at Madame Belinsky's shop on the Strand.

Located in a converted warehouse, the aged bricks and open spaces echoed of timeless traditions. Extensive renovations breathed life into the Russian Revival style popular before the revolution. Banji snapped her mouth shut and quit gawking at the opulent dress in the window. Heavy, white satin adorned with lace appliques, gold embroidery and iridescent beads glimmered under the recessed lighting.

Sensing someone stopping next to her, Banji briefly glanced to her left and smiled at the beautiful woman. Her glossy long black hair draped around her shoulders in spiral waves. All the styling products in the world couldn't force Banji's hair to do that.

The large brown eyes danced with merriment right before she said, "Hi! I'm Lulu."

Banji automatically smiled back. "I'm Banji. How did you know?"

"Boris sent me a picture of you and Sahara last night." She turned to look at the dress and said, "White's not your color. I'm glad you chose something untraditional. Let's go inside. We don't want to keep Madame waiting." She led the way to the carved, solid oak door and pulled it open. "Madame made my dress. It was a very traditional Russian dress with tons of embroidery and pearls since I was marrying Niko." She laughed and kept moving ahead to the center of the show-room. Annie wore more of a Cossack style with a long tunic in royal purple since Boris was giving away the brides."

"Santiago is from Argentina." Banji met Lulu's gaze. "I don't have a relative to give me away so my best friend Zala said she'd stand in and do the honors."

"You're either the bravest woman on earth or crazy." Lulu burst out giggling and holding her hand to her mouth. "Zala's been part of our family ever since she crashed *Caligirl* into Misha's dry dock." Her hand dropped away from her face, she wrapped her arms around her sides as unbridled laughter erupted. "He was so mad. She has no idea how close she came to dying that day."

A stout woman with steel-gray hair piled on top of her head in a messy bun arrangement, wearing a loose dress and an apron with a dozen pockets full of thread, scissors, and ribbons walked up to them. She smiled and her thick accent punctuated her words. "What are you girls laughing about?"

Lulu reined in her laughter and said, "Madame, this is Banji Preston."

"Ah, yes, I have the dress ready to try on. Come, you must change."

Banji gave Lulu a side eye and moved forward. "Come on, you got me into this."

They followed Madame Belinsky who stopped in front of a louvered door. One twist of the porcelain knob and the extra-wide door smoothly swung open to a large fitting room with wall-to-wall mirrors. On a dress form hung Banji's dress.

She dashed across the room and did a happy Madison-like dance in front of the dress. "It's gorgeous. I love it." She spun around and looked directly at Lulu. "Help me try it on." Her jeans and shirt disappeared in record time.

Madame Belinsky snorted and strode over to a white dresser. "You cannot try on the dress in that." She nodded at Banji's underwear and pulled open the second drawer. After rummaging a moment, she pulled out the appropriate undergarment and held it up.

"Here, this will hold the dress's shape. You are not wearing a gunnysack. Young women these days do not understand how to dress properly." She held out a black lace corset that looked like a remnant from two centuries ago.

Lulu giggled. "I had to wear a white one under my dress. Niko loved getting me out of it. It's good to make the guys work for it every now and then."

"Really, I hadn't thought of that but I like it." Banji smiled conspiratorially, "Lace me up, let's do this."

❧

That afternoon Boris and Misha scrutinized every aspect of the Betmunn car to their satisfaction. When they were done questioning Santiago, they nodded to each other.

Boris looked up at the sky and then back at Santiago. "Okay, it's good. We can go to the Riptide now. You will come with us."

"Banji has the Trans Am. I do not have a ride."

"We will bring you back later. Come, we go." They turned in unison heading the direction of the guest parking.

Santiago could either go with them or run the risk of insulting them and pissing off Banji. Her friendship with Cami was too important to risk. His long strides caught up quickly to Boris and Misha. "What is this place, the Riptide?"

Without looking back, Misha said, "It is good tavern for seamen. We go there after work to talk and drink very cold beer. There is wine for the women." He looked over his shoulder at Santiago. "No trouble, all good. You will like."

Santiago wasn't too sure about that but he nodded anyway. He was taller than Misha but not by much, wider across the shoulders than Boris. His long black hair was only a few shades darker than theirs but that's where the similarity ended. Their hair, moustaches and beards were neatly trimmed. Compared to them he was a wild man.

Misha looked across the truck cab at Boris and then over his shoulder at Santiago in the back seat. "You won't need that knife in your boot, but it doesn't hurt to have it. The docks can be rough after dark."

"It is an old friend. I do not go anywhere without it." Santiago met Misha's gaze. "You understand how it is."

"We are the same. We protect what is ours." Misha turned back facing the front.

The rest of the ride was quiet for the short time it took to get across town to the tug boat docks. Santiago sat back and relaxed while taking in the houses and store fronts along their route. Weather beaten was the only way to describe it with an oceanside kind of charm. That must have been what attracted Banji. She was attached to the sea. He could live with that.

Before he had time to form his next thought, they pulled up and parked across from a line of boats bobbing in the water and tied to the docks. He got out and waited for Boris to lead the way.

Misha stood beside him and nodded toward the boats. "Those are all Tugger's. Captain Annie and my brother run the company." He nodded toward the far end. "You see that sail boat? I built it for Boris and Sahara. That's Salvatore's Alessia."

Santiago met Misha's gaze and said, "You are master craftsman."

"*Da*, yes, like you."

Boris came around the front of the truck. Santiago caught the man's eyes taking in the street in both directions and the cars parked around them before setting off in the direction of a weathered wooden building. Yeah, they were alike in many ways.

He followed Boris and Misha through the doors into the dimly lit tavern and over to a long table. They pulled up chairs and sat down with Misha on the left side of Boris and Santiago next to Misha. Boris waved at the bartender then turned to the men at the table and said, "This is Santiago. He is with us."

Several of the men nodded in his direction. He gave a curt nod in return. It was enough for that evening. The waitress brought over three cold schooners of beer and set them on the table in front of Boris, Misha and Santiago.

Santiago reached for the wallet in his back pocket but stopped when Misha grumbled under his breath, *"Nyet."*

Misha picked up his beer and took a long drink. Santiago followed his lead. The men talked about the events of the day. Santiago didn't understand most of what they were talking about but it didn't matter. Boris had his reasons for bringing him to this place. The reason would be made clear eventually.

He was halfway done with his beer when the door opened and Niko walked in with his crew. Madison scampered alongside one of the men, her arm wrapped through his. The man kept glancing down at her and speaking. Santiago could not hear what he said but the smile and blush that lit up her face indicated she liked his comments. Santiago's lips curled into a knowing grin.

Madison saw him and steered her companion toward his end of the table. The man pulled up two chairs and she settled next to Santiago, leaned over and said, "This is Fedor. He works on Niko's boat."

Fedor met Santiago's handshake. Their eyes locked and Fedor said, "I watched and made sure Madison was safe."

"Thank you. Her sister and I appreciate that." Santiago released his grip on Fedor's hand.

Madison's head swiveled from Santiago to Fedor as he took the seat next to her. Her fingers gripped the edge of the table as she leaned forward looking at everyone gathered at the table.

"This is great. I wish I had a picture of it." She caught Santiago's ear. "Do you think Banji would like this place?"

"I do not know. We can ask." Santiago turned his attention back to the men on his right but he could still hear Madison talking with Fedor.

The bartender brought him a beer and her a wine cooler. Madison gushed, "Thank you. I'm so thirsty."

"You should have told me. We have bottled water on the boat."

"I didn't want to be a problem for anyone. You were all so busy working. I was fine." She lifted the bottle to her lips and gulped down several swallows.

Fedor lifted his hand and signaled the bartender for Madison's next round. He leaned close to her and said, "You can take many pictures of us at the party after the race."

"Are you all coming?" Madison scooted around on her chair toward Fedor. "That would be great."

"*Da*, it is family, we will be there."

Santiago chugged down the rest of his beer and signaled the bartender in the same manner as he'd seen Boris and Fedor use. All these Russians, deck hands, and tug boat captains were Cami's family and friends which made them Banji's. She had explained it to him but seeing it was reality.

He wasn't at all sure he wanted to marry into this.

CHAPTER THIRTY-EIGHT

IT WAS four days before the race and her wedding. Banji sat in the resort dining room chewing on her toast and drinking coffee. Lots of coffee. She was having a bad case of nerves. She hadn't proposed to Santiago, yet. Getting him to the restaurant on the pier was on this evening's schedule. Getting him to actually go was going to be the hard part.

He was still grumbling about his night out at the Riptide. Yes, he liked the family, no he didn't like drinking schooners of beer until his stomach was too full to eat dinner. Note to self, a tired and starving Santiago was a grumpy Santiago.

Alena strolled in and flopped onto the chair across from Banji. "I hear Madison has a new-found interest in a certain deck hand."

"It's probably the newness of meeting someone from far away." Banji kept chewing.

"We need to take her to Houston and get her a better dress to wear to your reception. It's too late to get one from Madame Belinsky."

"She couldn't afford one anyway. She's not telling anyone but I know she's only got the money she's been making at the boutique. Lloyd was a co-owner of her savings and money market accounts. He took it all."

"The wedding dress she picked out isn't cheap. How's she going to pay for that? And what happens if she doesn't wear it?"

"I took care of it. Gram wouldn't have wanted me to be mean to Madison on her wedding day." Banji took a sip of her coffee. "She's getting married if I have to bribe someone to do it."

Alena crossed her arms over her chest. "You sound like Lloyd."

"Get over it. She deserves a good guy. Cami swears Fedor is the pick of the litter. He's quiet, protective, and loyal as a Rottweiler. Madison will be safe from Lloyd and his schemes with her very own cuddly Russian."

"You are insane. I've always suspected it." Alena let out an inelegant snort. "There's nothing cuddly about any of them. They're all hard bodied, working seamen."

"That's better than the marshmallow soft sneaky creeps Lloyd keeps sic'ing on her. She's too kind-hearted for his games."

"Why would Lloyd even care at this point? He's already taken her money." Alena uncrossed her arms and leaned forward.

"Her grandpa left her a nice little trust fund. She'll be fine in a few years and he's waiting to siphon that off." Banji bit into the orange wedge on her plate. She was so nervous she was reduced to eating the garnish for something to chew on.

"When you're through devouring the parsley can we go find Madison a dress? We have to be at our fitting this afternoon."

"Is she even awake? She's been swilling down wine coolers since she discovered them the other night. Fedor probably thinks she's a lush." Banji picked up the sprig of parsley, bit into it and grinned at Alena. "That'll probably cost me extra."

"Yeah, she's awake. She called me before my eyes were open this morning. She wants to look beautiful for Fedor at the reception."

Banji swallowed the parsley, wiped her mouth, and dropped the napkin next to her plate. "Let me get my wallet." She rolled her eyes and stood up. "Where are we going to find this man-killer dress?"

Alena smiled broadly and chuckled, "The Galleria, of course."

∿

Shopping at the Galleria took the rest of the morning. They ate drive-thru burgers in the Trans Am on their way down Interstate 45, speeding back to Galveston in time to drop Madison at the resort and still get to the dressmaker on time.

Banji needed a nap and she wasn't going to get one. She was stuffed into the corset and standing on the platform in the show room for the final touches to her dress.

The bell over the front door tinkled, she turned to look and gasped. Santiago filled the doorway of Madame Belinsky's dressmaking shop. She was having a nightmare wide awake in the middle of the day. She reminded herself to breathe and sucked in a lungful of air.

His eyes widened and he threw back his shoulders. "What are you doing? What is that?" His hand waved in her direction and his eyes met Banji's.

Her fingers froze holding the burnt georgette overskirt in her hands. "It's a wedding dress."

"Why are you wearing it?" His brows knit and his eyelids lowered.

She chewed on her upper lip, exhaled and said, "Because it's mine. I'm going to wear it when I marry you." Where the hell was Alena when she needed her? How long did it take to put on her dress?

His forehead wrinkled. "I have not asked you to marry me."

"I was planning on asking you this evening when we go to dinner on the pier. Alena made the reservations already." Banji let go of her skirt, glanced at the wrinkles and brushed her hands over them smoothing the material. "But since you're here, would you like to marry me?" She looked at Santiago and did her best not to cringe. What if he declined?

The silence was oppressive. She glanced out of the corner of her eye at Alena who had stepped into the room and got zero help. Great. Worst case scenario, she'd have the most beautiful ball gown ever. She turned her attention back to the man advancing on her like a lion stalking a gazelle.

Santiago moved steadily toward her wearing the inscrutable look that could go either way. She really hated it when he did that. She took a step back, caught her foot in the underskirt, tripped and landed in a heap of tulle, lace, satin and burnt georgette. She sat on the raised dais and stared up at Santiago looming over her.

"*Si, Carida,* it would be my pleasure to marry you."

Alena breathed a sigh of relief and mumbled, "Oh, thank god, that's over." She fastened her gaze on Santiago. "What are you doing here?"

He grumbled, "Getting married."

Alena fiddled with the beaded lace applique on the left shoulder of her gown. "No, you only got engaged. Married comes later at the resort chapel after the race."

"Why so long?" His gaze stayed fastened on Banji.

"Because you have to get the marriage license tomorrow and our dresses won't be ready until race day." Alena looked at her reflection in the mirror and smiled. "What's your hurry?"

"I am not in a hurry." He glanced over his shoulder at Alena. "Gabriel sent me to get you. There is a problem with the qualifying times."

"That's crazy. Our times were fine yesterday." She turned toward him. He sent you here to spy on us, didn't he?"

"No. He wants to know what color your dress is. He says last time you were here you wore blue velvet."

Alena grinned. "It's too hot for velvet this time of year."

He touched the skirt of Banji's dress. What color is this?"

"Your favorite time of day. Sunset." Banji brushed her hands over the bronze-colored lace appliques decorating the dark copper skirt. "Do you like it?"

"*Ay, Carida,* only you would do this for me. Every day you take a little more of my heart." His moustache couldn't hide the smile that spread across his face. "It is beautiful like my bride."

"It's not done yet. Wait till you see it with the crystal beads added."

"I will only see you." He reached out, took her hands and helped her to her feet.

Banji put her hands on his shoulders, stretched up and pressed her lips to his. Feeling his hands gripping her at the waist, she ended their kiss before he could wrinkle her dress any more than it already was after her inelegant fall. "You can't see me in this dress again until the ceremony. It would be terrible bad luck."

He held both of her hands in his. "Of course, *Carida*."

Madame Belinsky stood beside Alena adjusting the layered black-lace bodice and listening. She sighed and softly said in her thick Russian accent, "He is very romantic man. I like."

Alena said, "Yeah, he's one of the good ones." She corrected her posture, put her shoulders back and stood up straight. "This black dress is going to be perfect next to Gabriel's tuxedo."

Madame Belinsky tugged at the bodice. "You need better undergarment. Come with me. I have something to hold this up." She pinched the top edge of the cleavage seam and tugged upward causing Alena's breasts to bounce. "Tsk, this will never do. Come."

Alena glanced at Banji, shrugged and followed Madame to the fitting room.

Banji's eyes widened and she stared up at Santiago. "Oh, lord. Madame Belinsky is going to lace Alena into a corset. Better plug your ears. There's going to be all kinds of cursing in two languages any second now."

Santiago reached for the front of her dress. "Are you wearing one under this?"

She slapped his hand away. "You'll have to wait and see after we're married."

"*Ay, Carida*, you torture me with this. I will not be able to sleep wondering how beautiful you will look."

She winked and said, "I have some herbal tea that can fix that."

"You could show me after dinner tonight." He put his hand on the small of her back and pulled her to the edge of the platform. "It would not be bad luck to see it."

"It doesn't go with what I'm wearing to dinner." She snickered and said, "You'll have to wait."

A squawk filled the air followed by Alena shouting, "I can't breathe in this thing!"

～

Santiago helped Banji into the back seat of Gabriel's truck and then took the seat next to her. Her dress was beautiful. The royal-blue silk clung to her curves enticingly, and the low-cut back made it hard to keep his hands to himself. The only thing saving her from being carried back to their room was the reservation that had been changed from two to five people. Since she'd proposed and he'd accepted earlier that day, it was now a party that included Madison, Alena and Gabriel.

He'd been telling himself for weeks that he wanted to marry Banji and he'd also awakened from troubled dreams where he'd been left standing alone at the altar. This was not the time to give up hoping that he could still have the life he'd worked so hard to get. It had always been just out of reach until he'd found Banji sitting on the beach along with the flotsam and jetsam washed ashore by another storm at sea.

Madison climbed in and settled in on his open side and closed the door. She looked past him to Banji and said, "Thank you for my new dresses. They're so pretty. Fedor's favorite color is the sky's clear blue in the early morning." She sighed then giggled. "He's a morning person."

Santiago had witnessed the two of them getting better acquainted at the Riptide. They made a very nice-looking couple. But that was only his opinion. He'd watched Fedor closely. It was his duty since Madison was part of his family and he liked her naïve view of life. He wanted to help her hang on to it a little longer. Reality would eventually intrude but not tonight.

Fedor was a man who appeared friendly and approachable, but Santiago had seen the steel in the man's eyes and noticed the way he'd put his arm over the back of Madison's chair when he caught a seaman at another table paying too much attention to her. He'd staked his claim and heaven help any man who got between him and his girl.

A tingle traveled up his back and the locket's image skittered across his brain. He turned an appraising eye on Madison. Could it be? Had she found the true love she'd asked for?

~

During dinner on the upper level of the restaurant on the pier over-looking the Gulf of Mexico, they drank toasts to Banji and Santiago's engagement, Alena and Gabriel's and Santiago's race, and to Madison's successful marketing campaign. Their window table afforded them a spectacular view of the Gulf waters in the evening's fading light. The wait staff boxed and wrapped their souvenir drink glasses while the manager thanked them for coming. Gabriel handed him a ten-pack of free passes to the races.

Santiago helped Madison and Banji out of the truck and escorted them inside the lobby behind Alena and Gabriel. The desk clerk waved and called out, "Miss Preston there's a delivery for you." She held up a bouquet of colorful flowers in a cut-glass vase.

Madison looked at Banji. "They must be for you."

Banji shook her head. "I don't think so. They have to be for you." She glanced at Santiago.

"Not me. I have something waiting for us in our room." He grinned at Banji. "You will like it."

Madison walked slowly to the counter glancing back over her shoulder several times. She took the card from the holder and opened it. A jubilant smile spread across her face as she turned toward the group. "They're from Fedor." She shoved the card into the middle of the bouquet, snatched it off the counter, and buried her face in the arrangement. When she pulled back and looked over the top of a red chrysanthemum indicative of love and passion, she said, "No one has ever sent me flowers. He's so sweet."

It was all Banji could do not to roll her eyes. Bennett and Garth must have been the most brain-dead men on earth. How hard could it have been to call a florist and send some daisies to Madison? Then a niggling thought struck her. She tugged on Santiago's suit jacket sleeve. "It's the curse."

"*Sí, Carida*. I noticed it last night."

"I hope it's true. She deserves something good for a change." She wiped the sentimental smile off her face and said, "And I already paid for her wedding dress."

CHAPTER THIRTY-NINE

THE NEXT MORNING, Alena and Gabriel had their hands full at the track while Banji and Santiago were at the court house getting their marriage license. The car was ready, the driver was ready, the track was clean, and the sky was threatening to unleash holy hell on the whole island.

Alena's phone buzzed. She pulled it out of her back pocket and checked the screen. "It's Remington." She answered, "What's up?"

"Thought you'd want the good news. Preston has been arrested by the DEA. It's all over the San Francisco news."

"Why?"

"Importing and shipping drugs in his antiques."

"Couldn't happen to a nicer man. I'll drink a toast to it this evening."

"One more thing. I have the connection between Bancroft and Preston. Preston was the go-between. Bancroft handed Preston a blank check. Preston filled in the amount and handed it to Santino Bosco."

"How do you know? It's not likely they took a picture of the hand-off."

"Preston wrote in the amount. It's his handwriting." Remington inhaled and let out a long breath followed by a smoker's cough. "Do you want the copy of the check? The bank has the original. You'll have to get an attorney to ask a judge for a subpoena to get an admissible copy."

"It's kind of flimsy but yeah we'll take it. It's a start. It really only proves Lloyd handled the money, but if nothing else it'll be good for giving him some sleepless nights and maybe an ulcer for being in on it."

"I'll overnight it to you at the house." Remington coughed again. "How's Galveston? I'd be stuffing myself full of fried Gulf Shrimp if I was there."

The sun came out from behind the clouds and struck Alena in the eye. "It's going to be another beautiful day. I'll eat some of those shrimp in your honor. Thanks for everything Remington, you did great as always."

"No problem, Al. Now, go win something. I'll send you my bill."

Alena laughed and said, "Bye. Catch you later," and disconnected.

She looked at Gabriel and Santiago. "The DEA has arrested Lloyd, and Remington found a connection between Lloyd and the man he hired to kill Ritter. I'll tell Banji when she gets back. I'm afraid the feds will take precedent over the state."

Gabriel squared his shoulders. "At least he'll go to jail for something. That's good news but you don't look too happy."

"What's going to happen to Madison? Lloyd Preston is her father. If he's convicted, the government can take everything he has."

"It's a good thing she's living at Santiago's. We can have our attorneys recommend someone to represent her if she needs it. She'll be okay."

Banji and Madison had morning appointments at the resort's private spa enjoying a massage. Tomorrow they were having their nails done.

Banji lay on the massage table adjacent to Madison. She was able to see her out of the corner of her eye. "Are you okay over there? You look like you're one second away from falling asleep."

"I'm good. This is so relaxing. Thank you for paying for me." She inhaled. "I love the scent of lavender."

"Glad you're enjoying it." Banji closed her eyes and inhaled. Yeah, it was lavender all right. She preferred jasmine, but anything to keep the little chatterbox happy and quiet. She'd buy a whole crate of lavender scented everything if it would buy a moment's peace.

Madison's voice drifted over the relaxation music being piped into the room. "My Mom would love this."

"Yeah, mine too."

"I'm sorry about all the things I did to you when I was a kid."

Banji stared straight up seeing nothing but soft grey acoustic ceiling panels. Being angry with Madison hadn't changed things. It was way past time to let it go.

Banji asked, "Why are you telling me this now?"

"I don't know. It's so peaceful here and I was thinking how much I like being your sister. I'd like it to stay that way."

"I guess we can try it and see what happens. Now, will you please shut up and let me enjoy my spa day?"

Madison giggled, "Tomorrow we get to have our fingers and toes done." She turned her head and met Banji's stare. "I've never had a professional manicure before."

Banji opened her mouth to tell Madison she was going to have her fitted for a muzzle but changed her mind. It wouldn't do any good. Instead she said, "Crystal Foxz is going to meet us in the chapel's dressing room with Lulu to go over the last-minute details. I want her to meet Alena. You can stay but only if you don't pester her with a million questions."

~

Crystal reached out her right hand. "I'm Crystal. Boris sent me your picture with Lulu and Sahara the other night. How did your meeting go?"

Compared to Madame Belinsky, Crystal Foxz appeared especially tiny. And she was enchantingly beautiful in an ethereal way that could only be described as charmed. Sable-brown hair fell in waves around her shoulders. She had a heart-shaped face, violet blue eyes that complimented her disarming pixie's smile.

Banji's professional smile automatically snapped into place as she shook Crystal's hand and stammered, "Good." She cleared her throat and tried again. "Very good, the story behind the locket is a real tear-jerker. I'm glad I could help with the translation."

Madison quietly sidled up to Banji's side and stuck her hand out to Crystal. "I'm Madison, Banji's sister. I cried and cried listening to what happened to that poor princess, but I got to touch the locket before they put it back in the bag."

Crystal's lips turned up in an amused smile as she shook Madison's hand. "It's nice to meet you."

Madison replied, "Your chapel is beautiful."

"Thank you." Crystal turned back to Banji. "I'm glad you chose the Nautilus Pearl for your wedding." She stepped over and sat on the nearest French style boudoir chair. "What do you think of my cousins, Boris, Niko and Misha?"

"My friend, Cami, is lucky to have them looking out for her. I won't have to worry about her as much."

"They might be a little rough around the edges but they're good men. They're my family." Crystal tucked her feet off to one side.

"You're really lucky." Banji didn't want to sound condescending. "I mean that honestly. Not having family is a lonely place to be."

Crystal smiled. "You're lucky, too. The guys tell me you're good people. I'd say your family just got bigger, if you want it."

Sitting around the dinner table at a trendy seafood restaurant, Banji sat back and closed her eyes. She didn't feel lucky. She groaned, "Really, Lloyd's been arrested for smuggling. That's great but it still leaves my mother labeled as a suicide." She opened her eyes and looked at each person seated at the table. "It's not fair. He's getting away with murder."

Madison volunteered, "I'll tell the police what I heard."

"That's not evidence and Lloyd didn't say he'd killed Genevieve. It was your mother talking." She looked down at her hand wrapped inside Santiago's firm grasp. "I know the truth and that's the important part. I'll give it to the police for their files and put it in the hands of fate."

Madison asked, "What do you think will happen to my Mom?"

Everyone at the table exchanged looks.

"Well, say something," Madison pleaded.

Alena offered, "Remington only said Lloyd was arrested."

"I should call her and make sure she's all right." She looked pointedly at Banji. "I know it sounds mean but I don't want her to come live with me."

"I don't blame you. She can see if Lloyd's sister, Marlene, will take her in. You don't owe her anything. She turned her back on you. They took your money and threw you out."

Madison put her hand over her mouth. "Oh, no. What's Fedor going to think when he finds out about my Dad? He probably won't want to be my boyfriend now."

Banji shot Alena a raised eyebrow and said, "If that's the kind of man he is, you don't want him."

Alena nodded. "Exactly."

Banji glanced at Santiago and picked up her wine glass. "Here's to better days ahead and winning the important races."

Raising her glass, Alena said, "Important races." She put her glass down. "I wish Misha wasn't the size of a Grizzly bear. He's a maniac behind the wheel. I'd love to put him in our new car but he won't fit."

Banji laughed with everyone else and glanced at Santiago. He looked fine but that didn't stop her from wondering what he was thinking. The pile of ugly baggage surrounding her kept growing. It wasn't fair to burden him with that. She wouldn't blame him if he wanted to back out of their engagement.

She shook off the unhelpful thoughts and smiled. Until otherwise notified, she was getting married the day after tomorrow.

CHAPTER FORTY

BANJI HELD her breath as Madame Belinsky fastened the last hook on the back of her dress. "It's beautiful."

"Very good." Madame nodded. "You will put on gold necklace and it is done."

"I have it." Madison held out the box. "I hope Alena gets here soon. We can't start without her."

"Alena's running late. Betmunn came in second and she'd not in a good mood." Banji brushed her hands over the semi-full skirt of her ballgown turned wedding dress. "Crystal said she wanted to see me before the ceremony. She should be here any minute."

As if on cue, there was a knock on the door and Madison snatched it open. Banji turned in time to see Madame execute a quick curtsy and murmur. "Princess Alexandria, welcome."

Crystal gave the woman a nod. "Madame, always a pleasure to see you." She gave Banji an appraising look. "Magnificent. Madame, you have outdone yourself."

"Thank you. Please come and take closer look. It is some of my best work." She swept her hand out motioning toward Banji.

They advanced on Banji who was tempted to step back but thought better of it considering the last time she did that she ended up on the floor.

Crystal said, "I brought you something borrowed to wear with your dress. When Lulu sent me a picture of it, I knew this would be perfect." She dug in her purse and pulled out a velvet covered jewelry box and opened it.

Banji's jaw dropped. "My god, that's gorgeous. You never see heirloom citrine stones that size. It's got to be at least 40 carats." Banji glanced at Crystal. "And the weaved-gold collar looks like vintage eighteen carat."

"That's because it is. With the matching earrings and bracelet, it'll be the perfect finishing touch to your dress." Crystal handed the box to Madame and unfastened the collar from the ties holding it in place.

"Why are you doing this? You don't know me."

"You are Cami's friend and that makes you part of our extended family." Crystal opened the clasp. "Turn around." She clipped the safety clasp together. There, all done. Now let's see."

Banji turned back and stared at her reflection in the mirror. The citrine gemstone in the diamond studded claw setting rested elegantly over the center of her chest. Placing her hand next to the pendant she asked, "Is this part of Princess Charlotte's collection."

"Yes, I'll tell you a quick story about it." Crystal picked up the bracelet next. "It was the only thing she wore the first night she spent with Vasili after she lured him to her hunting lodge."

Madison clapped her hands together. "How romantic. A hunting lodge rendezvous with her lover."

Crystal picked up the earrings. "That was just the first of many. She always knew exactly what she wanted." Crystal stepped back, her eyes skimmed over the finished result. "Lovely."

"Lulu will take wonderful pictures and they'll be in the best magazines." Madison chirped gleefully. "I can help her with your marketing."

Banji lost her smile. "What did I tell you about keeping quiet?"

"But I can do something really amazing with this," Madison whined. "Super amazing."

Alena hustled through the door and asked, "What's amazing? You can tell me while I get dressed." She glared at Madame. "I need to breathe so don't go pulling those laces like you're cinching a saddle."

Crystal giggled. "You can stand to be zipped into a fire-retardant jumpsuit for hours but not a corset. Now, that's amazing."

~

Santiago's hair and moustache were trimmed along with a shave from the resort's barber shop. He barely recognized himself in his new tailor-made black Tuxedo and dress shoes. Looking at him anyone would think he belonged here but he knew better. He'd never been in a place this grand.

Boris had confided in him that Crystal had spared no expense to make the Nautilus Pearl Chapel a magical experience. Captain Nikolai Rustov stood at the front of the chapel dressed in his traditional formal Russian coat prepared to conduct the ceremony.

Lulu had carefully concealed herself in the alcove with her camera. She would silently capture the video and photos for their wedding album.

Light from flame-effect LED bulbs flickered in crystal fixtures and reflected off the antique oval mirrors adorning the walls. It was easy to believe that the chapel was truly enchanted by the sea goddesses depicted in the seascape frescos embellishing the walls.

Banji stood at the front of the chapel waiting for him. The iridescent beads on her gown and the ones threaded throughout her hair sparkled and reflected the colors dancing in the faux-candle's flames. Her usually unruly hair was tamed into a fine French twist with a few loose tendrils to frame her face. One look and he'd fallen in love with her all over again.

Soft musical renditions of a romantic love song filled the space between them because Banji adamantly refused to have the traditional wedding march. Alena tugged on Santiago's sleeve and asked, "Are you ready?"

Before he could answer, Gabriel hurried into the vestibule and stopped next to Alena. "I left Madison waiting out front but we have a problem."

Her head snapped around. "What kind of problem?"

"Cami says we have to wait. The *Raikou* docked a few minutes ago and Zala is on her way. Misha's driving but unless you delay the service, she won't make it in time."

"Banji will kill me; I'll have to sleep with one eye open for the rest of my life, if I let anything ruin her wedding. Zala can have a drink and dance at the reception." Alena looked at Santiago. "Walk slow, really slow, that'll buy a little time."

"No. I do not want Banji to think I am not sure." He squared his shoulders. "We do this now."

"For a man who didn't want to get married a few short months ago, you're sure in a hurry." Alena wrapped her arm around his and tightly gripped the sleeve of his tuxedo. "I can't run in this dress and corset. It won't look good if you drag me up the aisle behind you."

He tugged her forward. "I will take small steps for you."

"Good. I can barely breathe as it is."

His eyes held Banji's as he walked up the aisle to stand beside her.

Captain Rustov nodded, looked at the open book in his hands and asked, "Who gives this man to be married to this woman?"

"I do, his daughter." Alena inhaled deeply. "I've known Banji most of my life and she's perfect for my *Papi*. I am confident that they will take good care of each other. She could not get a better man to stand by her side." Alena inhaled and exhaled slowly. "So, it is with confidence that I give Santiago, my *Papi,* to Banji in marriage." She released his arm, stepped to the side and stood between him and Gabriel.

Alena gave Niko the evil-eye and fussed with arranging her dress.

Banji hissed, "Hold still."

Her command was punctuated when the chapel doors swung open and Zala barged in dragging Madison along behind her by the hand. She marched all the way up the aisle wearing a look that dared anyone to say a word.

When they stopped, Zala pushed Madison toward Banji's far side and hissed, "Go stand there and smile." She grinned at Banji. "I pushed *Raikou* for all his engines could give me. It's a long way from Mykonos but I wasn't about to miss giving you away. It's worth every leaking gasket." She looked directly at Niko. "Go ahead and ask. I'm ready." She patted her emerald-green silk blouse into place.

Niko's brow wrinkled and he scratched his jaw through his beard. "Who gives this woman to be married to this man?"

"I do, her oldest and dearest friend." She snorted and mumbled, "And Madison does, too." She looked at Madison and pointed, "Her, right there." Zala nodded. "Okay, are we good?"

Niko gave a curt nod. "*Da*, all good."

~

Banji clamped her jaw shut tight. Her wedding was going down in history for being the worst of what not to do, thanks to Zala. At least she'd shown up. The blouse was good but the tan cargo pants and gladiator sandals weren't exactly wedding attire.

She came out of it just in time to hear Niko ask, "Do you take this man to be your lawfully wedded husband?"

What happened to for-better-or-worse blah, blah, blah? Never mind. "Santiago, his name is Santiago, and yes, I take him to be my husband forever and ever no matter what."

Niko shook his head and turned his attention to Santiago.

"Do you take this woman to be your lawfully wedded wife?"

The ensuing moment of silence stretched uncomfortably long. Alena glanced past Santiago to Banji and then back at him. She hissed, "Say something."

Banji watched his throat work as he swallowed. He inhaled, reached over, took the bouquet of peach-colored roses and white lilies from her and handed them to Alena. She wasn't going to panic. She refused to panic. It was going to be okay. The room tilted. Maybe it was spinning. She couldn't breathe. Her eyelids fluttered and she heard Zala mutter, "Shit, she's fixing to faint."

The strong arm behind her back and one around her waist kept her from crumbling into a heap at his feet. Her lips were too numb to giggle at the thought of landing there again. It was starting to become a common occurrence.

"Yes, she is mine. *Carida*, you are my love."

Banji felt herself being lifted into Santiago's arms and she forced her eyes open. He turned her toward Niko in time to hear him say, "By the power vested in me by the State of Texas, I now pronounce you husband and wife."

Alena mumbled, "Thank god." She waved the brides bouquet at Madison. "Here take this."

Gabriel thumped Santiago on the back and laughed. "You did it. Congratulations."

Madison sniffled. "I love weddings. Banji looks so beautiful. Do you think she's okay? She's never fainted before."

Zala put her hand on Madison's shoulder and guided her down the aisle. "She's fine. Brides faint all the time. They need to carry fans instead of bouquets. Come on, let's go find the champagne. I need a drink."

Lulu stepped out from the alcove and scurried to the vestibule. She pointed her camera at the strikingly bold man carrying his gorgeous bride down the aisle.

~

Santiago sat with Banji at their table in the reception room. He leaned close and quietly asked, "Are you feeling better, *Carida*?"

"Finally, I can feel my fingers and toes." Her lips puckered to the side and she muttered, "You scared me. I thought you'd changed your mind."

"I did not change my mind. I needed the right words." He took her hands in his. "As long as I live, we are lovers."

Niko sank onto the open chair beside Santiago. "I've got license for you to sign. Monday, I will file it at the courthouse."

"Give me the pen. I do not want Banji to change her mind and sail away with that Zala woman." Santiago held out his hand. "I think she is crazy."

"The *Raikou* is not going anywhere for long time. Misha says it has been neglected for years. Zala sent him pictures when she found it. It is miracle yacht made it this far. Someday her luck will run out." Niko shrugged.

Banji watched Santiago sign and reached for the pen. "I'm not going anywhere except home with my man." She scribbled her name at the bottom of the page. "There, I'm now Banji Aloysius Cordova." She pushed the pen and paper toward Niko and kissed Santiago.

Niko folded the license and put it in his inside pocket along with the pen. "Come, we will drink good Russian vodka and celebrate. It is very old tradition."

Banji challenged, "But we're not Russian."

"Close enough. You are friends of Cami, Cami is ours. She married strong Russian man. All good."

"Yeah, it is." Banji glanced around the room. "Where's Madison?"

"Dancing with Fedor." Santiago smiled. "I am glad you bought her a wedding dress. I think she is going to need it."

ABOUT THE AUTHOR

Nellie Krauss is an emerging author of contemporary romances. This is Nellie's fifth book. She is a Pro member of Romance Writers of America and San Antonio Romance Authors. Her cross-cultural stories are inspired by her experiences from traveling foreign countries, living in Texas and spending summers with Native Americans on the Pine Ridge Reservation in South Dakota. The Renaissance Fair is her favorite place to be when she's not in the Black Hills or at the beach. Her biggest thrill is hearing the roar and rumble of her Harley's engine on the open road. In her civilized life she is a Paralegal, a Nationally Certified Investigator, has a purple belt in Karate, is an NRA Pro-Marksman, sky diver, scuba diver, belly dancer, Harley Motorcycle rider, and off road 4-Wheeler enthusiast. She has travelled the Caribbean, the Bahamas and Western Europe in search of adventure.

.

Made in the USA
Middletown, DE
11 March 2022

62500624R00166